CAMILLE AND THE
RAISING OF EROS

Also by William Rose

The Strange Case of Madeleine Seguin

CAMILLE AND THE RAISING OF EROS

William Rose

SPHINX

First published in 2019 by Sphinx, an imprint of
Aeon Books Ltd
12 New College Parade
Finchley Road
London NW3 5EP

British Library Cataloguing in Publication Data

A C.I.P. for this book is available from the British Library

ISBN-13: 978-1-91257-313-4

Typeset by Medlar Publishing Solutions Pvt Ltd, India

www.aeonbooks.co.uk

www.sphinxbooks.co.uk

CONTENTS

PART ONE: CAMILLE

PART SEVEN: THE THREE

PART ONE

CAMILLE

CHAPTER ONE

A dream of feathers

She stirred; a heavy veil of sleep rose, fell back, then rose again. Waking caused her to tremble. Had it been just a dream? She wanted it back, but then, in the light of dawn and the rising reality of a new day, she recoiled from herself and her wish. For a moment she had felt a strange pleasure, something uncanny, a vision only answerable to itself. But then, turning her head upon the thin hard pillow, she whispered, "It's just a dream," and this, she thought, it must only be, and the thrill she had felt turned to an ache of self-reproach.

She pictured a stone in her stomach. It was smooth and white and round, and there it lodged, an impassive, unforgiving presence, scrutinising her thoughts.

Restless, she turned again and knew she must rise. The timings of the monastery, signalled by bells and so crucial for their lives, were now part of her being. But her body disobeyed. Her mind too, so well-groomed in the selection of thoughts, failed to comply. One renegade part, like an invader, had staked its claim and was not deterred by the advent of dawn which now with pale light configured the small, square shape of the window high up on the wall.

"Perhaps I am unwell," she thought, and she found comfort in that, but her wishes again defied her and the sensual presence of the dream, like a creature in its own right, cunningly called her back.

She allowed the lapse and reached out to touch the edge of her dream, a misty veil, drawn across, but as yet unsealed.

She drew it back.

She thought, "A dream is like a scene within a play. Was I the writer? Or was it written for me?"

With a warm feeling, she imagined being placed within a scene; to be there through the wishes of another. Yet as she eased herself and gathered the memory, grasping the light silken strands and drawing them to her, she knew that no other could have made this, but also how could she have done so herself? And how something could be so strange, yet feel so real? The atmosphere had made it thus. She remembered that as a child she had been enthralled by a magic show; conjuring tricks that had amazed her, yet it was the setting she now thought of. It had been an old theatre, tucked away in a Parisian street that hosted other small theatres and strange little curio shops. Inside, the curtains were musty and of heavy red velvet and the ornate plaster, peeling in places, was painted with gold and russet. The lighting by gas lamps eerily threw shadows across the few rows of seats, and on the seats the audience with intent faces which seemed to her so flushed now in the flickering light.

"It was the atmosphere," she thought, "and I now linger in the atmosphere of my dream, and I will not let it go, lest I lose it forever."

And so again, she allowed it to come.

There had been the sound, even the sensation of something fluttering. It brought a memory of the garden of her childhood

4

home. The garden had sloped down to the rear of the house, and right at the back, at the top, there was a little flat area of grass from which she could look down, through the shrubs and along the whole length of the garden, and there below was the roof of the house. And this little platform of grass was boarded on all sides by buddleia trees and honeysuckle that threaded through the shrubs, so that at the rear and sides there was a dense curtain of foliage. "Like the wings and curtains of a theatre stage," she thought, and again she recalled the magic show.

Sometimes, when she would sit in that very secluded place at the top of the garden, all would be quiet and still and then she would hear a flutter, and it would be the beating of the wings of a bird, striking against the twigs and the leaves, deep within the foliage. But no bird would be seen, and she could only know it was there by the sound. She thought how quickly the tiny heart of a bird must beat and how keenly its eye would be focused on her as it perched safely and unseen in its hiding place.

In her dream, she had also sensed the flutter of wings, though stronger, and it was in a place quite like that most private area of her garden. As a girl, her delight had been to contemplate nature—God's wonderful creation, but now all around her, in the dream, there was a difference, a sense of something new and strange. Nature was changing into a human form. She heard the wings and felt the turbulence they made in the air and then she sensed the presence. A figure stood next to her, and she dared not turn to look, though she knew it was so close. Then there was breath upon her cheek, and he whispered in her ear.

She gasped, shocked by the vision, and jolted out of her reverie. But now she was cornered by her dream and unable to escape its memory; through her very submission came a liberty, a surge of energy that brought warmth to her skin, spreading its heat through her body and up to the flushed cheek upon which he had breathed.

In defiance of her training and its insistence upon humility, she allowed a feeling that came to her like a visitor from the distant past, one that had become a stranger to her. She let it come, and so remembered the ruthless nature of the wish to possess, and she welcomed this and spoke aloud her conviction.

"It is my dream; I will not share it!"

And then with even greater courage, for her eyes were upon the plain, drab, walls of the cell that surrounded her,

"Nor will I confess it!"

Her struggle was no longer with the doctrines of her holy order. It was now her memory that she feared. Would its gift to her of the dream be withdrawn? Would it cruelly reclaim and withhold all that had been offered? He had whispered in her ear, but what had he said? She had no recall. Not even a suggestion—a communication so strong but undefined. And yet—it was hers. Hers and his, given only to her, with his breath upon her cheek, his whispered words tickling her ear, and the fluttering of wings that was now a commotion in her breast.

The frustration at words not recalled became a tingling in her body, so that she reached down under the blanket to a place that she had ceased to know but that through instinct offered relief. And having begun, she was claimed by instinct and was not deterred by a voice within that spoke with a singular comment, "Sister—this is lust." In lust, her mind was cleared of all that might diminish its brilliant images, and she saw the structure of his wing and reached and touched the thick bone, which, meeting the shoulder, was secured within the brown skin, holding the curve of long white feathers.

Her outstretched fingers combed the feathers which slipped smoothly between them, tickling the sensitive little enclaves where each finger joined the next, and then, reaching out again, she grasped the bone which gave the wing its power, as strong and subtle as a longbow, rooting to the body the main of the soft white wing. She felt the power, centred in his back and shoulders, that could raise the weight of the great wings and then draw them down, dismissing the air before them, and she knew that with just two strokes of the wings he would rise with ease and the earthbound would be as nothing to him. And since he was the creature of her dream and the sensations within her body were themselves rising and falling like the beating of wings, she grasped his hand and felt his arm tight around her waist, and they rose together, and the earth was no longer of consequence and her body was without weight or form.

When their feet once again met the ground, it was the moist, cool grass of her little private enclave at the top of her childhood garden, surrounded by shrubs and the scent of honeysuckle and jasmine. Her secret space. And now, placing her hands upon his arms, she wondered,

"Do I look upon his face?"

CHAPTER TWO

From an essay on J and his work

By Dr Paul Faucher (1935)

D r Jean-Luc Javert is one of our most esteemed colleagues and an early member of our Paris Psychoanalytical Society. He is nearly always only referred to as J. Why this should be is a mystery, but such aspects of the unknown fit him well. For a while, he was analysed by Freud himself, though as we understand it, he is now somewhat estranged from the master due to his dalliance and indeed, even some informal analysis, with Carl Jung. Such a tragedy that those two great minds, at first so creatively entwined, now leave us only to contemplate their difference. But this seems to trouble J far less than the rest of us. Indeed, he even finds it amusing and continues with his thinking in complete autonomy, drawing from both their works as suits him best, whilst interspersing their views with those of others, and with a profound addition of ideas that can only be his own. And he can mix the serious challenges of our psychoanalytic work with an unrestrained playfulness, so that in our most demanding and often rivalrous discussions within the Society, he can joke and have fun. Perhaps his impervious response to the rift between Freud and Jung is due to his irreverent nature—he is absolutely his own man and sees not the slightest reason to take sides. I must add though that he is no traitor to the movement and his belief in the aims of psychoanalysis is second to none. But there is something, and it can be another spur to his playfulness and humour: it is Freud's atheism. He seems to find it an ongoing source of amusement.

I can safely say, having benefitted considerably from his teaching and from his astute remarks when I was struggling with my early cases, that I know him better than most. The help he gave me was often through the medium of his own clinical and personal experience. And one thing became absolutely clear: J is not an atheist.

There was a case in point.

In the summer of 1920, fifteen years ago, he had as a patient a young woman, a girl really; she was seventeen years old. She had no wish to see him; everything was at the bequest, the dictation in fact, of her father. This father—the mother was deceased—had become preoccupied with the mental health of his daughter and feared she might lose her sanity. So he arranged a consultation with J and duly arrived with his daughter, the subject of his anxiety. As Professor Freud has so amply described, anxiety is the ego's affective response to a perception of danger. Of course, in ordinary life, the danger may be very real, and the anxiety is the warning, but in our neurotics it is all in their inner world—an unwanted impulse, an idea or a memory that threatens to make itself known.

This parent was anxious but his daughter, the prospective patient, turned out to be not anxious at all. Far from it, she was blissfully happy. However, this only compounded the father's view that she was about to be struck down by mental illness.

The wellspring of the girl's happiness was an adolescent adoration of God. She was completely taken up with Jesus, the Blessed Virgin, and every single angel in heaven, with whom she mingled during many happy hours of daydreaming. To cap it all, and to her father's horror, she had also formed an unassailable ambition to become a nun.

So J met both the father and the daughter, whose name was Camille, for the consultation. During a rather uncomfortable hour, he observed that whilst the father was displaying considerable anxiety the girl showed none and given that she was so happy and the father so unhappy he wondered whom he should really be treating.

This whole consultation was described to us by J at one of our Society meetings. Although from some years before, it was still absolutely fresh to him. To most of my colleagues, it was clear-cut and to interpret the girl's state of mind was easy. They approved of the father's wish to find treatment for Camille and all agreed that psychoanalysis should have been the way. She had clearly been struggling with the onset of adolescence and its huge upsurge of sexuality, and she had requisitioned the purity of religion and the virginal life of a nun as the perfect antidote; a complete repression and a turning around against her sexuality. A defence that we call a "reaction formation." A discussion ensued, with my colleagues competing to make the most impressive remarks and gain J's favour—such is his esteemed position.

J, as well as not joining in with the general diagnosis, was tantalisingly enigmatic and retained his reticence at our later meetings. When asked about the fate of the girl he was completely unforthcoming. It was only because I became a trusted colleague that he later disclosed to me the remarkable outcome.

After that initial consultation with father and daughter, J saw Camille by herself just one more time. He did then agree to see her again but much to the father's chagrin he made the appointment for two years later!

At the appointed hour, two years on, Camille, now aged nineteen, duly arrived and presented herself as definitely less ecstatic but still absolutely purposeful in her wish to become a nun, and not just that; she wanted to join a contemplative and strict order of the Carmelites.

To have retained her wish over the intervening years and, as J surmised from the interview, with only a little ambivalence, was impressive. J also mentioned to me that he would have been less impressed if there had been no ambivalence at all. The fact that Camille could now express some fears about the enormous commitment and sacrifice added a degree of reality to the situation, and convinced J that he could end the session by stating his pleasure at having met her again and offering his very good wishes for her chosen future as a religious. I believe that he even waived the fee since he had no expectation of payment from the father.

A year later, he received a letter from the girl thanking him for his encouragement, though interestingly, she referred to it as "his blessing," and said that she wished him to know that her time as a "postulant" was ending and she was about to become a "novice." She was resident at the Carmelite convent in Cordoba in southern Spain, and she remarked in her letter that he would know why that place was her choice.

He, in fact, understood her choice very well, remembering clearly her description of a family holiday in Cordoba when she was a girl. It had been very important for her to tell him of this. She was just thirteen. It was the festival of Corpus Christi, in the early summer, and her father and aunt had left her by the cathedral, so she might watch the religious procession emerge on its long trek around the streets of the old city. Rather than remain at the cathedral gates, she had followed her impulse to join in the procession. It wound through the narrow streets for what seemed like hours, but she was entranced. The surfaces of the streets were covered with twigs of rosemary and, as the thousands of feet passed over and crushed the twigs, the perfume of rosemary rose and drifted around the lovely old buildings and their decorated balconies and their funny little entrances with walls covered by Moorish tiles. She had followed the procession all through the streets, marvelling at the strength of those who, at their slow and steady pace, carried the enormous structure on which perched the monstrance, and the stamina of elderly nuns who kept pace with the fresh-faced priests, all singing as they passed by the many churches with their sacred ornaments displayed in the streets. She could hear the steady thumping of drums and the wail of the horns of the brass band far ahead in the procession. And the figure of the bishop in his robes, near the end, close to where she was, quietly walking and looking diminutive amongst the grandeur and opulence of the artefacts but with a presence which to her was full of calm, spiritual power. The procession finally wound its way back to the cathedral from whence it had come and within the magnificence of that building, raised amongst the pillars of a previous great Islamic mosque, she knelt and took part in the Benediction that followed and, embedded within the huge congregation, received the blessing of the Eucharist.

All this occurred whilst her father and her aunt, as rather overheated tourists, were exploring the nearby Castle of the Christian Kings. And when she met them afterwards, she told them nothing of what had occurred, only that she had stood and watched the procession.

Neither did she tell them, when two days later, on the pretext of an early morning walk, she had slipped out of their hotel and into the nearest church. She had no exact purpose in mind, it was just to savour something from the procession, but a Mass was being held and, discarding all inhibitions, she joined the worshippers. Walking boldly to the front, she knew in an instant what to do as perhaps, she mused to J, God was

13

calling her, and she received communion—she, who had no right to do so, having never been baptised a Catholic and this only her second time in a Catholic church. She told J ruefully that it was one of her "first and greatest sins," still to be mitigated, but was unable to suppress a hint of amusement.

All of this she hid from her family.

"It is my secret," she said, "and I wish to possess it—I will not confess it," and she remarked contentedly to J about her pleasure at her catchy little phrase.

As she continued to grow, through her teenage years, she would find a place, just for herself, in the garden of the family home. She described to J how she would go high up in the garden, which sloped downwards to the rear of the house, and how in that little space at the top, which was surrounded by shrubs, there was a rosemary bush which would exude its sweet odour in the heat of the sun and would remind her of the streets of Cordoba at Corpus Christi.

J told me he said very little to Camille in return, but he did venture that this special, most personal space that she found, firstly in her new experience of the procession, which was to be kept so private and secret, was also the space at the top of the garden, and perhaps it was also the space she felt compelled to seek in the still and quiet confines of monastic life. He added that he hoped it would indeed bring her fulfilment.

All this J recounted to me one warm, summer evening at his Paris home. We were sitting near an open window that overlooked some gardens and had enjoyed a cognac and a fine cigar after an excellent meal.

Having completed the introduction to his Camille story and remaining silent for a while, his tone became more formal. He needed to tell me, he said, that he completely trusted Freud's theory of sublimation. There was no problem with that. The baser sexual instincts, if all goes well, are transformed and expressed in higher forms, and the girl's religious ardour was no doubt, in part, a beneficiary of this process.

14

"But," he said, and for a moment I saw a trace of anger in his face, "this is not enough! Such a love of religion at so young an age, such intensity, and such intuition at the communion. This girl truly had a calling."

I have called this J's "introduction" to Camille. I did not know it then, but he would have far more to say about this strange case. For the moment, he was content to change the subject and as dusk descended we discussed, with much laughter, the more familiar subject of the eccentricities, foibles, and the occasional follies of our colleagues in the Paris Society, as well as the wider psychoanalytic world.

CHAPTER THREE

Camille and Sister Africa

"We live together, and we die together, but really we are strangers."

The thought did not dismay her. She had accepted the sacrifice of worldly relationships for a more profound relationship with Christ. It was their way. And it occurred to her that there was pleasure in the more distant observation of others, the gradual forming of impressions from which recognition grows, yet allowing unknown spaces.

And so it was with her—the African. And so much stronger than with all the others. Stronger and more mysterious, and she relished the thought. How does one with dark skin, surely from Africa, come to be serving Christ in the small Carmel monastery of Cordoba?

"She came across the sea; Africa is close," she thought, "but are they not of another religion there, the one that worships Mohammed?" Their ancient presence was all around in Cordoba. The walls of the monastery had many beautiful tiles that were in their style: diamonds and curls and stars, the shapes of radiating flowers, but always as a pattern and the attention to colour meticulous, bright, varied, and happy. The narrow streets of the city had many entrances to homes decorated with these, but most of all there was the cathedral. Once it had been the Mezquita, the Great Mosque, until the Christian Kings had driven the Moors from southern Spain. Then they had proved their presence by building their churches and cathedrals, and one was built within the huge mosque, so that at the centre was the Christian altar and nave with all the opulence and grandeur of a cathedral. Radiating around it there remained the structures of the mosque with hundreds of ornate pillars and arches of red and white.

The reclusive life of the Carmelites did not allow them to visit the cathedral, but it was still clear as a treasured memory for Camille from the fateful day when, as a girl, she had followed the Corpus Christi procession through the streets and ended with the people of the city, crammed in to the cathedral to receive the Benediction from the bishop. Then she had looked in awe at the Christian opulence but also at the difference in the structures of the Moors, glittering and receding into the distance of the huge building with repeated arches like the waves of a red and white sea.

And Camille wondered, "If the Moors went back to Africa, then in some ways Sister Africa is old Spain, and here she is again, but like the cathedral, she has slipped in, in Christian form." Camille thought of the dark-skinned woman as Sister Africa; she liked the name, though in their community she was Sister Julia of Saint Jerome, a name she would have adopted as a novice. Camille wondered whether Julia was an African Saint.

She did not doubt that Sister Africa was a true Christian. She had made her vows many years before. "Not old enough to be my mother, but an older sister," thought Camille with pleasure. She had known her to pray for many hours in the chapel and had often wondered at the grace of her movements which, more than for any other nun, conveyed the essence of their community: a silent, barefoot glide through the rooms and corridors, the dark skin of her face almost as black as the veil that surrounded it. In the darker rooms, her face would seem like part of a shadow or silhouette but framed by the brilliant white edging of the wimple beneath the veil. But also there were the eyes. Camille surprised herself as she realised how much she liked those eyes and then even more surprised to think "I love them."

Camille knew that she was different since her dream of the winged god; that love was no longer the simple pious and selfless quality that had brought her to Carmel. There were unexpected moments when she would feel a warm flush of happiness, but these were not from prayer or contemplation. They would not last long, but they would return, and she would feel them in her body. It was one of those that filled her as she thought of the eyes and pictured them very clearly—their colour a rich dark brown, surrounded by a white as clear as the starched edging of the wimple that framed Africa's face.

And then she dreamed again, and it was of her. It must have been her, and probably the dream was set in Africa, as much as one can tell in a dream. No voice said it was, but it was unlike anywhere else she had seen. She knew it was warm, very warm, and it felt vast; a great wide and flat vista, and she later marvelled at how such a place, never seen, could be seen in a dream. And there were sounds, and these she knew were sounds of jungle creatures. As a child, she had been taken by an aunt to the Ménagerie du Jardin des Plantes and had seen and heard such creatures and was so entranced that from each enclosure her aunt had to gently, but firmly, pull her away. The little Camille could only stare, and her aunt had laughed. "And so perhaps," thought Camille, "there is something here too about my aunt." But there was no jungle in her dream, just the wide, bright vista, with rocks in the distance, but with jungle sounds, screeching, calling, warning, declaring, so that the air was full of them. And then too there was the African and she was running, clothed in a smock of red and white, the colours of the pillars in the great Mezquita mosque. The cloth was flat against her body as she took strong and muscular strides that lengthened until each stride seemed like a great leap. Then, by her side, in perfect unison, stride for stride, was a great cat, a lithe, long-bodied creature, and she remembered from picture books that this was a cheetah, the fastest of the wild beasts.

When she awoke, she was full of the very being of Sister Julia, and the sounds and smells and the vision of Africa were so vivid that she believed they were now her inheritance too. But most of all she felt full of the alien wonder of the wild beast. The sinews of its long body stretched as they squeezed out the power and the energy and she sensed, with some fear, that she had come close to a stranger and that the stranger was pure instinct and that this was the same element that powered the flight and the ardour of her winged god.

As she slowly and without attention donned the intricate layers of her clothing, nothing mattered, but the sensation of her dream and an experience of her body that involved sinews and motion and that cared little for the bell that would soon be calling them to Divine Office.

CHAPTER FOUR

Camille in her cell

They lived to the sound and rhythm of bells: the sound of great bells, resonant and commanding, and pretty tinkling handheld bells calling them to worship, to prayer, to rest, work, and contemplation, the rhythm of their daily lives.

And when she heard the bell for evening contemplation, she had always been happy, loving this as her own moment of time and her time to be alone. But now there was a change and she no longer felt alone in her cell, because now there was Sister Julia, the African. Camille thought of Julia, alone in her cell along the corridor just a few doors away and wondered, "Is she also thinking of me?"

She pictured her with the black veil covering her head and shoulders and beneath that the brilliant white of the wimple, and with pleasure she thought,

"The black and the white together—her and me."

And again, she knew that somehow, she loved her African sister in a way that differed from common love. And then her mind drifted in a manner that had taken hold since her first dream. The thoughts were of the physical, though at first she had denied this. It had not been long since the bell had signalled their evening solitude and thinking of this she declared, "The shape of the bell must be female and the inside, the clapper, surely male—it rattles around inside," and she laughed aloud and then abruptly brought her hands to her mouth to stifle the sound that had broken the absolute silence of the hour. She felt fear now, but still there was pleasure in the mischief of her thought.

"Would Jesus mind?" she asked and looked across at the only ornament in her room: a plain, dark wooden cross upon a bare wall, just visible from the flame of a candle burning on a small oak table below it. The candle flickered, as it often did, bothered by the draught that slipped beneath the heavy door before searching for its exit through the little barred window, high up, facing the garden but too high for Camille to reach.

"And no one must see in. We are Sisters of Carmel. I chose this. I chose to be barefoot, to be silent, to worship the Virgin, to remain a virgin, to be the consort only of her Son, our Saviour." But at this, her dream returned and she saw the figure of her winged god, rising, the wings gracefully, powerfully, and perfectly defeating the air. She remembered how he had held her and raised her up so that both hovered like great birds as high as the tops of the trees, and as she thought of those great and beautiful cypress trees in the monastery garden, her body felt a heat, radiating through it and along each limb and into the flushed cheeks of her face, even tingling her scalp, and she knew that it was anger—a rage at that little barred window that gave no view of the darkly beautiful trees and let no one look upon her within.

She crossed her arms, grasping the rough material of the smock which she wore at night and with one fast and fluid movement, fuelled by rage, drew it over her head and to the side so that she stood naked, the garment dangling from one outstretched arm.

She threw it to the floor. "I have no mirror," she thought, and a lesson from her schooldays came into her mind. They had learned English and had been given a poem to study: the English poem, "The Lady of Shallot", who was captive and cursed so that she could only view the world outside her tower through a mirror.

"But I have no mirror and cannot even view myself."

Nothing in her little cell reflected anything. The walls were flat white with a dusty wash, peeling in the corners. Upon her bed, the blankets were grey. Her little pillow, so flat and hard, now seemed grey too. The floor was of hard, dark slabs of stone: no reflection, not even of the candle flame. And so she looked directly downwards. Her eyes searched over her body. For years this had been a cursory inspection, a brief necessity, an irrelevance to the life that was led within the culture of her order. The body, hidden by the ample and flowing brown robes, the modesty of the cropped hair beneath the black veil with the white band across the forehead; her face framed like a little painted icon.

But now she looked, and as she did her hand rose to touch, first her chest, where she felt her heart beating, and then, carefully, she lifted each breast. "How heavy they are," and was surprised at this and was now engrossed in her search. Her hands ran over her thighs and reached behind to her buttocks and then returned and rested upon her stomach and there beneath was the soft, dark place that, after the dream, she had entered herself.

"And now," she thought, "it would be like a young girl crossing the threshold of a sumptuous room that belongs to others—to the grownups perhaps."

She felt very young, yet the soft hidden place was not of a child. And again her feelings swung back, and she feared that threshold. With dismay and guilt, she whispered, "I may not enter that room!"

She bent down and grasped the smock, wringing it between her clenched fists and then, looking around at the sanctuary that had now become a prison, she cried, "But I love my life here!"

She remembered when she first came to her cell and how she was entranced by the beauty of its very plainness. There was no imposition then; its gentle purpose was to hold and rest her in her devotion to Christ.

Again, she threw down the smock, but this time she followed it. Falling upon her knees and clasping her hands together, she knelt naked and begged for forgiveness and then laid her whole body, head to feet, face down, prostrate on the cold stone floor before the little wooden crucifix.

****

But there was to be no redemption for Camille that night. She dreamed again.

The air was very clear, the sky a bright blue and the clouds as white and as high as can be. She was on a great grassy plain that stretched out around her as far as she could see. She was with the African. Camille was dressed in a summer frock of white linen edged in lace and Africa wore a smock of bright colours—red, blue, and yellow, and wore wonderful big earrings of silver and as she moved her head they chimed with the sound of the little bells that summoned them to prayer. It was so peaceful, and she could only hear the bells and the rustling of their clothes in the breeze. Camille was amazed to be there in the great open with Africa in her native dress, and she gazed at the long legs that stretched out from the smock, and she looked up at the smiling face with no cowl to frame it and the crown of short, black curly hair. This freedom to look and be seen frightened her, as if it were evidence of the true being of her companion and this was too much to receive. She felt small and submissive and very young in the dream. And she looked at Africa with an awe that gradually turned to deep satisfaction, because Africa knew everything and Camille thought, "Of course, she is a goddess," and she knew she was again dreaming of the gods.

They sat for a while and then the goddess rose and seemed to grow taller and taller until she towered above Camille and then once again sat beside her and became her true size. She reached out and plucked from the ground some blades of grass and laughing turned to Camille and tickled her nose and cheeks with the grass, and it felt as when her winged god had tickled her ear with his breath. The two women, the mortal in her light summer frock and the goddess with her smile and shining teeth, gazed at each other. Camille felt the love in the eyes of Africa and felt its power, and its power was greater than anything that had been before, greater even than the love of Jesus, so great that she felt her very substance dissolving in the look that came from the wide, dark, smiling eyes. And with dissolution came fear.

As the fear came, she saw a new look come into Africa's eyes, a sharpness, and instead of love, there was suspicion. The look that had shown such loving knowledge of the other now expressed a different knowing, quizzical and coldly separate, and then the change was complete, and there was sheer hostility.

Now it was dusk, and a wind came that turned the long grass into a multitude of tiny, hissing whips and there was a howl, and the ground shook beneath her. Africa was gone, and instead she saw the shape of a figure moving towards her, far away but charging and becoming huge as it bounded closer, crushing the undergrowth beneath it and letting nothing be in its way. She saw the hair upon the naked body and the great thighs, thrusting the body forward, covered by the hair of an animal. The cloven hooves pounded the ground, and the eyes

25

became visible, piercing and fiery, and on the forehead the little curved horns above a snout and lascivious mouth with lips drawn back from the teeth. Then it was upon her. It leapt, and she awoke in terror.

Camille knew she had screamed, and her scream would have echoed through the corridors. Some would have heard. She lay uncovered, her blanket crumpled upon the floor and the sweat of her fear now turning her body cold in the night air. She reached for the blanket, throwing it over her body, and in despair she said the words aloud, "Why did she not protect me?"

CHAPTER FIVE

From an essay on J and his work. Eros and Psyche

By Dr Paul Faucher (1935)

At first, J was in a splendid mood. As light-hearted as I have ever seen him. There always seems to be something irreverent in his "joie de vivre," as if it exists in opposition to the more exacting formalities of life. It need not be in the actual content of his conversation, but its suggestion hovers playfully around him. It is not mere frivolity though, and his sense of purpose and consideration towards his patients remains second to none.

I should perhaps note something of J's appearance since I find it as full of character as the man himself. He is large, tall, and certainly, as a young man, would have been muscular. As to his age now, I am not helped in this by his enigmatic relation to it, but he is surely now in his seventh decade. Though he enjoys good food and drink, his waist still fits reasonably within the waistcoat that he habitually wears, and in which resides a heavy timepiece secured with a larger than usual silver chain. His suits are clearly of excellent quality but well-worn and often crumpled and there is nearly always some disturbance to the arrangement of his collar and necktie, so I guess that in these, his more mature years, he rarely bothers with the use of a mirror. His forehead and crown have lost the hair which, judging from that which still meets his collar, was once a sandy colour. His face has the pigmentation which comes with age mixed in with freckles which must have been a particular feature in his youth. His nose is small and rather round, and upon this there always rest circular spectacles with horn frames. His mouth too is small and to say the lips are thin would do him a disservice because of the connotations, so I would say instead that he is slim lipped. He is also always clean shaven. When seated in an armchair, which is often the case when we meet, he likes to rest well back with his legs fully extended whilst his hands remain constantly expressive.

Yesterday evening he wished to continue to speak about his patient, the young woman, Camille, but it was in the context of two of his great loves—mythology and art. It was after our supper and I should record that J's housekeeper, Madame Bernard, is a magnificent cook and our meal had been one of her finest achievements. Indeed, after the meal, J summoned her to the dining room so that we could both thank her profusely and she left us no doubt happy but quite disorientated by the enormity of the gratitude. Such is J when in an especially fine mood. Then the servant girl entered to clear the table and was completely nonplussed to receive an extension of the gratitude for which she could not fathom a reason.

That evening it was I who was meant to describe a patient. This was our manner and had been for some time. Twice a month I would visit J in his apartment in L'avenue des Gobelins to discuss my work and to benefit from his guidance. What had originally been a more formal consultation had, over time, developed into a most pleasant social occasion. We would first enjoy a meal cooked by the excellent Madame Bernard whilst conversing about general matters. I must admit that given the eccentricities and sometimes bizarre nature of some of our colleagues, our conversation would often be reduced to gossip and was no less pleasurable for it. And after, with cognac and cigars, we would engage ourselves with the more serious subject of my work with my patients.

This evening was not to follow such a familiar course. During the summer months after dinner we would sit out on J's balcony, but now the failing light and the sharp edge of a winter breeze persuaded J to move us inside for our discussion, with the compensation of sitting before a warm log fire in his study.

"Do you know your myths?"

Well, I know a few of them, and that was the nature of my answer.

J continued, "Freud and Jung make good use of them, though in different ways. With Jung they are a live issue—given that they reside in the collective unconscious, we all share them. I say to you, 'Do you know your myths?' Well, I believe that whether or not you think you do, they are there in your mind somewhere because these universal truths live through us. The Greeks and Romans gave them their narratives, and so did the Old Testament. Different races and cultures have their own stories, in different forms but with the same truths. Freud believes that they are inborn too, but it is personal history rather than universal mythology that is his medium. The myths are a bedrock of his theory though, Oedipus, of course, as the main one.

"Well, my patient Camille Beauclair, who may or may not have picked up a few of these tales at school, she could never quite remember, suddenly found herself right in the midst of them. Indeed, one particular myth took her over—like a possession by a demon—or an angel."

I had to interject here. "So your treatment of Camille did continue—even though she became a professed Carmelite? Surely not possible!"

"It's another story and I will tell you all about it, Paul. Yes, I was to be of use to her again, but tonight I want to talk about Camille and her particular myth.

"It all started with a dream, a sexual dream, which woke her up in more ways than one. It certainly awakened her sexuality, probably for the first time in her life. You remember, when she first came to see me as an adolescent girl, all she cared about was Jesus, and when she saw me later, just before she became a novice nun, it was all still channelled into religion. A pretty girl too. I couldn't help thinking that somewhere there was some very nice young man who was missing out. I nearly said it to her but, as you know, I also had a respect for the depth of her belief.

"Her myth was Cupid and Psyche, though some creatures from other myths slipped into her dreams too. That was the main one though."

J flicked the ash from his cigar into the fireplace with some irritation.

"I shan't call him Cupid! The Greek name Eros is much better. The trouble with Cupid is that it gets mixed up with all those horrible little cherub creatures flying around in Mannerist paintings. Ghastly little flying babies. And the wings! The wings of Eros should be magnificent, a vision of virility, not pathetic little things that wouldn't grace a gnat.

"And Eros is no baby—he's a god of love, a beautiful young man. Yet some artists paint him with the wings of a Dodo. No wonder the poor creature became extinct.

"No problem for Camille Beauclair though, or Sister Constance as she now was. Her Eros flew magnificently and took her up with him. Her dream had all the symbolism of sexual intercourse that we know from our patients: the liftoff, the rising height of passion and for her, a gentle and very satisfactory landing. Of course, after such a dream she could never be the same. It opened her up to her body, and her femininity rushed into her so that she became suddenly open to all aspects of her libido. Very soon after, she fell madly in love with another nun, one from Africa, and I dare say that the exotic difference was all part of what she was reaching for. In a sense, Africa rose up within her."

I was astounded by this and fascinated to know how J had continued his contact with a Carmelite nun and received from her such intimate details; the kind that are normally entrusted to the analyst only in the quiet haven of the consulting room. However, J was clearly sticking to his assertion that this particular evening was mainly for mythology.

"The thing about Psyche is that she is such a hapless girl. She stumbles from one mishap to another. Such trials and tribulations, and Camille was to play out this role perfectly. But such suffering too—it's a painful process, breaking out of the shell. Psyche is of course mortal, fallibly so, and her Eros is a god. It never goes too well when the gods and humans get together, which they often did, father Jupiter being the arch seducer; disaster was the usual outcome. I'll keep you waiting as to the end of Camille's story, but there were certainly troubles along the way.

"Anyway, Eros falls in love with Psyche and moves her into his castle. And what a place and what a life she leads. Magical, invisible servants cater for her every need and then to bring things to perfection, every night the winged god visits her, and they make wonderful love together. Just one thing though, Eros forbids her to look at him. I think we can take it that this is not out of shyness and at some stage, Paul, you and I must put our heads together to try to understand the meaning of that. It happens elsewhere—Wagner's Lohengrin does allow his betrothed to look at him, but she must not ask him his name. Same sort of thing. Of course, she does, and that's the end of it.

"Well, despite the prohibition, Eros and Psyche still manage to make love without looking at each other and then in the mornings he flies off, no doubt to interfere with other people's lives with those infectious arrows of his.

31

"Well, Psyche has sisters, and in these stories sisters are usually dangerous. Envy and jealousy of course and we know from our work with analysands just how deep-run and murderous is sibling rivalry.

"Psyche can't help but tell her sisters about what a wonderful life she now has, though she could also use a bit of human company. The sisters are madly envious. There are a few paintings of this. Our own Fragonard has done a nice decorative one of her laying out before her sisters all Cupid's gifts. One can imagine what they are thinking! They find the obvious way to spoil her pleasure. 'Surely you must take a quick peep at him when he is asleep, for goodness knows what kind of creature you are sleeping with.' She does, and he wakes and flies out of the window, and she is abandoned. The winged god, her wonderful, magical lover had gone. The magic castle went too. Psyche was left with nothing.

"And that's what my Camille feared. She loved her dream Eros so much, but her dread was that she could never keep her secret amongst the sisters in her own life—the monastery nuns. Her pagan wishes were forbidden, but the thought of their loss was awful for her. And she now had the problem too of her love for a real figure, Sister Julia, the African. The pressure was mounting."

J's cigar had now reached its end, and I sensed the change of mood in him. He looked mournfully at the dying cigar before abandoning it to the fire, as if in that moment he was sharing some of Camille's growing despair. He clearly did not wish to speak more of her that evening and seemed as well to lose interest in the tale of Eros and the unhappy Psyche. We turned instead to discussing a recent presentation by one of our colleagues on the compulsion neuroses and though our conversation was interesting and of some use to me, the zest that had so invigored us earlier had faded, along with heat from the fire. J, in keeping with his now more melancholy mood, had allowed it to reduce to barely glowing embers.

It was late as I walked home and cold; my usual pleasure in walking alone through the empty streets was spoiled by the absence of company, and I thought of Camille and the struggle she must have had, like Psyche, to hold on to her transforming young god.

I thought of J too and how his emotions were affected so deeply by his memory of hers.

CHAPTER SIX

Camille with her Sisters

Recreation was their rest from the meticulous routines of monastery life. It was also a time to converse. They lived so much in silence; inner voices responding to devotional texts or silently reciting more personal prayers. But at Recreation, there was conversation as ordinary as their cloistered lives would allow. At such times the faces of nuns would have expression, could suggest emotion, sometimes perhaps more; there could be laughter, but all feelings tempered by a chastity of thought as well as deed. A chastity within their Sisterhood that required a reservation and personal reticence, so that there was small room for intimacy and any passion would be saved for their communion with Christ.

Here at dusk in the community room she sat with the others, twenty of them now, but sometimes more or less according to the duties and observances that were in place as well as deaths and the arrival of novices. They sat in small groups. On this evening she had made no choice, but taking a remaining empty chair she was close to Sisters Josefina and Gertrude. There could never be only two together. Such exclusivity was too great a challenge to their absolute devotion to God.

As the three conversed she had little to say, and she felt a discomfort that irked and grew and which she believed she should not allow but could not resist. She looked at it and accepted it. It was boredom. She watched the face of Sister Gertrude, observing the involuntary twitch that repeatedly contracted her left cheek and eye and which was often accompanied by the sound of a spasmodic sniff. She wondered whether it had always been the left side. She thought that was so and considered the fact that in the years she had known Gertrude, and they had arrived in Cordoba at the same time, the twitch had remained and repeated with unabated insistence. Indeed, she contemplated the possibility that it may now be worse. Meanwhile, Gertrude in her relentless high-pitched voice was recounting her most recent hours in the monastery garden.

"Where I flew with my winged god," thought Camille, and the thought only served to increase the sense of banality. She chose, as a remedy, to abandon polite affectation and to study the facial contortions with a complete and open focus. It seemed to her an act of ruthlessness and another new presence in her range of feelings. She understood it to be aggressive and did not care. She was pleased, and she stared. She thought Gertrude noticed; despite her insistence in describing the growth of the monastery vegetables, there was a flash of recognition in her eyes that was immediately disowned. Camille looked down at her lap, and upon her hands resting in each other, the palm of one holding the fingers of the other and she considered how often she sat in just that way and resented it and pulled her hands apart. Sitting up straight, she stared hard across the room. There, at the other end, the eyes of Sister Julia, the African, returned her gaze.

Sister Gertrude had paused for a moment in her speech, allowing Sister Josephina to offer a few words and to thank

36

God for the rain that had been needed for their garden. It had been so very needed. For some of the nuns, the garden was a joy, a place of ordinary life and earth and seeds and growth, and a place of the spirit where God's love for his natural world could be shared and nurtured. Sister Josephina spoke more quietly than Gertrude and for a moment, listening to the soft assurance of the words, Camille's boredom receded.

"It is what I still value," she thought, and then Gertrude struck up again. She spoke of the coming Corpus Christi procession that would wind its way through the narrow ancient streets of the town. Camille remembered the thrill and the beckoning that had compelled her all those years ago as a girl to join the procession; free of her father, ecstatic with the colour, the music of the band, the singing of the priests and nuns, and in the hot air the sweet smell of rosemary crushed underfoot. And Sister Gertrude in her relentless high-pitched tones was now proclaiming the restrictions that would prohibit them from the procession. Only a glimpse from many yards away, with the outside gate opened to allow the barest look as the procession passed by. She had so loved to be part of it.

"Now, just crumbs," she thought and looking up, Gertrude with the twitching face struck her as the embodiment of restriction, and thus she allowed a new feeling. She watched it begin as a hint, then a suggestion, gathering power and identity to become, as she acknowledged, hatred.

With no concession to the conversation, she rose. Aloof and disdainful, and observing only the one figure that mattered, she strode the length of the room, and with no forethought but with absolute clarity as to what she required, she grasped an empty chair, lifting it clear of the floor and swinging it firmly into place just inches from the African nun.

Over the years they had hardly spoken; just the hushed impersonal words of ritual and observance. Now nothing was planned, what would be would be, and the words that came were clear and loud so that many heads in the room turned and inclined towards her. But her attention was solely upon the dark face, framed by the white band of the wimple and the eyes that met hers held her gaze steadily and offered no expression. Camille spoke in French. In the monastery, there were three other French nuns, and sometimes they would forego the usual Spanish and briefly share the intimacy of their own language, but this was rare. Camille spoke now as she would speak to a girlfriend met in the streets of Paris, and with no introduction, just a simple expectation that she would be understood, and she was.

"We have such little time to speak, and when it comes, we say so little."

There was a pause and then the reply in a soft contralto, "If we have little to say, it is because we are listening for the voice of God."

The gaze remained, the face open but still impassive. As communication it offered nothing.

The two nuns who had been seated with Julia had now to adjust to this intrusive addition to their group. Sister Marie Elizabeth, an elderly and arthritic woman whose painful spine required her to bend almost double and spend much of the time looking downwards, forced her head up, looking for the source of disturbance. Sister Mariana, large and from local peasant stock, tried immediately to return the conversation to Spanish.

"We were speaking of our Sister Julia's arrival, twenty years ago, and how blessed we are that she is amongst us." She then smoothed the folds of her gown to restore order where she could.

Camille ignored her. She was now aware that she was dramatically subverting the customs but cared little. Once again, she addressed Julia directly, and again in French.

"Somehow, I knew that you would speak my language," and the sound and meaning of her own words warmed and encouraged her.

"From where do you come and how did you find yourself here? Can you tell me your story? Can I tell you mine?" And then to her own complete surprise, "Perhaps we will find that we have travelled together."

In response, the look remained calm and impassive. For an instant, Camille questioned its nature, whether it was truly steady or whether there was fear at showing feeling.

Julia said, "God has willed me here, and it was He who planned my journey. He beckoned, and I followed." And there was perhaps a hint of expression, maybe humour, and the eyes widened.

"And from where did He bring you to Cordoba? How far did He travel with you? For me, it was from Paris and, yes, I believe that it was He who brought me here though there was much for me to do myself. Surely, it was the same for you."

The two other women were now compelled to only observe. There was already something different, a more personal engagement from which they could only feel excluded.

Sister Julia, seeming calm and in her soft contralto said, "My will was not in this. I was brought to Spain as a slave. I came from Senegal."

Sister Marie Elizabeth, her body bent with pain and her eyes directed back upon the floor, muttered, "Mary, Mother of God, save us from the sins of men." The large Andalusian nun, Mariana, could not follow the French and twisted self-consciously in her chair looking around as if for help. Though other conversations had resumed in the room, heads were still inclined towards them.

"And did you escape from those who enslaved you?" Camille was earnest in her enquiry and her fascination, immune to the reactions around her. The very tone of her questions, the loudness of her voice, the directness to one other that excluded the rest, the original suddenness and speed across the room to be with and to confront Julia, all defied the communal rules.

"I became free. It was hard. Thanks be to God."

Recognising the words "thanks to God," the Spanish nun loudly repeated them, trying to restore the collective.

Camille persisted. "To the outside world, I am Camille, though here I am Constance. You here are Julia, but I call you Sister Africa."

Camille looked defiant as if this latest expression of her individuality would need its defence. Still, she gave no glance to the others in the room. All other conversations had ceased. Some of the women were now even turned towards the couple. There were looks of worry, puzzlement, disapproval.

"And in Africa, what did they call you then?"

There was a pause; the eyes had widened again with surprise and this time with no trace of humour.

"Diatou."

"I love you Diatou, and I love you too as my Sister Africa."

At this moment Camille was suddenly returned to the reality of her surroundings. She was unsure for how long, but she felt that she had been taken up and transported to a different sphere. She was certain that the nature of her love for Africa would bring her punishment and penance. In her new defiance, she brushed this aside, and she tasted the power that came with it. "Who can question the nature of my love?" she thought. "I have said aloud that I love you, yet is it not that which binds us together here?" And for a moment she felt invincible.

Knowing that the attention of all was now upon her, she turned and addressed them.

"And, dear Sisters, is it not love that draws us all together and that has brought us to this place and to the life that we have chosen?"

She knew that she was now playing with them and the sense of liberation and power was still growing. She thought of her winged god and felt that through his embrace she had received his strength. She delighted in the thought and was

40

emboldened. She wondered whether he would visit her that night. She would tell him of her adventure.

"Dear Sisters, I have found a love that I thought not possible and I thank you all from the depth of my heart, but most of all I must thank our Sister Julia because she has brought with her the magic of her African country, which was unknown to us until she came. It is her gift to us."

She saw the other women struggling with their uncertainty. Any impulse to judge and condemn her for abuse of the conventions was itself subverted by her new proclamation of love. Her elevation of Sister Julia seemed to express a forbidden affection, yet could they begrudge such warmth shown towards one who was unlike any others and who, as some knew, had uniquely suffered?

And Julia, still with the impassive look, the eyes no longer wide but lowered, the body upright, remained poised. And now, as Camille looked upon her, she saw the beginnings of a smile and then the smile became distinct, broadened, and Julia who had once been Diatou, looked up and rose to her feet. The smile was wide and the white teeth flashed as she raised her head and she seemed to Camille, who sat before her, to grow and the brown cape spread wide and above it the headdress almost touched the ceiling. Sister Africa was now gazing down upon her, as a goddess in the heavens might regard the speck of a mortal, and she heard, "Come with me, Camille," and entranced, she rose from her seat to go with her, to any place that that should be. But it was not towards Julia who was now receding, moving away, her back towards her, no longer huge but smaller and disappearing. And the voice again, "Come with us, Sister," and the tug upon her arm, the hand upon her arm moving her firmly in the other direction, to the door that led to the cells; there were voices, soothing in tone but unwelcome, because she knew that they were removing her from Sister Africa and there was no strength now and no winged god came to her aid. Her only sense was of where she

41

was and where they were taking her. She felt the familiar wall of the corridor that led to the rooms in which they slept, and she knew that all of that strength, the wonderful vigour with which she had declared her love for the dark sister, was gone and the weakness that replaced it was an awful failure, like a death. And then she wondered, "Have I died? Was Africa my angel of death who came to call me?" And she decided it was indeed the case and it was why Sister Africa was there, and after all it was welcome because they would surely meet again; Africa would finish her mission and together they would travel to her death. This was her thought of comfort as she felt them put her to bed; the voices were soothing, and now she was grateful to them. There was a hand there to hold, and she felt a warm palm upon her forehead, and she whispered the words, "Blessed Mother," and she heard the words, "Bless you Sister."

CHAPTER SEVEN

The Great Silence

A knock on the door would surely have been heard by others. In the silence of the night, the softest of human sounds would travel through the corridors and throughout the old building. The walls themselves would prick up their ears and whisper to one another, "A sound—at night, whilst our sisters sleep—it is not possible."

But here she was. She stood barefoot on the cold stone floor and without light. There were no windows in the corridor; just the dark, silent, impassive walls containing the sleep of the nuns and keeping them safe. On the landing above there was a large window with its curtains slightly open, so that a thin ray of moonlight just outlined the staircase and the shapes of the cell doors against the matt black surrounding them.

The nuns called it the Great Silence. It remained as that from Compline, the night prayer, until dawn. Camille dared not make a sound, and she had brought no light; even the smell of a candle would be alien within the rest time of the convent.

She was thus motionless and stood for many minutes, feeling the chill of the pre-dawn air through the thin smock that she wore for sleeping. She was afraid. Her intention threatened her sacred vows and broached the rules of the convent, broke them terribly, but to return now to her cell would also be terrible. She looked back to where, in the dark, her own cell door must be. She knew that to grope her way back and enter the lonely little room would be her failure and the source of even more despair, but her entrance to the door before which she now stood seemed barred to her. Gradually she turned to go back, then stopped. There was a cry that echoed through the corridor followed by a whimper, and then the jumbled utterance of a voice in sleep. She thought that the words were in English—Sister Maria, the Irish Sister perhaps. The sudden advent of sound stirred a bolder impulse. Why should she knock? Turning back to the door, she grasped and turned the handle and stepped inside. The hinges were quiet, and the door clicked softly into place as it closed behind her.

Camille stood still and absolutely silent in one corner of the small cell. The window was larger than that of her own room, but the moon was behind a cloud and her eyes took time to make out the shapes of the few objects there. The main one was across the room against the wall, in the bed beneath the window. She thought, "If I was my winged god, I would step lightly across with my wings held back, and I would kneel by the bed and kiss the figure sleeping there and then I would command the window to open and fly us both out into the night."

But all she could do was stand. She watched as the moon returned from behind the clouds. The slight moonbeam touched the floor near her feet. She thought that as the moon moved minutely, slowly across the sky, the beam may become nearer and she stood still and waited. And yes, the light came closer and moved onto the wall. Still, she waited. The chill of the night remained, and the floor was cold beneath her bare feet, but she remained motionless, and underneath the window,

44

in the bed, there would be Sister Africa, though in that place there was complete darkness. She stood there for an hour, perhaps longer. She had arrived but knew not what to do, only to wait and watch for the light of the moon to reach her, as if that would bring an answer. And eventually, her whole figure was within the moonbeam, and though the light brought no warmth, it was as if the cold had receded.

Then from the darkness came a voice, "You will be ill from the cold. You will need to come here, or else you should leave."

Camille heard the sound of a blanket being lifted, and she felt all the strength leave her legs so that she floated across the room to the hard, narrow little bed and to the warm body and the arms that encircled her.

Julia pulled the blanket over them, and their faces were together.

PART TWO

SISTER AFRICA

CHAPTER EIGHT

Sister Africa's story

They whispered in French. For Camille, it was her native tongue. Africa's French was strange to Camille, sometimes interspersed with words she did not know and in an accent she had not heard. They had no clocks in their cells; the time was told by the bells that each nun in turn would ring, signalling and summoning them at frequent and regular times throughout the day. As a result, the nuns developed their own sense of time which could be remarkably accurate. Camille sensed that it was close to four o'clock. At five, the bell would ring to raise them from their beds and summon them to Matins. The sisters would emerge from their cells and she would need to be safely back in her own cell. She had just an hour.

And yet Africa whispered in her funny French accent, "You wanted to know my story, so I will tell you." She paused. "Then maybe, Sister, you will stop staring at me whenever we meet." It was said with humour and, as she said the words, Africa touched Camille's head and stroked the short, cropped hair.

And again with humour, "Bless us Sister, for we could get into much trouble for this."

"I am already in trouble." Camille breathed the words almost to herself. She remembered the details, the sensations and thoughts, and her actions during Recreation. It was two nights ago. She had remained in her cell since then. It had been a command from the Prioress, and for the moment they considered her to be sick.

"How else can they see it?" thought Camille. "Yet I see it just as a strangeness and perhaps, a new honesty."

She knew that evening had been the strangest of times for her and she had been full of fever and that the forces within her inner world had infected the outer more than ever before. The body now lying beside her, warm and manageable, had become a frightening giant then.

"We have little time," said Camille to Julia.

"And my story is long," replied Julia, undeterred and seeming not to care. "You thought we shared something. Perhaps, we shall see, but you cannot have had my life.

"My country is called Senegal. It is in Africa. There is a big river in Senegal, near to the top when you see the map, and above us is a country called Mauritania which has a lot of desert. But I lived with my family near the river in Senegal. Where we were, we looked out at the ocean. Have you heard of my country?"

In the dark Camille gently shook her head.

"There were many Arabs across the river. We had our own village, but as I grew up, I would see the Arabs sometimes come amongst us. I knew some feared them, but I knew not why, and when I asked my mother and father they told me to hush as if it was a bad secret.

"We were not wealthy, but our lives were happy. Yes, as I think back past the terrible day. When I think of that day I ask, 'How could I ever have been happy before?' But I know that I was. My family was big. I had brothers and sisters, four of each and there was me, right in the middle. And I loved being in the middle. Sometimes I felt held like that, in the warm arms of my family."

Camille, lying close to Africa, felt that she too was now in such a place.

"Sometimes, being in the middle, I could hide and pretend that I wasn't noticed; I liked that very much but not for too much time as I also liked them to notice me."

Africa breathed a chuckle and moved so that she now lay on her back, though her arm was still around the shoulders of Camille who lay on her side, facing her. She had forgotten about the daybreak, and she felt warm and lulled by the soft tones of Africa's voice and the strange accent and the occasional words of Africa's own language.

"So, if I also wanted to be noticed that could happen too, since I would shout and play, and I had all these sisters and brothers who I could make laugh or make angry."

Camille said, "I have no brothers or sisters, I was alone."

Africa paused, perhaps because she was thinking of Camille, or perhaps herself and her story.

"Our village was near the sea and we would often be on the beach. But sometimes we would go to where the trees and the bushes were. In our part of the country, we had those because we were away from the desert and we lived near where the great river joined the sea. We would play there and also gather fruit and nuts. But we knew too that it could be dangerous because we had some of those animals living there, the ones that you have in your books. You would have looked at pictures, but I really saw them."

A memory was close by in Camille's mind. It was very close, though she searched and could not find it.

"One day when I was small, maybe I had been born for seven or eight years, I was with my oldest brother. I really liked him and thought that he was wonderful. He was already a young man, and I heard people whispering about who it was in the village that he would marry, or even a girl in another village.

"We were walking quite close to our hut in a place where the trees grew close together so that the sun could not get through, and it was dark, and it was quiet too because the trees kept all the sounds very soft. Then we saw him—Gaynde—standing there between two trees so that his shoulders touched each one of them."

"It was a cat?" Camille moved a little to signal her question, but she already knew the answer—she had remembered what alluded her—it was her dream. The dream of Africa racing with a big cat.

"It was Gaynde, the lion. I always felt safe with my brother, and I thought he was like a god, so though I was scared to see the lion there between the two trees and staring at us, I believed we would be safe. I turned to him and reached out to take his hand, but instead of taking mine he gave a fierce whisper—'We must run!'—and he did; I was so shocked that I just stood there, with the lion as close to me as the door is to us."

"*Our* danger is what is beyond the door," thought Camille.

"For a moment my brother stopped and looked behind him to where I stood, and again he said, 'Diatou, run for your life!' Then he was gone. I heard him shouting to me to follow, but that was all, and I was so shocked, more by my brother leaving me than by the animal, that all I could do was stand, right there in the same place. I was crying then. I don't think that I made a noise because I thought the lion would hate that. And then he came from between the two trees and they brushed his side as he came through them and all the length of his great body. He came towards me and then he stopped very close. He was not looking at me now, but around us and he sniffed the air. He was so close that I could smell the animal smell on him and even feel the heat from his body. He was watching everything very carefully, just the way that animals need to, and I knew then that he was not going to hurt me and my fear changed to a different feeling. It was still there, but I think that now I was also excited. And he very carefully and slowly walked in

52

a circle, all the way around me and I could see that there was a special strength in his shoulders and back and I could see the muscles moving like little waves under his skin. I thought of all that power that he needed when he made his leap to kill an animal. But he did not have that need. As his body passed mine his tail moved like, I do not have the word …" "Twitched and flicked," thought Camille, "and though he looked ahead, I knew that he could still see me, and then he was once more between the trees and into the bushes, and he was gone.

"I had cried and felt dazed but also, for a moment, was in another world, like a dream.

"When I came back to our house, I walked in, and my brother was there with some of my sisters, and he looked at me and laughed and rubbed my head with his hand as if we had not seen the lion. But I knew then he was no longer the brother I had loved and worshipped and that when danger was close I had not mattered, and he had cared only for his safety.

"As I grew older, I knew more that it would always feel strange between us and though it was not clear to me yet, because I was still very young and not experienced, I had a sense of his shame and that when he saw me, he thought of his cowardice.

"I was so sad—he had been my hero. This was my shock, and it left a big hole in my life.

"My father and brothers were fishermen, like the apostles of Jesus, with their boats and nets. Later there came the time when I was starting to become a woman and by then my eldest brother had left to marry a woman in another village. I thought he must be pleased that he need not see me and be reminded of his shame.

"One day, when the sun had become low in the sky, my other brothers and my father were in their boats to catch mackerel and a fish we call Yaboy. In our sea, our ocean, we could have storms that would come quickly and be very great. The wind would start and lift the waves high into the air, and it was near the end of our season of rain when we knew the sea could not be trusted. But my father had always been a fisherman, and he knew the sea and the storms. He said that the storm was a big angry god, but he knew about his ways and that he would not be caught by his rage. So he went to fish with my brothers, though the angry god was stirring. My father was a man who always believed he was right, and he was sure they would return before the great waves came. But this time the angry god was in such a fury and rushed in faster than we had ever known before. I ran down to the shore with my mother and my sisters, and we saw their boats a long way across the water. They were not coming to the land because the great sea would not allow it, and we saw the boats thrown up into the air as if they were the shells of nuts that we crack and throw away, and then no longer could we tell the rain from the waves or the sky from the sea and the boats were gone.

"I threw myself on the ground and so did my mother and my sisters and my mother tore at her clothes and her hair and screamed in her pain and the wind took our cries and cared nothing for us, so that the sounds from our mouths were lost in the storm. We could not move, though the rain made us like we too had been in the sea, and the wind in our clothes whipped us in a way that I would know later, from a human hand.

"When we came back to our hut, the sky had cleared and there were stars that could be seen in the sky. The wind calmed, and all around us the trees and the shrubs and the huts of our village were as they had always been. How can they be like that, just the same, when for us everything had changed, and we were there in our hut, now only girls and women?

"Just one of my brothers was found, on a beach, not even close to our beach, and he was the only one we could bury.

"It was a terrible thing for my family. All the men had gone. My eldest brother was living away and the others had drowned. My mother grieved terribly—she had lost her husband and her sons. But she was also very scared and did not know how she would survive. She had only her daughters. I was not the oldest but the next in age, and I had just become a woman and my two younger sisters were still girls.

"Then my eldest brother came to see us. He had always changed for me, after the lion, but now he was more different. I saw that his body had become fat. When I was small, and I used to look at him, I loved to see the strength in his arms and his thighs. I was just a child, but I knew that these were the first feelings that we feel as grown women when we want a man."

Camille had never heard another woman talk of the body of a man and about desire in such an ordinary way as if it were so natural. But also she thought of the strength in the great wings of her god lover and then, with a chill, her dream of the horned, half human creature with its huge limbs, racing towards her and unstoppable.

"My brother came and stayed for two nights, and there was much talking between him and my mother. One time I had been outside amongst the trees gathering the baobab fruit. We were very poor now that my father and my other brothers had drowned, so it was a great help to find good food that grew near us. I had the fruit and I carried it in a basket; I was so pleased to have found the baobab, so I rushed into our hut feeling happy and proud, and there were my mother and brother sitting close together and talking, but as I entered they stopped, and my brother looked down, how do you say; with suspicion?"

"It's called furtive," whispered Camille.

"And even my mother was furtive. My dear mother but in truth, can she still be dear? My brother then looked up and smiled at me, but it was the same smile he always gave me since he betrayed me and left me with Gaynde. And I thought, it just came into my mind, he will betray me again and I knew that they had been speaking of me.

"My mother turned away and began to tidy the pots and the things for cooking that were all laid out in a corner of our hut.

Unlike my brother, she looked grim and had no false smile. I put down the fruit that I had gathered and my brother in his lying way said, 'Well done, Diatou, for looking after our mother.' But my mother said nothing and still looked away, just moving around the pots.

"It felt very strange and bad, and I did not know how to stay in the room with such a feeling. I did not feel loved, Camille, and I felt ashamed."

Camille heard her childhood name used, her worldly name, and thought of Africa's name, Diatou. She thought, "She remembers my name, from the Recreation, when I told her." And she was surprised to hear Diatou use this name and it felt good. She had not heard it said for many months. "I like my name," she thought, "and now I must use her real name as well."

"Why should I feel ashamed?" said Diatou. Her voice was husky and louder with anger, and Camille again feared that they would be heard. She placed her hand upon her friend's arm. Diatou's other arm remained around her. On a warm impulse, she turned her face and body towards Diatou in the bed and nuzzled into her shoulder with her forehead.

"I left the hut. I just turned from them and left. I knew that something bad would happen—something bad would happen to me and I knew that I was alone. My brother, the young god," and again her voice rose with anger and now also with contempt, "he had left me alone and frightened before, and again I felt that aloneness. Was I a bad person? Why should I feel like this? And ashamed. As I walked away from my home, not knowing where to go, I looked down at my body, at my legs and my skin, my feet which were moving, and this body that I had always loved I no longer liked, and it seemed to me like the body of a stranger and a body that no longer loved me.

"My brother left that day and my mother still did not speak to me. In the evening, in our small home, my sisters spoke to each other and to me, just things about the day, but my mother's face stayed just the same, without smiling. She made the food

56

for us and spoke a little to my sisters, but she said nothing to me and I too could say nothing. That evening we ate the baobab that I had brought home, but I was not thanked. I could eat nothing. Soon my sisters became quiet as well because they sensed that something very strange was happening.

"It was like this for days, until the very bad day came. My mother had sent my sisters away to do a task in our village, so that I was at home with her. And then she spoke to me again. When she spoke, I thought, just for a moment, that once again she would love me, but I knew too that all had changed. There was still no smile and she looked away as she spoke. She said that she must leave for a while to see my sisters and that I should wait there. It felt strange, but I did what she told me, for in those days since my brother's visit I had felt as if I was just in a dream and nothing was the same as before.

"And then they came for me. They walked into our home as if it were they that lived there. The same Arabs that I used to see in the village when I was small, the traders in goods. Yes, they were traders. My mother had sold me, and I was the goods.

"There were three of them, men of course, and they had their clothes that are very different to ours. Our men and women wore loose clothes that wrapped around with bright colours and sometimes the men would only wear a cloth around the waist, and the women would have their breasts bare. I was then just a woman and had breasts that were new, and I could see that the men in our village liked them and I was very proud of them, so sometimes I wore nothing above my waist. But since my brother's visit, it was different. They had made me feel ashamed and outside of their talk, and since then I wore the dress that many women wear. These men, the Arabs, wore long robes and little hats. They had beards, not like the men in my village. One of them, who I would know more than the others, had the biggest beard. It was very black and right down to his chest. I could tell that he was their leader. Does a big beard make a man a leader?"

Julia's voice was hushed as she said this, but the words were whispered with contempt and were followed by more that were in her native language. Though the words were whispered, they were uttered with such force that Camille was again conscious of where they were and how forbidden it was. She had become increasingly entranced by the tale of Diatou, told in her soft voice, and lulled by her warm body and embrace, but now the voice had become more strident. Camille also now searched for the sense of time that she could always rely on, but to her confusion and anxiety, it was gone. From the corner of her eye, she looked to that small place on the wall of Africa's cell where she knew the window was, fearing the slightest lightening of the dark square that would show the hint of dawn.

"This one with the biggest beard, his name was Kaleo, spoke French. We knew French in our village because the French conquerors of my country had been with us for many years and had taught us, and many Arabs could speak French too. Kaleo did, but not the other men. They did not think I was worth speaking to anyway. They had just come to collect their goods, their new possession. Kaleo said, 'You are going to come with us now. Your mother will have money to buy food for a year—maybe she will then sell us some more of her daughters.'

"He turned to the two others and spoke to them in their own language. I expect he said the same thing, for they all laughed. I saw that one of them was looking at me in the way the men in the village have looked since I became a woman, but the way he looked at me was different, and it was that word you told me—furtive—but worse than that. It was bad, it was all bad, and I said, 'I will not go!'"

This Julia said out loud, much louder than before and Camille, again startled and frightened they would be discovered, placed a finger upon her lips. For a while her finger lingered, feeling and tracing the outline of the top lip. "Perhaps it will sound like she is just calling in her sleep," hoped Camille. There had been many times when lying awake in her cell, she had heard, echoing through the corridors, cries, even the shouting, of sisters in the midst of troubled dreams.

"I thought then—I can escape, I can run faster than any of these swine! I will go and join the big cats amongst the trees—I will find my Gaynde. That is what I thought. I will join Gaynde who spared my life, who walked all around me and then back into the trees and he will protect me because he will want me to be free like him. It was a crazy thought, but I pushed the big bearded one away, and I leapt just like a cat towards the opening of the hut. I knew that anytime I could run faster than these men in their stupid robes.

"The man with the eyes who had looked at me in the bad way was so sure I would not escape; he knew I would try, and it was his pleasure to stop me. As soon as I pushed with all my strength so that Kaleo stepped back, bad eyes was in the doorway and waiting. He was pleased to have the chance to take hold of me. He wrapped his arm around my neck like a wrestler, squeezing me very tight and then he pulled one of my arms behind me, and one of the others took the other arm, also pulling it behind me. They forced my hands and wrists together and I felt them binding them with leather, wrapping it round and round my wrists, very tightly so that I cried out with the pain. Then he, with the bad eyes, stood in front of me while the others held me from behind. He waited for a moment and I could see the pleasure on his face and then he reached for my dress, held it and then pulled down with all his strength so that the cloth was ripped from top to bottom, and then he tore the sides away from my shoulders and stood there in front of me, looking.

"They all looked, the three of them, and they talked in their own language and they laughed, and though I did not know their words I knew that they were saying: 'We have fine goods here.'

"They took me, and I never saw my village again. It was afternoon and it was a time when I would see others, men and women, sitting near their huts and there would be children running between them. But now there were none. They were all hiding inside or gone away from the village. They were all scared, and they did not want to see this terrible thing. I thought, 'Am I the only one to not know this would happen?' Maybe, or maybe just the sight of the Arabs was enough.

"If I had shouted, still no one would help me. All three of these men had knives underneath their belts, and I could see that Kaleo, with the big beard, had a gun too. It was placed underneath his belt so all could see.

"In our Wolof tribe we are divided, and we cannot marry those who are not like us, and in my village our ancestors had once been slaves. So, amongst the Wolof, there are many who believe they are better than us and who despise us because we are the offspring of slaves. The people of my village were frightened of their history, that they could be slaves again, so they hid away in their huts and did not save me. And because of our past, my mother knew she could easily sell me to the Arabs.

"I had nothing with me. They pushed me out of our hut and across the compound; I wanted someone to come rushing out, to pull me back, to say that I was not a slave, that I was Diatou and I was free, but all were hiding. I knew then that my life would change forever."

Camille felt the warm, soft body next to her harden. Julia twisted in the bed, withdrawing her arm. It pulled the blanket away from Camille and she felt the chill of the air upon her back. She thought again of the fast-approaching daybreak and the short, bleak passage back to her cell.

For a few silent minutes Julia sat up in the bed and then, slowly adjusting the blanket, she laid back down, her arms once again encircling Camille. Their faces in the dark were now very close together, and as Julia moved to the next part of her story her voice was hushed, almost to a whisper.

CHAPTER NINE

The spirit of the cheetah

"The Arabs took me through the compound and out of the village; there was another one of them there waiting and keeping their horses, but also sitting on the ground were two women and, because they looked so unhappy I knew that they were captured too. They were not bound like me and they looked tired like they had done much travelling.

"I soon knew why they were so tired, because we were not to be the ones on horses but were to walk whilst the men rode and cursed us if we were slow. It was very hard. We were still near the sea, and I could see the seabirds and sometimes hear the waves, but we came closer now to the desert, and I knew that we would be heading to the north which was more the land of the Arabs.

"On the second day I stumbled. I am very strong, but I was tired and my foot hit a stone. The one with bad eyes, I knew his name now, Salem, was very pleased to hit me with a leather strap for falling.

"As I rose, I looked up and beyond him and I saw Tene Mi. He was far away standing on a hill and in our country Tene is almost white and, because we were near the desert, he was hard to see. But one of the other women, she was called Amina, she too was looking at Tene. Even when we began to walk again, she turned her head to look, but the Arabs noticed nothing. Tene Mi was high up on a hill and could look all around, but he was just watching us."

"What is Tene Mi?" asked Camille.

"He is the fast cat with the long body, and he runs faster than any other animal."

"We call it cheetah," said Camille, and she thought again of her dream of such a creature, with Sister Africa racing alongside.

"I wanted to run like the cheetah but where could I run? The men were so sure that we could not escape they hardly looked at us. But if one of us was slow, they would turn their horses around and ride back and curse and beat us. And most of all they beat Amina. They beat her with leather straps they used for binding their belongings to the horses. They all beat her, but Salem was the worst.

"Later, on our second day, Amina had been weeping and had been very slow and then she fell. She rolled all the way down a sandy hill and Kaleo, the leader, had to go down and pull her back onto the track. Then he passed her to Salem who beat her very hard. It went on and on and I thought he would never stop, and then Kaleo shouted at him and he stopped, but he spat at her. Then we moved on and Amina could not even dare to weep.

"Amina's sorrow made them even more cruel to her. At night time one or two of them would drag her away, out of our sight, and when they came back she would be crying and then another would take her, and it would happen again. Salem was always one of those.

"The other girl, Demba, and me they did not touch, though bad eyed Salem always looked, and he would have touched

62

me I know, but Kaleo was always there. I think they thought us the best goods, so we had to be kept in a special way.

"But not Amina. One morning when we woke, she was gone. We were still not far from the shore, but the desert and the scrub came down to the shore, and there was nowhere to hide. This was why the men did not need to bind us. That morning when we woke up, we were lying near to the beach. It had been very cold in the night, but we knew that the day would be hot. We woke and saw that Amina was not there. The Arabs were awake as well and they saw this too, but they seemed not to care; they rose and tied their blankets to the horses, just as they did every morning.

"They led off and we followed behind, but instead of following the line of the shore they moved in towards the land, to where the ground became higher, up a hill with sand and stones. We all came to the top of this hill and we could see all around and there, in the distance, was the tiny shape of a person—a woman.

"It was very small, and now the sun was rising and already very bright and shining on the sand and the stones; the light was in our eyes so that it was hard to see. But there was this tiny shape and in the shining of the sun—how do you say?"

"It is the glare," said Camille.

"Our skin is very dark, and they had taken her clothes so that Amina, in the glare, was just a little black shape against all the bright white of the sand and stones. We knew it must be her and I saw it as if she was not on the land of the desert but a great white sea and that she slowly moved up and down, just as something that floats on the sea, far away, moves up and down on the waves. Then she would disappear because of the hills in the sand, and then we would see her again.

"The Arabs spoke to each other in their language and there was laughter. Then we moved off again, down towards the line of the shore where it was easier for us to walk and easier for the horses. But bad eyes Salem did not come with us. Instead,

63

he slowly rode his horse towards the tiny black figure in the distance.

"That was a very hard day for us. The sun was hot, and though Salem had gone towards Amina the rest of us moved on at the same speed. But most of all I feared for Amina and when Salem would reach her, what he would do to her, the two of them alone in the desert and without even Kaleo there to stop him.

"That night, when we stopped, there was no Salem and no Amina, so that we said to Kaleo, 'Where is Amina? Will we see her again?' And Kaleo just shrugged his shoulders as if he did not know or did not care. But I had seen that we were goods to be traded, and though they had soiled Amina terribly, she was goods as well and they would not waste her. I knew too that because they were keeping me and Demba as new, they were giving all their cruelty to Amina.

"We have religion in my country, which most of all is from the prophet Muhammed. We also have the Christians, though not so many, and this came from those who conquered us and especially the French who also brought their language, and we learned their words. We also keep our own history and in that history are other gods and many stories of those gods and spirits. And even when we are Christian or of the Prophet, when we talk or think about the trees or the rivers or the desert and all the creatures, we still think of those old gods and of the spirits. We were taught that these are not the true gods, but they do not leave us."

When Julia spoke of the old gods, Camille knew that she must also be speaking of her winged lover and also the great horned creature that had rushed at her and scared her so much. And she was surprised because she had never thought of this before, that these, that had come into her life through her dreams, were the old gods, though she also lived as a bride of Christ, devoted and sworn to be faithful to the Christian God. Now, listening to Julia who once had been Diatou, she felt even more that she could allow this; that there need be no contradiction, and she wanted to hear more of Julia's old gods and spirits which were the same as hers though in strange and different forms.

Julia said, "There is a very special spirit who lives in the big cats. When I met the lion, it was there too—if that is what you believe." And there was a little laugh from Julia, and for a moment Camille became anxious that her friend was only joking about the spirits, but Julia continued.

"We had seen Tene Mi, what you call the cheetah, staring at us as the Arabs drove us along, so he was watching, and he could see how much we were in pain and he could see most of all the suffering of Amina.

"That night I could see that the men were restless and wondering why there was still no Salem and that he should have come back many hours ago. They spoke with their voices low, even though we could not understand.

"In the morning, very early, Kaleo left us and rode away to where we had come from. The other two stayed with us, and I could tell that we would not be moving that day as Kaleo had gone to search for bad eyes and also for Amina. He rode away quickly, and I could feel that there was bad temper amongst our captors and perhaps as well, there was fear. They had been so sure of themselves, so in control and confident with these women as their captives and their slaves. Every night they forced their pleasure upon Amina and so they felt even more powerful, but now one of them had disappeared, and they were no longer so sure.

"I hated them and I also feared them, especially bad eyes Salem. I could see only evil in him. I hated Kaleo too, but I saw that he would not join the others at night time with Amina but would sit alone with his thoughts. He was their leader and he was the cleverest. He was religious too, and I would see him pray during the day, but not the others.

"He was gone the whole day. He would move much faster now because we were not all together at walking speed and I thought he would be back before the darkness came.

"It was nearly the night time when we saw him. We saw the shapes come slowly towards us, the two horses and their riders, and I felt very sad because there were only two and so Amina must be lost or killed by bad eyes. And the riders came closer now, but there was something strange. I could not believe it—Kaleo was upon one horse, but it was not Salem riding next to him. Though it was almost dark, Kaleo's robes were pale and so easy to see, but on the other horse the rider and the darkness seemed as one and it was as if a spirit of the night rode towards us.

"When they reached us Kaleo dismounted, and it was Amina who slipped down from the other as if she had ridden many horses in her life. Kaleo did not look at her, but he found a blanket and threw it towards her so that she could wrap it around her body. It was now becoming very cold as it does at night, but there was also her need for modesty. He spoke to the others, and I could see that they were dismayed and anxious as if something strange and frightening had happened; one became angry and shouted until Kaleo gave him sharp words and then he was quiet.

"Amina came to where I sat with Demba and she did not look as before. She was proud again and also very calm. I could not understand or believe this way that she was so calm, and I said to her, 'Amina, what has happened out there in the desert?'

"Amina answered me, 'Tene Mi saw that I was there and that I was escaping and he watched over me. He watched all the time from the top of his hill, and he saw the slaver riding towards me. He watched as the slaver reached me and as he got down from his horse. He saw him with his whip and knew that he would hurt me very badly, and then he came. He is the fastest of animals, and he came across the land with the speed of a great arrow and his teeth were as sharp as the blade of a knife, and with one leap he took away the face of the slaver.

66

Then he turned to where he lay, and his teeth went deep into his head and dragged him away. I did not see Tene Mi again, but I know that he is still protecting me.'

"Amina turned to look at Kaleo who was still talking to the other men. She said, 'He knows too.'

"Afterwards, when we travelled, there was a spare horse and we all rode. There were two women on one horse and the other behind one of the Arabs. But it was not just the spare horse. There was a change. We were still slaves to be sold, but Kaleo was no longer cruel to us and would not allow the others to be cruel. There were no beatings now and never again was Amina taken away at night. It was not in the religion of Kaleo, as it is not in our religion we share here, but he knew in some way that there was an old god who was watching and that Tene Mi had killed bad eyes and spared Amina and that Amina was very close to the spirit of the cheetah."

"What happened to Amina?" whispered Camille. "Where is she now?"

"We were sold to rich families in Spain. Mine was near Seville. Amina was sent to Granada. When our boat arrived in Spain, all three of us went to different places, to our new owners. We never met again."

They still lay close together with Julia's arm around Camille and Camille on her side. She realised that her eyes had stayed closed as she listened to the tale of Diatou and Demba, and of Amina, and she opened them to look at her friend.

With alarm, as she looked at her face, she saw the beginning of daylight playing upon her features. Daylight was their danger. As soon as the bell for Matins sounded the corridors would be full of the sisters hurrying towards the chapel.

"I must go," said Camille.

"Yes, you must—and my story is not finished—and I do not know yours."

"I don't have a story," said Camille. "I didn't have a mother."

Camille stood in the centre of Julia's cell, her bare feet upon the cool stone floor. There was now a pallid square of light from the window dissipating the darkness that had kept them safe.

She was amazed at what she had just said. The full force of its meaning overwhelmed her. As a fact, she knew it to be true, but never had she felt the catastrophe of it as now, and she stood helpless in her emotion as the bell sounded, echoing through the corridors.

"Go!" hissed Julia, and with a huge effort Camille reached the door, pulled it open and in her night time smock ran through the corridor towards her own cell as fully-dressed sisters passed her, staring at her and at the door to Sister Julia's cell that remained open.

PART THREE

ISSOIRE

CHAPTER TEN

From an essay on J and his work.
A letter from the Prioress of Cordoba

By Dr Paul Faucher (1935)

One evening, in November of last year (1934), J chose
to tell me more about the strange case of the young
Carmelite nun Camille Beauclair. I was relieved that
he was now returning to the subject. We were both left in a
dejected state last time, whilst he mournfully compared the
emotional and practical struggles of Camille to those of the
mythological woman Psyche.

We had supped well and his housekeeper, Madame Bernard,
had once again triumphed with a dish that was her speciality,
a magnificent bœuf à la Bourguignonne. We had thanked her
with as much energy as we could muster given the enormous
size of the meal and the excellent wines that had accompanied
it. J is renowned for his love of fine wine, and the quality of his
cellar and I do believe that in selecting a 1922 Lafite Rothschild
he had marked this out as a special evening. Whether it was
because of his intention to speak more positively of Camille or
whether the good food and wine evoked his love of a narrative

I cannot say, but it was soon after our repast and with an enormous Partagas cigar comfortably burning, that he continued with his tale of this remarkable case.

As this also served as his consulting room, we were surrounded by his many books and against one wall there rested his analytic couch and the button backed chair in which he would sit, out of the view of the patient, but giving full attention to their free associations.

The chair was unusual for though it was button backed and in a conventional soft green velvet, it had no arms. We analysts do like to feel securely contained by our chairs. Our physical comfort is of prime importance in helping us tolerate the sometimes extreme distress expressed by our patients. A good strong chair with sides is a help and nice big arms are excellent for supporting an elbow when we are smoking. Quite where J rested the hand that held his cigar, I cannot imagine, but he did confess to me his reason for choosing such a chair.

"It is a nursing chair, Paul," he declared, and clearly this amused him. "We are, after all, nursing our patients and in their deep unconscious we are the mother feeding them from her breast. Perhaps I take the symbolism too far, but it allows me to share something of her experience."

I know as well that as the arms of the nursing mother must be unencumbered by her chair, so too must the thoughts and actions of J. He would allow no less. Only such a liberal analyst could have the capacity to engage with such an extraordinary case.

He padded across the thick pile carpet to his desk and returned with a letter. Deep in thought, he gazed at it, his fingers caressing the paper, and for such a time that I wondered whether I would ever know the content. Then at last he handed it to me. The letter, which still exists in his archive, was headed:

To: Dr Jean-Luc Javert, L'avenue des Gobelins, 5th Arrondissement,
   Paris, France.

From: The Reverend Mother, Marie Cecilia, Prioress of the Carmel-
*   ite Monastery of the Holy Resurrection, Cordoba, Andalucía,*
*   Spain.*

We know that the orders of reclusive nuns can be most restrictive and completely hive off their chaste charges from the ordinary world of, well, the word that comes to mind is, men! So, for a man, even one of J's professional reputation and status to have received this letter was in itself miraculous! But I should not mock.

The exact transcript of the letter is thus:

April 26th 1929

Dear Dr Javert,

I write in unusual circumstances, and when you have read this let-
ter, you may well understand that it has required a search within my
own soul and much prayer and caused a suffering of a kind that is
unfamiliar to me. I fear that I may be transgressing the bounds of my
position in Carmel and making a decision that will prove to be grossly
flawed. If that is so, I will have to suffer the consequences and penance
will be due and I can only hope that my atonement can protect the
Sisters in my charge, their future, and the future of our monastery
from at worst, divine retribution, and quite possibly the dissolution
that can follow such disruption of tradition.

We have a casualty in our house. There have been those amongst
us, even Sisters who have proclaimed their life-long service to Our
Lord and made the commitment of Solemn Profession, who find
the demands of our order to be too great. For them, the withdrawal
from their vows can only be attained through the most arduous and
complex process, and instead of this, there is illness. My sadness is
that there have been terrible illnesses. The human body, we know,
can be the source of the greatest obstacles to a spiritual life and the
conflicts and weaknesses that beset us can ravage that body, so that
the despairing soul can no longer continue its quest. But sometimes

73

the body remains whole, and it is the mind itself, no longer using the body as its excuse, that bears the sickness of the spirit.

We have with us in Cordoba, within our holy charge, Sister Constance. In her life before Carmel, she was Camille Beauclair, and I believe that this is how you will know her. Can I expect you to recall all those patients whom over the years you have treated? Well yes, in this case I can. All before the Lord are equal, but we are but human. I am well aware that some find a space and reside in our minds and hearts more than others. This is my own experience of Sister Constance, and I believe that I am not alone. She has been a special presence for us in our house.

In the midst of her current torment and confusion, Constance names no one but you, speaking your name as if you are the only source of redemption. If only she were beseeching Our Lord to bestow such relief. It has been our task to encourage her so, which, as a Sister and Bride of Christ, should be her natural course, but to no avail. If it were not for the fact that we have failed in this, I would not be writing to you now. She has, even to our great dismay, refused the Confessional.

There have been occasions during our history when the mental suffering of a Sister of Carmel has been so great that the removal to a hospital for the insane has been the only outcome. It has fallen upon me once before to sanction such a course, leading to such grief within myself and within our community that I never wish it to be repeated.

Knowing that we have previously been ready, as the final resort, to use the doctors of the insane asylum, I believe that we must surely be prepared now to use another lay resource for one, who, I fear, is now close to such a fate.

We have, in our records, our internal debate and response to the application of Sister Constance when she first asked to join us. This is normal. There is so much to consider when a young woman wishes to pursue a life solely devoted to Christ, a course that requires all the so-called pleasures and reassurances of a worldly life to be forfeit. No longer can she have a family to love and visit; she will never have *children; she will never love within marriage as other women do. We have these records, and there was little opposition to her admission to our order and to her joining us in this life. Indeed for five years, three of which have passed since her final vows, we have been blessed that she is amongst us.*

From her initial supplication to us we know that Dr Javert, a doctor of the mind, helped her greatly in making her decision and that she even felt "blessed" by him and that he showed much understanding and sympathy towards her calling, one that had great opposition from her family. And it is the name of this same Dr Javert that she keeps repeating, with a yearning in her voice, that shows that she, at least, believes only he can be her saving.

I believe that you must be this same Javert, with your address and practice in Paris, the city of her family and childhood. If I receive word that you will consider treating her, I will make enquiries of our Carmel monasteries in France. I trust that one may accept her into their community. Such transfers between our houses do sometimes occur, and I feel some hope that even a return to the country of her childhood may attract God's blessing. We hope that He will look down with favour upon our endeavours to help a Sister who is so greatly in need.

You will of course find this to be a most unusual case. I see no way that you will be allowed within the living areas of any Carmel house. There are extremes of illness when a physician has access but here, with no physical ailment, only a sickness of the soul, I see no access being granted. Indeed, even as I write I feel my own misgivings and question my decision to write to you.

Your communications may well be through a screen, and you will never see the patient you are treating.

You will understand that we care greatly for her and pray for the time when we can welcome her back into our midst.

Respectfully, yours in Christ.

Marie Cecilia

Reverend Mother of the Cordoba Carmel of the Holy Resurrection

There was another letter that arrived a month after this, confirming that Sister Constance was to be transferred from the Carmel institution in Cordoba to a monastery ten miles from Issoire and two hundred and eighty from Paris. The letter included a sincere apology that it could not be closer to Paris but the Prioress at Issoire had been the only one who was amenable to the plan. Accommodation could be arranged for several weeks in the nearby town. If J were to write to Mother Geneviève, the Prioress, arrangements could be concluded for him to begin the treatment, though there would be strict limitations as to any physical interaction.

"Well," said J, "When we analyse the patient on the couch, we never see their face anyway."

He walked across the room to the bureau, and the letters were placed safely back into their draw. Then returning to his seat, he resumed his favourite posture, legs outstretched with head relaxing into the padded comfort of the chair and continued with his tale of the young nun.

CHAPTER ELEVEN

The journey to Issoire

The Carmelite monastery of The Holy Mother of Bethlehem lies in a gentle wooded valley in the Auvergne, ten miles from the town of Issoire and two hundred and eighty miles from Paris. In winter swift streams rush down from the surrounding hills and through the woods until they join the Allier River which from its source in the Massif Central, will eventually rest and ease itself into the Loire. In the summer the little torrents are reduced to shallow sparkling streams, skipping over the rocks and smooth stones and swirling around tangled tree roots.

It was early summer when Camille travelled from Cordoba to Issoire and the weather had been warm and dry. For the last part of her long journey the small carriage, drawn by a single horse, had travelled away from the town alongside such a stream. Through the window Camille watched its course as it reached close to their narrow track and then sped off out of sight to quickly return, bubbling and bending its way around tree and rock.

Then it was gone, suddenly and for good. With no farewell, it slipped away amongst the trees, and the carriage swung aside on its own course into a lane that was wider and smoother until, with a command of the coachman to his horse, there was the rustling of leather harness and the groaning of springs and they came to a halt.

"We have arrived at last," said Sister Josefina.

Camille had not spoken to her companion since they disembarked from the train. Throughout the whole journey, they had been mainly silent. This was their way and the hours and reading of the office would also be maintained even when travelling. Camille was glad of the silence; she could find no worth in speaking. Josefina was there as a companion in Christ, an older nun who could take charge of the journey and speak to others when required, but Camille could only see her as a chaperone.

"They cannot trust me to be alone," she thought and felt a wave of annoyance. She kept her gaze fixed firmly upon the window.

A call came from the coachman who had descended from his seat and was unstrapping their bags from the rear of the carriage.

"We are here now, Sisters. God bless you and say a prayer for me and my family."

"Is he serious?" wondered Camille, "Or is he mocking us?"

Josefina had no such doubts. "We will pray for you and all whom you love, and we thank you for our journey."

The driver knew they preferred not to be watched. He regained his seat and, feigning distraction, leaned forward to give his pony an affectionate slap to its hindquarters.

"He looks away as a man might feel he should if he came across a woman undressed and bathing." These words were spoken quietly but audibly by Camille, and though they were addressed to her companion she was as much speaking to herself. They produced in Josefina a nervous laugh, before a gently reproachful, "Hush, Sister please," but Camille's mind was already away from there and remembering her dream.

She pictured the horned creature that had terrified her so as it rushed towards her. Now she watched it parting the reeds of a river bank to peer through and spy upon a bathing girl. Camille had learned to take these imaginings and scenes from her dreams for granted. They came of their own accord, at times with the power of a vision. She had tried to turn them into actual visions seen by the physical eye and had almost realised this. But not quite, not yet, so she was content to let them be the theatre of her imagination. And it was passive. She did not conjure them up, they arrived and departed as they pleased. Recently, she had started to think about and even analyse them, and she thought maybe this one had come because of their coach journey by the stream and all that water, slipping and gurgling between the grassy banks.

"Just the place for a river nymph to bathe," she thought, "And yes, the girl must be a nymph."

Camille did not really know about nymphs, but there had been something in a book once, and she thought that they must be spirits of the forests and the streams and this also made her think of Julia, Sister Africa, and her lions and cheetahs. She allowed herself to slip further into the scene and studied the horned creature in the undergrowth and was startled to find it gazing straight back at her.

"Goodness!" She wondered whether she had said the word aloud and looked around at Josefina. She thought that perhaps she would blush for it felt so real and she could see that she was assuming the part of the nymph.

"What white skin she has." She marvelled at how white it was, just like alabaster, and the hair was a light burnished brown, "Like mine I suppose." And she remembered the long hair that she had as a girl, just like that, like the nymph, and how it had grown so long, right down to her waist. As a young woman, the time had come for her to cut her hair shorter and she had done so with a thrill at her new status, but also sadness at the symbolic loss of childhood. And then, for the monastery, her hair had been cut close to her head. She had not minded; she had welcomed it in fact as a gesture, declaring her devotion and her resolve not to be troubled by vanity and worldly desires. But now she looked with pleasure at the naked girl with the white skin and the long, burnished hair that descended over her shoulders and rested along the curve of her spine. The girl was facing away, standing in the water just up to her calves and was gazing intently downwards.

"She is looking at her reflection," thought Camille, and she felt pleased about this. There had been no mirrors in the Carmel of Cordoba, and there would not be any here in Issoire; of that, she could be sure. Sometimes she had caught, just for a moment, the blurred image of her face in the reflection of window glass and even flickering in the water of the bowl in which she washed. This amused her—the water of the bowl, and now here on such a grander scale was the nymph, a creature of the river, standing in the water and gazing at her reflected self. The nymph was so attentive and preoccupied that she did not see the horned creature that had no interest in her reflection but only her exposed white body. Camille felt an impulse to call out a warning, but then she knew that this scene was not for her to change. And the creature, so terrifying in her dream, had become now just a little more familiar and so accepted, and from a less known and darker part of herself, there came a thrill of expectation that mingled with the fear.

Then the creature suddenly made its move. It burst from the undergrowth and with dreadful leaps was crossing the small meadow. Camille now saw it in its full form and was amazed at the sinuous energy and the power of the great strides. It was no longer crouched in stealth but had unfolded its whole body. She saw the animal hair covering the legs that thrust the body forward and felt the ground tremble at the impact of its cloven hooves. The face and chest were coarse but human, and for an instant she saw the eyes, transfixed upon their prey and glowing red.

It was the instinct of the hunted that shocked the nymph from her reverie. She turned. In an instant, her body, so gently absorbed in contemplation, became a figure of utter tension, crouched and intent on nothing but survival. Exactly together, as in a crazed dance, creature and nymph leapt. The hunter leapt towards its prey. The leap of the girl was a great dive as she drove herself through the air away from the shallows, cleanly piercing the surface of the water. In one graceful movement led by the outstretched hands, her head, body, and legs slipped away beneath the surface.

The creature landed with a huge splash in the shallows. It flailed around, tearing up mud and reeds from the river bottom, hopelessly searching for the girl who was now far away and safe in her own element.

There was a loud, sharp sound and Camille was expelled from her reverie. Josefina had exited the coach from her own side, slamming the door.

"The door of my mind is closed, shut upon me," thought Camille, and her vision was gone.

The carriage door her side was pulled open and there looking up, her face earnest and concerned, was her companion.

"My dear Sister, you have been so tired and quiet. But we must meet your new Carmel family. Are you ready now?"

"As if I was an invalid," thought Camille. Without self-awareness, she performed the movements that she had made countless times before: the stroking down of her habit, the hands then reaching up to the wimple above her forehead and around her cheeks, feeling for any adjustment that was needed. She then caught herself, "As if I fear that a strand of hair might show." And as she stepped down from the carriage, she imagined herself as the river nymph and with this came a welcome, heightening of her own senses. Resting her feet down upon the gravel, she felt enveloped by the rich smells of the shrubs and the conifer trees that surrounded them. Then, as they swung open a little wooden gate, they stepped into a garden of flowers so beautiful that she felt that this must be of the gods and that she was surely a nymph.

"How beautiful this is; how lucky you are," said Josefina. And for the first time since they had left the train, Camille answered her, "Yes, it is beautiful."

"Here," Josefina said, "you can find peace and join us again in the devotion we share."

Camille turned to look at her. She was a slight woman, short in height, and Camille was much taller so that the other nun's face was upturned towards hers. Pale, round, and open, the face was full of emotion and the eyes were moist with tears.

As if waking from a dream, Camille was suddenly returned to the reality of her life. This was her Sister in Christ, Josefina, showing her love and compassion and this was the Sisterhood and the caring that she had so deeply valued: the beautiful garden of Carmel.

She softly but audibly spoke,

"Am I lost, Sister? Have I abandoned myself?"

And Josefina, hearing a tone return to Camille's voice that had been missing since that evening Recreation when they had carried her, fevered and almost unconscious, back to her cell, was overwhelmed by a sense of salvation and wept.

"Dear Sister Constance, please come back to us."

For a moment, Camille was once again the calm, devoted nun who had graced the Cordoba Carmel; the one who, through the grace of her being, even gave succour and strength to her sisters.

"This is a Christian garden and it welcomes me. Gardens have always been kind to me and I will get better now. Fear not, my dear Sister." And she fully wished to embrace and hold Josefina close to her, but she knew that this was not their way.

The two nuns carrying their small travelling bags walked through the garden and towards the house that was to become Camille's new Carmel home.

Often as Carmelites, they would be barefooted, but for the journey they had worn sandals and the gravel crunched under the flat leather soles.

The old house was large with three stories and an adjoining chapel that was of the same style and materials, so that all could be seen to have been built together; the garden too, with its huge exotic shrubs, rested secure in its maturity. Vines and wisteria covered the walls, curling round and brushing against the leaded windows, even rising to those on the top floor. Camille observed the bars on the windows of the ground and first floor, but not at the top, though the branches of the wisteria were still robust when they reached there and right up to the eves. It was a haven for birds and as she looked there was the flash of wings, and a black shape darted from the shadows to disappear into a nearby tree.

There was a thought forming in her mind about the top floor window, the wisteria and the bird, but this was interrupted as the great weathered oak door swung open before them.

The sister standing in the open doorway was a stout, elderly woman with wire spectacles. She gave the familiar greetings, respectful and with humility, cheeks touching and hands on arms.

"Bless you Sisters, and welcome to our Carmel. I am Gertrude. Come and take refreshment, your journey from Spain has been very long."

And so Camille, stepping just behind Josefina, entered the Carmelite monastery of The Holy Mother of Bethlehem, Issoire. She felt the warmth on her back, the sun still upon her as she reached the door and then, like a slap, the chill upon her face as she entered. Outside all had been brilliant and now, as the door swung closed behind them, the change was such that she could only make out dark shapes.

Shutters were across the nearby window, there were no curtains in this Carmel, and the air was musty despite the added heavy scent of incense. The two nuns instinctively removed their sandals to go barefoot and the floor they stood on was of stone and was cool.

Gradually Camille's eyes adjusted to the change of light, to see that they were in an entrance hall of dark oak panelling with a high ceiling. She was surprised to see a painting there, a portrait of a Carmelite nun—Saint Teresa, perhaps. It was a large portrait and because of the lack of light it was indistinct. The tones seemed mainly in brown.

There was a wooden bench along one wall and a strange thing that Camille noticed. Upon the bench and at the far end, away from the slight light that filtered through the shutters, in deep shadow sat the large, motionless shape of a figure. They walked past and Camille, sensing that she must not look, heard the sound of the swinging cloth of a habit, and felt sure that the figure had risen and was following them.

Gertrude led them to a large room with white distempered walls, very clean and with two great scrubbed, wooden tables, and cooking utensils hanging or shelved along the walls. There were plain wooden chairs, and Gertrude gestured to them to sit.

"I will make you tea now, and we have soup that will just need to be warmed."

She looked at Josefina. "It is so rare for us to have visitors and especially all the way from Spain. Bless you. You will be refreshed and ready for your journey back tomorrow."

Camille observed the words only being spoken to her companion. She was the reason for them being there, yet she was ignored. "They must all know about me," and she knew that she posed them a great problem; the life of Carmel was not to be disrupted.

On an impulse, she turned to see if the shadowy figure was still there. It had gone. It was just the three of them; she and Josefina sitting whilst Gertrude bustled, making the tea and warming the soup that they then ate with thick slices of bread. Gertrude spoke in French which was natural for them all; Josefina had been selected as the companion as she too was French-born. Gertrude described her daily routine at the Issoire Carmel, and Camille knew that this was her introduction to the ways of the new house.

"I expect that it is much the same as in Cordoba. We rise at five in the morning and then an hour later we have Matins and the readings; after that is our time in solitude for prayer. At half past seven, we have Mass followed by Lauds and Terce and then a very welcome breakfast." At this reminder of food, Gertrude purposefully crossed the kitchen floor to a bench where she could cut more bread. She continued as she wielded the bread knife.

"Then we begin our work—I make sweets," and she chuckled at this. The Carmelites were known for their making and selling of confectionary and Camille had learned to do this in Cordoba. As a pleasure to the senses, sweets were a Carmelite product that surprised many lay people. Camille had also served at the little revolving wooden box that received the donation and then delivered the sweets to the outside world, so that nun and recipient had only contact through their voices and could only imagine the face of the other. Silent work was a vital part of the day, though nothing approached the importance of prayer. Prayer was the main work of the Carmelite nun. Its aim was to reach through the walls of the monastery, to be part of the healing, spiritual breath of the world.

"We have some time for prayer at mid-day, and then we have our dinner." Gertrude seemed more animated and enthusiastic each time food was mentioned. Camille wondered whether she had made the kitchen her domain and how that might rest with the principle of non-attachment.

"The afternoon depends. Some might still work, some will pray and contemplate, and it is a time too for our reading, food for our souls."

"Food again," thought Camille, who was now becoming distracted and was looking around the large kitchen.

"Vespers is at four o'clock after tea, and after Vespers we go to our cells where we can pray in solitude. Supper is at six!"

This was declared with a tone of triumph as Gertrude returned to their table with more bread and soup.

"And then, Recreation."

Camille, still examining the room, registered these last words with a wave of discomfort. It brought her back to the evening of Recreation in Cordoba. Josefina had been there, and she knew it would be in her mind too. She deliberately looked away.

"And finally, Compline, our night prayer and our time to examine our conscience."

Gertrude paused here as if that was exactly what she was doing.

"And then the Great Silence begins."

It was during the Great Silence that Camille had stolen her way to the cell of Julia, her Sister Africa, and to the warmth of their embrace in the narrow cot with the rough blankets and the soft, rhythmic resonance of Julia's voice as she told her story. And with the memory, she felt she would faint with longing and with despair at their separation.

Through the tears, there was a movement that caught her eye. It was a mouse in the far corner of the kitchen, and it stopped still under the shadow of a chair. She watched it. With remarkable speed, it skimmed across the stone floor and under the large iron oven. She wondered how it had found the space; the oven seemed flat upon the floor. They had mice in the kitchen at Cordoba, and she remembered that one of the Sisters was too frightened to enter the room, yet she was obliged to take her turn at cooking. For that Sister to be in a room with an invisible mouse was a far greater hardship than a long fast or a penitence of cold nights alone at prayer. "Such terror at a little thing and yet sixteen of our Sisters from Compiègne chose the guillotine over obedience to the Revolution, and Our Lord chose to be crucified." And then she thought about torment and the agony of the crucifixion and the many, many statues she had seen, and the paintings reproduced in the religious books of her childhood, and how the agony of Christ with the near naked, hanging body, the loincloth almost slipping from the loins, the blood dripping, the hair long and lank, had fascinated her. It still did. "It is called the passion of Christ," and it had been her passion too. She did still love the figure, her very own Jesus, but then into her mind came the winged god, handsome, also nearly naked but with a body that shined with vitality; the wings, the motor, and symbol of the freedom of flight. "How has Jesus changed to this?" And she thought of these, her two men, and how the one body was destined for pain and the other seemed only for pleasure.

Absorbed so deeply in her thoughts, she was no longer listening to Gertrude or to the conversation with Josefina that ensued. Until she heard a new voice, one that ended the drifting train of her thoughts, as if an iron door was slammed against them. It was the tone of the voice, not loud but with complete authority and absolutely directed at her. Instantly her eyes located the source, and she looked up at the figure that now filled the space before her. Deep in her thoughts, she had not noticed the silent entrance. The shadowy figure of the vestibule was now there and to Camille, still seated, she seemed immense.

Geneviève of the Resurrection, the Reverend Mother, was certainly a tall woman and the veil added to her height and the brown habit skirt from shoulder to floor increased the natural power of her presence.

Camille gazed up at her face with the unabashed fascination of a child examining a new object that had entered its world. The eyes that focused clearly upon her were a deep brown. The face was not of a young woman, yet there were no lines. Camille, now imbued with the pagan gods, saw the lips as full and sensual. "Not a nun's lips," she thought and then suddenly realised that the words being spoken to her contained no greeting.

"Sister Constance, come with me." And the tall figure turned, leaving the room with the full expectation that Camille would follow.

She did so, through a candlelit corridor, the air thick with incense and the figure leading her seeming yet more immense in the gloom, the swaying cloth of her habit lifting the air around her so that the candles flickered and shadows leapt around the ceiling and walls.

Camille, who was now imbued with the wild African spirits of Julia, thought, "Yes, she is a big black panther." And as she followed the woman that strode before her, she felt as small and vulnerable as the mouse in the kitchen and wondered, "Am I to be her prey?"

At the end of the corridor, there was a door to the left. It opened. Camille mused, "Did she push? Or did it open at her will?"

They were now in the light, but there was no sun. Her arrival to this new house of Carmel had been through the idyllic garden, and how she loved gardens, and with the warm early summer sun upon her. The breeze had been soft and restful, the scent of the shrubs nature's balm. But now she stood in a simple office that only received the plain light from a window facing north. There was a chill in the air and all was austerity. There was a large oak desk that strangely rested in the middle of the room and a dark mahogany chest of drawers by the side of a wall. There had been the one painting in the vestibule of the house, but here the walls were without imagery, save for a small wooden cross bearing the figure of Christ. Camille viewed the familiar, pain-wracked body.

The large woman sat down behind the desk, and Camille knelt before her in the expected way. Despite her initial feelings of awe, she was now more composed.

"I am Mother Geneviève. I have accepted your arrival here through my respect for Mother Marie Cecilia of Cordoba. Her letter interested me, and it implored so much I could hardly say no. You are dearly loved by your sisters there and they fear for your soul. So they send you to me, to your native France, and expect it to help. And there is also this strange request about a man."

Mother Geneviève rose, stepped across to the window and looked out. There was no flowered garden there, but a lawn stretched out for a long distance with great stone containers filled with shrubs, and both close to the house and far away there were statues. Camille saw that one was of a nymph and another, the details of which she could just perceive under a lone tree, was of a creature, sitting cross-legged, with horns and cloven hooves and playing the pipes of Pan. "Just like the creatures of my dreams," and she was astounded to see them there at a house of Carmel. But then, perhaps before Carmel others had lived there and the artefacts, so alien to a House of God, had been left behind. "Too heavy to move," thought Camille.

Geneviève turned back from the window to face Camille. She was close and towered over her.

"The request about the doctor of the mind—I find now that I cannot accept it."

In this moment Camille fully realised how great were her expectations of once again seeing the doctor, the wise friend who could understand and explain the confusion that threatened her very existence. The thought of not seeing him filled her with dismay.

"You are a Sister of Carmel. You have devoted your life absolutely to prayer and service and subjection. We want no pride here, no false selfhood. You want, Sister, a special treatment. A man to visit you and to cure your mind and with no spiritual intention. We want no man here who is not a priest."

The last words were accentuated and Camille sensed their hostility, and towards men.

"I was impetuous in allowing such a visit. Your Mother at Cordoba writes a persuasive letter. But we are servants of the Lord and exist for Him, not ourselves. I have been told of these strange behaviours of yours, these aberrations, the lack of faith that you have expressed in your actions, the outright flouting of our fundamental rules. Are these not all self-serving? You answer to God, Sister, and you are in complete abeyance to Him. We live for a truth and a simplicity of life that cannot allow, does not wish to allow, these flights of arrogance and worldliness. To undo these will be the task in your stay with us. You will see. It is this that will truly help you, and your peace and joy in service will return. It is simply a matter of pride."

The Prioress turned and beckoned Camille to stand. She moved from behind the desk and stood close to her. Camille saw that her body, though large and covered with the thick cloth of the habit, was firm and rested on a bone structure of perfect proportions.

In the midst of her distress, Camille still thought,

"How interesting. That under all that cloth, one can still sense the shape of the body." And she knew that her mind was drifting again, even in the presence of such authority. "Perhaps because of it," she mused.

She could also smell the woman who was standing so close to her. There was a sweetness to the natural smell that belied the grim nature of the words that had just been spoken.

She looked at the face and saw that the mouth was moving, so words were being spoken that she should be listening to. As she began to hear again, she judged the face and found that it was magnificent.

And with the spontaneity and impulsive response that had come to confound her Sisters of Carmel and was still a conundrum, even to herself,

"Mother, you are beautiful."

The words of the Prioress stopped. The mouth ceased to move and the lips closed together. They were full lips but were now compressed and the mouth a straight, thin, hard line.

The expression was frozen until she gave her response.

"And now you bring your pride into our house to infect us!"

The eyes of the Prioress moved from Camille to the crucifix where Jesus writhed against the wall.

"I was like you." The tone of her voice was restricted as if she wished no one else to hear.

She paused, and Camille already amazed at such an utterance, expected to hear no more. But as if it was an opportunity, unwelcome but compelling, Geneviève continued.

"My family was as wealthy as any in Paris."

She paused again, staring at the crucifix.

"My parents, my mother, had no sons, no other children, just myself to inherit it all. It was such a surprise to me, in no way expected, but I came to like it, even to celebrate it. God? Well, I cared not for him, and anyway, I was called a goddess. Men, and women too, treated me so, but of course mainly the men. Ridiculously tall it is true, but nevertheless 'the greatest beauty' and one of the richest in all of Paris. But what do these mean? Beauty, riches, they are nothing—poultry offerings that serve only to confound. I was made to see through it all. My life turned. It became so terribly cruel I thought I had been singled out for tragedy, but I know now that my catastrophe was my saviour. You will find this too, Sister, we will help you be rid of your profane thoughts. Your faith will return. It really is very simple, my dear."

With a gesture, seeming so out of character and surprising to Camille, Geneviève reached out her hand and placed it, just for a moment, upon her shoulder.

Camille had realised in Cordoba that her difference, the feelings and thoughts that had filled her soul, sometimes so welcome, sometimes so distressing, affected others so that they too acted in unexpected ways. She knew that she made a disturbance, that there was a wild force that they feared and which they viewed as both her personal tragedy and their challenge. But in more subtle ways and without conscious thought, it could change their behaviour. Mother Geneviève would never have made such physical contact with any other nun.

She accepted this and was calm as she observed it. She was calm too, as she said, whilst looking downwards,

"What was the catastrophe?"

The intimacy that was now invading the forced neutrality of Geneviève's life was challenging any denial. But she had no way to express it. Most of all, it was her body that spoke. Her shoulders dropped and a shadow left by tragedy passed across her face.

Ready for an answer Camille looked up, but the Prioress remained silent and Camille knowing her discomfort, turned away, she too fixing her gaze upon the crucifix.

At last Geneviève spoke, and now her composure was reclaimed.

"When we join our blessed Carmel, we close the door on such things. Does our life before even matter? I think not. Was it even I who lived it? It is only now that matters, Sister."

She stood with her hands clasped together beneath the great sleeves of her habit; the long, beaded crucifix rested solidly against her chest. She was, once again, a woman of certainty.

"I have something for you, Sister. This will be your one personal possession in your new Carmel. She moved behind the desk and from one of the draws she produced what seemed to Camille to be a tangle of cords. She placed them upon the desk and then carefully and methodically untangled them, pulling out and extending each of the strands, spreading them out across the surface, so that Camille saw that each of the cords was knotted at intervals and every strand was joined to a short leather handle.

The Prioress lifted the implement and slowly, as if in contemplation, wound the lengths of the cords around one arm, organising them as a neat coil. She then moved back around the desk to where Camille stood and handed her the scourge.

"This is your possession here Sister, and I expect you to use it as I use mine. It has helped beat the pride out of me and yours will do the same for you."

CHAPTER TWELVE

From an essay on J and his work. J continues: Saint Teresa

By Dr Paul Faucher (1935)

J had returned the letters of the Prioress to his bureau and was ready to continue with the tale of Camille, who was now Sister Constance. He had adopted his favourite position of comfort in an armchair before the fire. Night had descended, the heavy velvet curtains were drawn, and the lamps were turned low so that the light, coming mainly from the coal fire, cast a flickering warm glow and long shadows that merged with the darkness of the room behind us. The smoke from his Partagas curled before us, then rested poised for a moment before leaping into the fireplace and the vacuum of the chimney.

"If we are talking about Camille, you ought to know something about the Carmelites." And at that J gestured towards a small, framed photographic print upon the wall. Since I had never noticed it before and as it was impossible to see any detail from where I sat, I felt compelled to leave the comfort of my chair for a closer look.

It was of a marble statue, large in size, with the camera angled towards it from a position below. There were two figures. One, a woman in nun's attire with her robes a mass of material, flowing and descending to reach a platform of rocks upon which rested one bare foot. There she lay, collapsed, her head fallen back upon her shoulders, her face a consummate vision of ecstasy. An arm rested upon the rocks with the hand hanging freely and the fingers loose and extended. By her side, slightly above, a male figure with wings of ruffled feathers and a face of youthful beauty, smiled kindly whilst holding an arrow between forefinger and thumb, delicately poised to strike.

As I observed the photograph, J padded over to one of the many bookshelves and returned with a large, cloth-covered volume.

I dropped back into my chair, lit my cigar and gave him an appropriate, questioning look. He had placed the book on the floor and was studying with satisfaction his own cigar and the evenness of the glowing ring of tobacco burning beneath the hood of white ash.

"Clearly, you haven't been to Rome. When you do, you must visit it. It's in a church that was first of all a chapel for the Carmelites, back in the early sixteen hundreds. Very fitting. Now, of course, it's a grand place and this statue by Bernini is its greatest treasure. Indeed, a treasure for us all.

"Camille's brand of Carmelites started with her, Saint Teresa. She had her own views as to how they should best serve God—complete devotion to prayer. She was a mystic and there she is in the statue, receiving and merging with Him through his emissary, the angel. In goes the arrow, right into her heart and there she is in a trance and in ecstasy.

"Some might say that this is only to do with some fantasy of the sculptor. But he based it on her own words."

Here J reached down and, thumbing through the pages, found the extract to read.

"I saw in his hand a long spear of gold, and at the point there seemed to be a little fire. He appeared to me to be thrusting it at times into my heart, and to pierce my very entrails; when he drew it out, he seemed to draw them out also, and to leave me all on fire with a great love of God. The pain was so great that it made me moan; and yet so surpassing was the sweetness of this excessive pain, that I could not wish to be rid of it."

I interjected. "But surely …"

J cut me short.

"Yes, of course, we are psychoanalysts, and we don't even need Freud for this, though it helps. It's a phallic penetration leading to a monumental climax. But the Catholics don't view it that way, and they have a point too. Anyway, however you see it, there was a process of conception and birth, because out of this experience she founded a new order of Carmelites known as the 'Discalced.'"

I did not know the term.

"It means, simply, without shoes. It sounds more like a nickname; it is really, but it stuck. And it's a very good name for them because it gives you the essence of their creed. Complete austerity, bare feet, hard beds, no contact with outsiders, self-mortification, and lots of prayer. Everyone knows the nuns' dictate—poverty, obedience, chastity—which sounds enough, but if it's possible to take that further the Discalced Carmelites do.

"I understood young Camille's wish to join the barefoot ones. To her, it was the purest way possible. If she was to devote her life to Christ, this is how it should be—complete devotion and innocence. Think, Paul, what an amazing thing this is. You and I will rise tomorrow; we will choose our breakfast, perhaps even the time we take it. We will see our patients and usually we are well paid for it, and those fees keep us warm and comfortable with good wine and the best seats at the theatre. And we will have in mind our plans for the summer vacation. We are both single men, but I have fond memories of women I have known, and you have, well, I don't know what you have, and it's none of my business, but whatever it is, it's your choice!"

Perhaps J, who indeed knows little of my private life, was savouring his own memories as he took a deep draw from his cigar and exhaled a rich cloud of blue smoke in which I imagined seeing exotic and erotic visions. The cloud spread, paused, and then followed its predecessors up the chimney.

"But for the Carmelite nuns, there is no choice. Everything is completely regular; discipline prevails. There is no alternative to this and they take their vows, this is how they will live until they die, it is a truly remarkable thing. I admire such dedication and devotion. To be honest, Paul, I think I envy them. In comparison I see myself flitting around, devoted instead to the moment and the whim."

I should state now that I am writing here a considered account of a man of great stature who, in his own way, has made his own devotion to the understanding and care of the human psyche. Hardly a so-called "fly by night". However, J was clearly enjoying, in a playful manner, comparing his lifestyle with Camille's.

"Think, Paul, of the consternation that was caused when Camille, Sister Constance, began to be increasingly inconstant. This was contrary to all these rules, the obedience, the dedication to Christ, the absolute routine.

"And manifestly, it all started with her Eros dream. He dropped down beside her, breathed upon her cheek and all that young woman's erotic sensibility, her libidinal sublimation into service and prayer, turned carnal. Camille discovered she had a body—and then she had a breakdown! This does not surprise me. Make no mistake, this young woman was not mad—in no way—but she did have a deep wound in her psyche, I'll speak more of that later. And she was very sensitive and full of feeling. Really, the victim of her own qualities. You see, her all-important attachment to monastery life was utterly torn by this fresh self-discovery, and it was more than she could manage. The attachment then went straight on to the African nun, but that became erotic too.

"Camille began to behave in ways that broke the order of the monastery. She refused confession and failed in duties and observances. She was distracted, dissociated, and then she became physically ill with a fever that went on for days. It was during the fever that she was repeating my name and that's when the Prioress wrote that letter to me. After the fever she became calmer but still seemed in a world of her own and then she was accused of intruding into another nun's cell, the African's no doubt, during what they call the Great Silence. It's a lovely term isn't it, very evocative, it lasts between their final observance of the evening and the first of the morning, and it has to be that—absolutely silent.

"Penitence usually follows such misbehaviour, but Camille remained unrepentant and was also becoming increasingly mute. The Sisters truly cared for her, but there must have been some relief when she at last left for the monastery at Issoire—and to see her doctor!"

J paused for a while. There was some re-fuelling of the fire and then the need to replenish our glasses. He rose from his seat and a huge shadow leapt across the ceiling as the fire revived with a burst of flame. Leisurely, he moved to a far corner of the room, his shadow merging into the darkness. He returned to the light, a decanter in his hand and poured the brandy.

"But we must keep sight of Camille and the great myths. They had, after all, invaded her dreams and started all her troubles, and most of all Eros and Psyche. In the myth, we have already seen the problem of the sisters. For Psyche, it was siblings who were deeply envious and would ruin her bliss with Eros. But for Camille too, the sisters were a great problem. A discovery of her pagan, winged god would end in disaster. The nuns would decry such fantasies as blasphemous. To Camille, her trusted and beloved Sisters in Christ became a threat to all that she was now holding dear—the winged lover of her most private dreams and her love and desire for the African who resided tantalisingly in her cell just a few doors away. She kept it all to herself and confessed nothing, but whenever she looked at the images of Christ in their chapel she thought of Eros. To counter this she forced herself to think only of Christ's suffering, but there he was, almost naked on the Cross, completely physical in his agony, and she began to desire him too. When the sisters knelt together in prayer, she could only think of the African, Sister Julia. From where she knelt, she could watch her all the time, always under cover of prayer, and always fearing discovery.

"In the myth, the sisters are a temporary problem. After their destructive meddling, they horribly destroy themselves; they are victims of their own stupidity and envy. But Psyche has to face a far more formidable foe—the mother! And so did Camille. For Psyche it was the mother of Eros, the great goddess Venus, furiously resenting any love her son might have for a mortal, and to boot one that even challenged her supreme beauty. And for Camille, it was her new Mother Superior at Issoire who furiously resented just about everything. She was to be a formidable foe indeed."

J had become considerably energised by his subject. He poured more brandy into our glasses and then moved his armchair slightly back to accommodate his stretched legs that were extended before a fire which now burned with its own enthusiasm. I believed we were in for a long and fascinating evening.

I should remark here, for those who might come to read my account of J and his professional life, that it may well seem that it is turning instead into a story of the trials and troubles of Camille Beauclair—Sister Constance. But that is as it may be. This case was so savoured by J and was so close to his interests and researches that it overshadows all else. And I must confess that though I had expected to be writing more about the machinations and development of our Paris Society, I was as happy as J to be taken up instead with the life of the nun whose journey through her young life reflected so many of the conflicts that we, as analysts, try to understand. I had gathered too that there was to be reference to an esteemed colleague. Princess Marie Bonaparte, one of our founders and one so close to Freud himself, was to play her part in Camille's story.

But for now, I rest my pen. There was, after all, to be no more Camille this evening as J, perhaps in a spasm of professional guilt, decided that we really should discuss two of my own patients. Despite my disappointment, I had no grounds to protest. No doubt, we will visit Camille at our next meeting, and there is the prospect of hearing more of this ominous new figure, the Prioress at Issoire.

PART FOUR

GENEVIÈVE

CHAPTER THIRTEEN

Mother Geneviève's story

The inheritance

The armchair of plush, purple velvet was more comfortable than any she had known. Geneviève eased herself into the seat and could hardly believe it was allowed as if expecting some retribution for tasting such luxury. But it was allowed. She had been ushered into the room. The pomp was outside her experience. That morning an elegant carriage had arrived for her at the convent home with a footman in full regalia who, with great decorum, had helped her to her seat. The carriage smelled of leather and perfume. The horses were completely black, four of them, and they had raced through the countryside. She had ignored the window, being so deeply involved with her thoughts and still astonished and confused by the summons that had brought about her journey. But as the carriage neared the city and buildings began to replace trees, she looked out.

She had only visited Paris once before. The trip had been organised for the girls by the convent, and they had spent a morning at the Louvre, walking round in an orderly fashion, chaperoned by the nuns. She wondered whether the nuns had attempted a route that would only pass by the religious paintings. There had been glimpses of other scenes as they hastened through—blue skies and muscular men and the white breasts of plump women. But one painting could not be avoided. It was on their main course through the gallery. Another group of children had gathered around the far doorway causing a congestion that left her group, with their two nuns, to unavoidably contemplate a very new experience. The painting had an unusual oval shape and its strong colours evoked another world, so different to the small, dark and heavily varnished scene of the crucifixion that hung in the hall at the school of their convent home. A man and a sleeping woman were in a wooded, mythological scene. Behind them, the sun was low beneath a turquoise and golden sky. Both figures lay upon the ground amongst the trees. The man leaned over the woman and lifting the cloak from her naked body, he gazed upon the white flesh which radiated light against the dark background of the undergrowth. She had golden hair and her skin was white whilst his was brown, and little horns peeped through the dark hair of his head. Geneviève was then thirteen, and she looked with fascination and trepidation at the prospect of her own womanhood. Already, her body was changing, and things had been said in hushed reverent tones by the nuns. She had come to understand this coming metamorphosis as the start of a service, that to be a woman was to be in abeyance, to have a fate without a destiny. Yet she saw a dormant power in the body of this female. She was not sure whether to look at the woman or at the man. They both shared the state of nakedness, but otherwise there was only difference. She had hardly known any men. She scrutinised the painting, knowing that any moment they would be moved on. The other girls whispered and giggled. Something instinctively warmed her body and flushed her cheeks, and she could not tell whether this was pleasure or pain. It was no easier to look at the woman than the muscular man, though the sensations were different. Did she like the pale flesh? Is this what she would become?

"I suppose, I must," she thought, though the figures of the nuns, who were her teachers and guardians made such a different prospect. Geneviève had not seen bare breasts until one of the girls, mature before the others, had offered hers, proudly, for her friends to see and even to feel. Now Geneviève was developing herself, but the female figure before her, in the painting, and in such an opulence of femininity, filled her with awe.

"Come girls!" And the pathway now clear, the group was whisked on to other pictures and themes, yet for Geneviève there was only her response to that one painting, which remained throughout the day and for days to come. That day, in front of Watteau's "Satyr and Nymph," she was born into a new body, and its sensations were strange though not unwelcome.

These were her memories as now, eighteen years old, the carriage bore her speedily into the heart of the city. All around, there was a bustle of life and livelihood that she had never seen before. It excited her. It was a crisp, bright day in spring and as the carriage, now sedately, moved along a grand boulevard she felt a wave of happiness.

Suddenly the coach swerved away from the road, so that her body was squeezed against the padded wall and she felt the pleasure of allowing the force of the movement and the feel of the leather through her clothes.

They came to a stop and from the outside the door was opened. The same footman had descended from his seat above and lowered the steps and then stood to attention. Geneviève set her feet upon the gravel of a large courtyard. Another stationary coach, equally black and glistening, was nearby. A different footman approached her and bowed.

"Madame, the Countess sends her welcome and is so eager to see you again. Please follow me."

At the mention of her mother, the Countess, Geneviève physically felt her excitement change to anxiety. Her mother was a stranger to her, yet in her mind she was a figure of grandiosity, a status all the more evoked by her remoteness.

The house she now surveyed was everything that such a figure would require. The long driveway had led to a courtyard that was at a slight angle to the house, so she could see that behind it were silken green lawns that ended in a cluster of tall poplars. The facia that they now approached seemed to Geneviève to be full of huge glistening windows; even those on the third and top floor of the house were large and such a contrast to the small and forbidding shuttered windows of the convent and its school. The eves reached up into their highest point at the centre of the facia, perpendicular to the main entrance, and beneath them was a rococo frieze: a tangle of cherubs, bare-breasted nymphs, flowers, grapes, and foliage. On each side of this were identical huge heads of male figures, horned and bearded, all to remind Geneviève of her visit to the Louvre. Indeed, as she surveyed this great house, she felt now as she had then: a sensation in her body which she knew brought her closer to becoming a woman.

They walked across the courtyard and as they reached the wide steps before the entrance, one of the great double doors swung open and a new figure, a man in his late twenties, immaculately dressed in black, stood waiting. His greeting was made without the need for his eyes to meet hers, and with complete decorum.

"Please follow me, Madame. The Countess will join you soon."

It was he who had led her to the room in which she now sat, slowly allowing the luxury of the purple velvet chair.

She was facing a painting that she would come to know as a work by Fragonard. It caused her to think again of the visit to the Louvre when she was thirteen and the transforming effect of the painting she had seen there. Though she had little experience, she could see a similarity between the Louvre work and the one she was now viewing, though the subject was not of mythology and the voluptuous nudity was replaced by a delicate breast that peeped out above a lace chemise.

Paintings lined the wall, and the room was of such an enormous length that those furthest away were indistinct despite their size. Facing the paintings, were immense widows dressed in ornate pelmets, and heavy curtains of pink with grey and black motifs. The windows looked out upon the lawns and close to the house, the geometric patterns of perfectly kept flower beds.

"Not a petal or a blade of grass out of place," she mused, and compared the view to that from the windows of the convent school: a mass of buddleia trees and brambles that were cut back just once a year by the gardener who, she noticed, had always kept his eyes averted from the classroom windows and the girls sitting within.

There were six windows along the wall of the great room and six paintings that faced them. At the far end were double doors which now were thrown open. There again was the elegant dark-suited figure who, having entered, stood expectantly to one side.

Geneviève watched and waited but no one emerged. For a moment she thought that it must be an invitation for her to exit and she began to rise, but then through the door, slowly and with obvious pain, came the tall figure of a woman whose ill health was unmistakable. So too was her effort to mask her disability. Despite the ornate stick that steadied her she held herself erect, the head proudly poised above the shoulders, the neck still long and the gaze, even at that distance, directed immediately at the girl in the purple chair.

As this formidable figure moved slowly and resolutely towards Geneviève, passing each of the paintings, the dark-suited man withdrew, closing the large mahogany doors behind him.

Geneviève had only seen her mother twice before. The first was a vague and distant memory, she was probably three or four years old. The impression had remained of a figure of awe and magnificence. A beauty, apparent to even one so young and the clothes were of such rich colours. She remembered especially the pale blue of the dress and how it seemed to reflect the light and the sound of it rustling at every movement. And the abundance of jewellery: the necklace, the rings and bracelets that twinkled. And she wondered whether they had also tinkled, for it seemed to her that they made the sound of little bells. It was such a contrast to the plain black and white of her other mothers, the Sisters to whom she had been entrusted from birth. Her mother's orbit had entered her quiet and plain universe like a brilliant star. She had been told then that this was her mother, but she had no memory of words between them. Perhaps there were not any, and the visit was brief. Within minutes, the magnificent figure, the bright star, had left her childish narrow skies and all that was left was an empty space filled with darkness. She remembered that they allowed her to stand and wave as the carriage departed and that she had waved so hopefully and received nothing in return, just the blank shape of its rear, gradually receding. Over the years, the empty space became an accepted part of her being, lodged painfully beneath an otherwise natural vitality.

Now the figure of her mother, moving resolutely and slowly through the great room, was halfway towards her.

She thought of the second visit. She had begun to see the bodies of men and women through new eyes as it was soon after the school trip to the Louvre. She was ushered into a room where her mother was waiting, standing by an empty fireplace.

The nuns lit no fires until the advent of winter, and this was a cold autumn day.

Her mother was wearing furs, but the front of her coat was open, and Geneviève gazed at the graceful bare neck and the opulent bosom that was contained in the emerald green silk of her dress. The sensations of the Louvre painting returned, and she stood there, stupefied.

Her mother had asked her questions: "Was she happy? How were her lessons? Was she behaving?" The questions soon ran out and the woman, her mother, clearly had no patience for silence and soon called for a nun to escort her away. As she left the room, she leant towards her daughter and placed cold lips upon her cheek. Geneviève remembered the rich floral smell of the perfume and heard again the rustle of the dress and the tiny chimes of the jewellery.

And now she was here again, painstakingly stepping towards her, and the years since had ruined her. "She has been ill," thought Geneviève, and her surprise and discomfort at this left her sitting mute and still.

The Comtesse de Bolvoir was now close enough to speak.

"Do you not rise to greet your mother? Have the nuns taught you no manners?"

And then she was there, standing in front of her daughter and Geneviève rose, uncoordinated, confused and embarrassed and utterly unable to say anything.

But nothing was necessary or expected. The Countess moved the last few steps to an adjacent chair, steadied herself with her stick, and slowly and painfully sat down.

"I'm dying."

This was not addressed to Geneviève but to the window. The Countess gazed out at her manicured lawns.

"This is why you are here. I have utterly neglected you, I know. My selfishness knows no bounds and this I know too. Somewhere in my heart I may have loved you, but you were

111

sent away at birth and that was it. Perhaps we are both victims. Paris loves a scandal too much and I was too proud."

Geneviève was still standing, and her mother turned towards her.

"Sit down girl."

She obeyed.

"My God, you are big. I'm tall, but your father was very tall; you've got it from him, and the red hair. Don't ask me about him. I loved him only for days, but I liked tall men, and he had good looks. You have too, so you'll do well, I've known artists who'd sell their soul for a woman with your hair."

She ended the scrutiny of her daughter and gazed instead through the window. Geneviève could only look helplessly at the woman who was now dictating her future.

"You will succeed me as my only heir. My illness will kill me within months. My dear, you are about to become one of the wealthiest women in Paris. Possibly the wealthiest. All that poverty of the nuns, you won't know what to do with yourself, will you? Anyway, he will help you." And with her head, she gestured towards the double doors through which had exited the elegant, dark-suited man. The audience was over.

Within the society of fin de siècle Paris, Marguerite, Comtesse de Bolvoir, had attained both fame and notoriety. Her arrogant beauty and aggressive intelligence had eased her entry to the most sought-after inner circles. She was a frequent guest of the great neurologist Jean-Martin Charcot, both at his home and his clinical sessions at the Salpêtrière Hospital. His work with hysterical patients under hypnotism suited her tastes for the uncanny and the alternative states that so interested many of her artist friends. Stéphane Mallarmé, the finest poet in France, kept a seat for her, close by him, in the tiny flat where he hosted his salon. And there were as well her many affairs, along with dark rumours of her service to a high priest of the occult.

Geneviève knew none of this and it was beyond her imagination. Yet after her brief visits, something of the aura of her mother was left behind to inhabit a place within the girl's psyche. A certain knowing with no name or words to describe it that just sometimes, on restless nights, could dictate the mood of a dream. Such was the legacy of Marguerite de Bolvoir to her daughter, along with a mansion in Paris and a fortune.

Marguerite slowly lifted her body from the chair and stood, searching for whatever slender remnant of faith she might have in her limbs to support her. Painfully, she took the first steps on the long journey to the door before pausing, without turning, to speak again to her daughter.

"Morel will show you to your room. Welcome to your new home, Geneviève."

Was this the first time her mother had used her name? It was welcome but felt strange; as when one is called to by someone unseen and in the moment, unrecognised. Then there was just increasing distance; an interminable period as the ill woman made her determined passage past the huge paintings whose figures frolicked or posed contentedly, fixed forever in a moment of time that mocked the mortality of she who had owned them. And Geneviève became lost in time, unable to move and without autonomy, simply a slave to the situation that now overwhelmed her. She knew that she could only respond to a summons and so waited. She saw the heavy mahogany doors open and the figure of her mother dissolve into the shadows beyond. The doors closed, and she was alone and in complete silence. The only movement was from a fine aura of dust as it passed through a pale ray from the sun that, for a moment, escaped the cover of a cloudy sky and slanted through the window onto the muted colours of an oriental rug.

Still she waited, and in the strangeness and stillness of her surroundings she lost even the familiarity of time passing, since she could no longer sense time, and it felt that the passage of

113

her mother to the doorway had been eternal and though the doors had now closed, time remained without limits.

And then the summons came but from a different door, much closer to her at the other end, and it was the dark-suited, elegant man.

"Madame, the Countess has requested that you should be shown the full extent of the house which is now your new home. But first, if I may show you to your rooms and introduce you to your personal maid who will help you to unpack. My name is Morel and I am the secretary to your mother, and my service is also to you in any affairs in which you may need my assistance. I am nearly always at hand."

Morel turned and made towards the door and the dust that had so slowly drifted in the light and in the perpetual moment, swirled and dissipated, and Geneviève rose, finding the security of the strength of her legs as she paced after the secretary, attaching herself with relief, to one who knew the way.

CHAPTER FOURTEEN

The young heiress

Édouard Morel, the secretary, was a faithful servant. Geneviève had no doubts. He had watched over the affairs of her mother for the last five years since the death in 1893 of the elderly Count. Before, he had been a talented young staff member at the state offices of the Count, an auditor, with special responsibilities and his duties had sometimes required him to visit the grand house.

On occasions, the Countess had, as she put it, "borrowed" him from the Count. The house staff, imbued with tales of her amorous reputation, were eager to find evidence of such exploits with the elegant young Morel, but to their disappointment, found none. Instead, the Countess simply valued his care of her finances, particularly in respect to her substantial collection of art which included many works from the so-called Symbolist movement. He was no expert on art, but was finely tuned to financial trends and to good sense and would help order her affairs and undertake calculations with ease and calm. The minutiae of such details were an irritation to the Countess, but on occasions they imposed themselves as a requirement. At such times she found that a simple advisory liaison with Morel would bring relief. When the Count, or as she referred to him, 'My ancient husband,' slipped from the disabilities of old age into a senility of mind and body and then into complete torpor, the Countess took charge of all the finances, before handing them over to Morel. On the death of the Count, she gave Morel his own quarters in the house and made him her private secretary.

In the last weeks of her life, the Countess was racked with pain. Geneviève was completely unable to comfort the mother who had deprived her daughter of any such care. She could only look on as doctors came and went and as Morel slipped into her mother's room with the laudanum which, even for a woman of such resilience, was now essential.

In the early hours of a June morning in 1898, Marguerite, Comtesse de Bolvoir, died. Geneviève, suffused with guilt at her inability to even observe the body and having not seen her mother for five days, could only look on as Morel made all the arrangements for the funeral. At the funeral itself, she carried out the actions that were required of a daughter, but without sentiment and completely without grief. The black hole that had formed in this otherwise vibrant young woman could not be emotionally filled by the passing of a mother whose absence was its initial cause. Geneviève, though shocked by her mother's death, felt empty.

The burial was made easier for her as it was short, plain and without oration or any religious ritual. The Countess was known to have a life-long contempt for the Christian Church and had made sure that it would have no retrospective claim upon her soul. And few were there to witness the body's laying to rest. Due to deaths and infertility, the Bolvoir family had rapidly diminished, and in attendance there were only two nieces of the old Count along with a small number of those who, as representatives of wealthy and titled Parisian families, had decided they should be present.

There were as well, two elderly men whose appearance seemed different. There was an air about them, perhaps of informality, that caused them to stand out, though within the gathering they stayed at the back as if outsiders. Geneviève found something appealing about them, she knew not why, and her interest was raised further when Morel whispered in her ear, "They are artists."

As the gathering dispersed and condolences were given, the two men took their turns to engage her. The first was very tall. Geneviève found some comfort and an unusual warmth of feeling in being able to look up at him as she spoke. He seemed kind and asked her about herself and her plans, a question that was difficult to answer as she had none. He was not perturbed by her uncertainty and conveyed his belief that she would make the most of her opportunities as a young heiress in the world's greatest city. He departed, leaving Geneviève with the sense that something more should have passed between them.

She was then approached by the other "artist", a man whose good looks were not diminished by age and whose elegance was articulated by the curl of his fine grey moustache. Though she liked the twinkle in his eye, she sensed a certain physicality, an erotic knowingness, that caused her unease and brought back the memory of her mother's visit to the convent home and her open fur coat with the fullness of her breasts in the green silk dress. The man introduced himself just as Félicien and said that her mother had been a champion of his art and that she had also been his friend and that he would always love her. It was the first time that Geneviève had ever associated her mother with the word love. He added that he had travelled from his countryside home in Corbeil and that due to his ill health, was unlikely to come to Paris again.

Arrangements had been carefully made for Geneviève's fortune to be held in trust for three years until her maturity at twenty-one. In the main, Morel administered her affairs, but he was keen to encourage her involvement. Twice a week they would spend from mid-morning to lunchtime sitting together, first of all in one of the reception rooms and then later moving their meetings into Morel's office. It was easier as all the papers were there, but Geneviève also loved it snugness, especially in the winter when, with a fire fully burning, it became the warmest room in the great house. It matched the warmth of her feelings towards him. She had never known the care of a father, and it was a pleasure to receive guidance and advice from a man who had such a reassuring presence.

By nature, Morel was not outwardly warm, but she knew that he was there for her completely. He seemed to have no others in his life and to exist for the maintenance of the house and family estates. Except for one exceptional difference: Morel was a swordsman. On three early mornings a week he would journey to la Salle d'Armes Coudurier, his fencing club in Saint Germain, and remain there for two hours, returning in time to resume his duties and on some mornings, for his meetings with Geneviève.

Morel's influence spread wider than financial affairs. Geneviève increasingly realised that he had a remarkable ability to notice everything and this was matched by a power of memory which seemed to reduce the keeping of records to irrelevance, though he remained fastidious in such matters. But the power of observation in the moment was his most striking ability. There were many occasions when he would point out the slightest aberration in the maintenance of the house. He would register the wilting of a single bloom in a flower display and immediately have the servants change the bouquet. His observations were even directed at the person of his mistress. Geneviève need never be concerned about a failure in her appearance. The absence of even the smallest button from a coat or sequin from a dress would be noted and reported. And for Geneviève, this was completely welcome. The young woman, who had spent her whole life in the care of nuns and who had worn the simplest of clothes and lived the most sedate of lives, was joining the highest echelons of Paris society and was increasingly feted due to her intelligence and beauty. She needed Morel not just for the accounts but for his vision of her new position. For Morel, it was his responsibility to maintain his mistress in the high status she had inherited. Fashion, style and the more arrogant requirements of that position would not normally have been his concern, but this was for the wellbeing of Geneviève. He carefully registered the latest fashions and trends and calmly and respectfully offered her his recommendations, which she nearly always followed.

Morel, though still relatively young, had become the ordering father as well as the containing mother and his vision of her as the most exceptional young woman in Paris was a substitute for an actual mother who could inspire by example. With such help, Geneviève thrived.

Paris responded with growing expectations. There were the formal balls, which were splendid occasions that required extensive training in dance, the lessons all arranged by Morel. There were the soirées, the salons and the dinner parties. Here Geneviève easily held her own and even began to excel. Though lacking in experience, she had a charm, wit, and intellect that claimed a place within the most selective of address lists.

In sexual matters, Geneviève had little experience though she had enjoyed the caresses and been brought to climax by several of the girls at the convent home. The example and prohibitions of the nuns barely suppressed their adolescent libido. But her most powerful experience had been with one of the Sisters.

She had only noticed Sister Brigid at services in the chapel, or whilst passing in the corridors. She was tall and slim, though not as tall as Geneviève, who at sixteen was already the tallest in the convent and its school. Brigid's face was very pale and without expression, though her eyes were clear and grey and sometimes, when the light was a certain way, they would be green, and this was how Geneviève knew her. Otherwise, she was of no consequence, until at the age of sixteen she entered an English class for which Brigid was the teacher.

She now discovered the Sister was of Irish descent, though her French was fluent. Her voice though was flat and as inexpressive as the facial features framed by the cowl and the headdress. But the grey-green eyes remained clear and often rested upon Geneviève. The parentless girl, so pleased to have adult attention, welcomed this and was filled with pride when, one day at the end of the final lesson, she was asked to remain in the classroom.

The nun quickly pursued her intentions. There was a small room, leading off from the classroom, in which textbooks and paper were kept. She took hold of Geneviève's hand, a gesture that, though unexpected she found pleasing, and firmly led her into the anteroom. Without a word but with a gaze from eyes that now seemed only to be green, she stripped the girl of her clothes, down to her stockings and shoes. Looking intently and impassively only at Geneviève's face, she loosened her clothes, allowing the main part of her dress to fall away though the intricate headdress remained, and with one hand upon herself and the other upon Geneviève, she brought them both to climax.

The girls in the convent were used to submission. The nuns themselves lived such a life, submitting unquestioningly to the rules of their order, and in turn expected obeyance from their young charges. It was in such a spirit that Geneviève, surprised and disarmed, accepted the actions of Sister Brigid, the results of which, though surprising, were unquestionably pleasurable.

But it was the action that followed that was to make a lasting mark upon the girl's life.

Sister Brigid corrected her dress but gave no indication for Geneviève to do the same. The clear eyes that for just one moment had flickered over the body of the girl were once again turned upon her face. She said,

"Wait here."

She then left the room, returning immediately with a thin switch of the kind that was always kept in classrooms. There were nuns who used them to discipline the girls, usually upon their hands, and there were nuns too who never used them and use became far less frequent as the girls grew older.

With no hesitation Brigid struck Geneviève across the stomach, then the shoulders and breasts, so that she screamed and turned away, crouching in a corner of the room. Then, with meticulous accuracy, she continued the blows upon her back and buttocks.

It occupied just a minute of time. Geneviève, so much in shock that there were no tears, remained crouching, expecting further blows. All was silent. Eventually, she dared to look round and found that she was alone. There was no sign of Sister Brigid.

Nothing was ever said. The nun remained as impassive as ever in their lessons. Geneviève was never again asked to stay behind. But what remained was an association of pleasure with pain and with punishment and do as she might, it became an ever-troubling content of her dreams and fantasies until in time it was accepted and no longer resisted.

That she was attractive to men as well as to women became amply clear to Geneviève in her new life. It carried a thrill, and it did not take long for her to move from a position of surprise and modesty at this new attention to a more sophisticated playfulness that increased the male interest yet further. A year on from her mother's death, Geneviève, in the remarkable position of a young woman with considerable wealth and moving towards her independence, was discussed in the most elegant drawing rooms of Paris as being the greatest prize that a male suitor could claim. She, however, was in no hurry and simply enjoyed the attention.

Physically, men were an unknown entity to her. But the intimacy, inevitably invested in the care of her mistress by her principal maid Sophie, did on occasions of the evening bath lead the two, after a gentle drying with towels and extensive hair brushing, to sometimes make love, at least for an hour or two, in Geneviève's bed. This also allowed conversations in which the maid could describe her many experiences of heterosexual love, thus providing Geneviève with some initial education in such matters.

Nevertheless, physically and emotionally, she remained separate and simply enjoyed manipulating the space between her and the young men she met, a space that she realised she controlled and that they could only traverse as far as she wished. As she increasingly exercised her power, she became adept at allowing movement towards her, the amount depending on her mood and the man in question, only to then firmly close the door.

What could not be discussed with Sophie was an unease lurking in the background of her most personal fantasies, in which power also featured. It was mixed though with her memory of Sister Brigid, and it placed her, not in the ascendance, but in a place of subservience and pain. It was an unease that could be largely discarded within the etiquette and courtesy of her social life, but in her most private moments it could slip into her mind; a shadowy, sinister intruder.

CHAPTER FIFTEEN

La Belle Époque

Those years in Paris that ended the nineteenth century and brought forth the twentieth, teemed with cultural and artistic life. The time would later become known as "La Belle Époque." The city had good reason to consider itself the cultural centre of the world. Artists came there to live and work from all over Europe, and some even made the pilgrimage from America. Not only artists but also the patrons, who with canny foresight, took home paintings and sculptures that would form the basis of great collections.

The soirées and salons, hosted by wealthy residents and those of artistic and intellectual renown, claimed the afternoons and evenings of each week so that a diary could overflow with such appointments. First though, one had to be invited and without doubt the favour of such invitations was a mark of cultural status. Geneviève, at first unsophisticated but always bright and engaging, was increasingly welcomed and valued as a guest. Her natural interest in affairs, particularly in respect to the arts, overcame any criticisms that could be made about her inexperience and she soon turned her naivety to an advantage through her very openness about it, along with her obvious wish to know more. It became clear that she, the unacknowledged daughter of a notorious mother, was bringing a new quality to the house of Bolvoir, whilst at the same time maintaining its affinity towards the arts which had been so cultivated by the Countess. And Geneviève, at the age of twenty, could celebrate the excitements of this "belle époque," blending them perfectly with the innovations and discoveries that were natural to her age.

And a woman of such age needs friends to join in her adventures. Such a one, two years younger than Geneviève, lived quite near, just north of the river in the Avenue d'Iéna and close enough to the newly-built Eiffel Tower to experience its iron-wrought grandiosity and its new declaration of Parisian pride.

Princess Marie Bonaparte, known informally as "Mimi," lived there with her father Prince Roland Bonaparte, her grandmother Princess Pierre, and a household that included Mimau, a faithful nurse from her childhood.

Geneviève's introduction to such wealthy families in Paris had not been through the structure of her own family, which was no more than skeletal, or through the influence of her mother, whose friends came from a more darkly select group and who anyway was deceased. It came through her sudden appearance as a daughter to the Countess, a woman who had always been considered childless. This inquisitiveness was tempered for some by a degree of sympathy for an orphan girl cared for, as it was rumoured, by one of her servants. Admittedly, Morel was known to have served the Count and Countess well, and amongst the male gentry he had forged a reputation as a brilliant swordsman, a quality that allowed him an acceptance not otherwise available to one of his position. This of course was less of a factor for the ladies of society, whose main interest was whether Morel had indeed been the lover of the Countess. In fact, the Countess was far too shrewd to allow such diversions with one who cared for her finances. She had never mixed business with pleasure.

Princess Pierre, the grandmother of Geneviève's friend-to-be, had been an acquaintance of the Countess. It would be an exaggeration to say that they were friends, but they knowingly shared a ruthless strength of purpose. Princess Pierre, the daughter of a copper foundry worker had, against all conventions, married Prince Pierre Napoleon Bonaparte, the nephew of Napoleon 1. Their first child was Prince Roland. The finances of the family were not on a firm footing, and she had actively planned for her son to make a marriage that would bring them greater wealth and security. The source of these would be the twenty-year-old, Marie-Félix Blanc, the daughter of François Blanc, an entrepreneur who had amassed a fortune, most notably through his casinos. An astute businessman, his response to a gambler "breaking the bank" of his casino in Homburg, was to celebrate it with full publicity, thus transforming a great loss into a gain, as he renewed the illusory hopes of his clientele.

Much of the Blanc family fortune was left to his daughter, Marie-Félix. Princess Pierre, through careful planning and scheming brought about the marriage between the heiress and her son Roland. Eighteen months later the young bride, Marie-Félix, gave birth to a girl before dying from an embolism. This daughter was to become Geneviève's friend Marie. Marie was to receive three-quarters of her mother's estate on her maturity at twenty-one. In the meantime, the finances of the Bonaparte family were stabilised and Marie, being the daughter of Prince Roland, had the title of Princess Marie Bonaparte.

Princess Marie and Geneviève were thus two young heiresses waiting for their maturity, though Geneviève was the older by two years. Her own position, having only distant relatives, was much freer than that of Marie who, though she had no mother, had to contend with the forceful personality of her

125

grandmother and the spasmodic presence of her father, Prince Roland, whose attention she craved but rarely received.

Geneviève's personality was also more outgoing and confident than that of Marie, though her friend had a sharp and insightful intelligence that often caused Geneviève to pause for moments of deeper reflection.

Their first meeting was one morning in January 1900, when Princess Pierre, in regard to her acquaintance with the late Countess, called upon Geneviève. Princess Marie, her granddaughter, came with her.

The visit lasted for an hour and Geneviève engaged well with the old lady, sensing perhaps their shared difference, as both had grown up unaware of riches and status to come.

Mimi, Princess Marie, sat quietly, allowing her grandmother the space to conduct what was in fact an interview. Whilst doing so, she looked around the drawing room absorbing the elegance of the artefacts, many of which had been collected by the Countess, until her gaze rested upon a group of prints that were displayed in the unlit space between two windows. With her grandmother and Geneviève still in conversation, she rose and walked to where the pictures hung.

The imagery was uncompromising and very new to her. Each of the three prints, which were all in black and white, showed a scene from Parisian life but not as Marie had known it, or even guessed at. There was an unquestionable reality about the scenes and, though she was taken aback, the depictions of an existence so dissimilar to the elegance and politeness of her own, awoke a desire in her for something more primitive and an interest that would have greater consequence in later years. She experienced a sensation, often described as "butterflies," in her stomach.

The first image was an interior scene with four women. In a commanding position, looking affluent and dressed in black, and for a moment Marie thought of her grandmother just across the room, sat a portly, elderly woman. She was scrutinising the body of a girl who stood naked before her and whose dress lay, only just discarded, on the ground around her feet. Against the rear wall, with its portraits and striped wallpaper, was a couch upon which rested a bare-breasted girl with flowers in her hair, who was surveying the scene as one who had previously been a participant. Another semi-clothed girl stood in the corner by some curtains, watching. All the figures were compressed closely together, adding to the intensity of a scene which Marie could begin to only intuitively understand. She saw the artist's initials, FR.

The next picture showed a woman portrayed in profile. Her luxurious dark hair curled around shoulders that were exposed by the low cut of her dress. She sat with her arms upon a table, holding in one hand a fan and with the other raising the crumpled male figure of a puppet, dressed as a clown and helpless before her gaze. Marie looked more closely and then looked away, for it seemed to her that the puppet had the face of a skull.

This picture had the full signature of the artist.

Above these two was a three-quarter length portrait of a girl. The background was dark, suggesting only the night, and she leaned against a wall waiting whilst, with staring eyes, she gazed past the viewer. Her clothes were loose around her thin body and a necklace hung unevenly against the pallid skin of her chest. She had, fixed above her forehead, a tiny black hat and its attempt at fashion caused Marie to feel only pity.

Geneviève and Princess Pierre had paused in their conversation. It had largely been about the Great Paris Exposition of 1889, for which the Eiffel Tower had been built. Geneviève was sad to have missed it, and Princess Pierre had offered words of consolation—that the forthcoming 1900 exhibition would be even more extravagant and wonderful.

In the quiet moment, they both turned towards the third person, Marie, who was still closely observing the pictures. She noticed the silence and turned.

Geneviève, whose aesthetic interest easily rested upon the more familiar physicality of women and who had been enjoying the intimacies with her maid, Sophie, liked the look and shape of the young woman. Marie was dressed in dark colours that emphasised the slim and slight nature of her body. Her hair and eyes were dark too, and she showed a nervous alertness which was attractive and compensated for her introverted nature.

"The pictures are signed by Félicien Rops," said Marie. "I have not heard of him, but he clearly knew your mother, as one is dedicated to her."

And at the mention of the name, Geneviève was at once reminded of the elegant, elderly artist at her mother's funeral who had introduced himself simply as Félicien.

And completely to her own surprise, she said,

"Yes—he loved my mother."

Whether it was the sheer spontaneity of the statement or its interjection into a polite conversation or whether, as had been initially the case for Geneviève, the word love was too strange a word to be associated with the Countess, there followed a complete silence only broken by the rustle of skirts as Marie returned to her chair.

This incident had three main results. One was that Geneviève realised, more strongly than before, that she knew too little about her mother and it was time to find out more.

The consequence for Marie was that in that moment she was nudged towards a wider experience of the world and, most pertinently, of its more hidden elements.

And for them both, the dominance of the grandmother was, for a moment, forgotten, creating a space in which the two young women could begin to be friends.

****

Geneviève could not always rely on the company of Marie who was prone to illness or, to be more exact, to anxieties about becoming ill. And she would also sometimes excuse herself simply on the grounds of reading an interesting book.

For Geneviève, this was not a problem. She made no demands on people and was usually happy with events as they materialised throughout the day.

One repeated meeting point became the dinners given by the Villeneuves, who were Marie's aunt and uncle. These were occasions which, on a good night, included clever minds and interesting characters. Here, Geneviève learned a lot and also benefitted from Marie's more erudite nature and experience.

But usually, the two young women would simply enjoy having tea and conversation at each other's homes, though Geneviève had to contend with the frequent absence of her friend who would depart for the country, often for reasons of supposed ill health.

Thus going out together for major events was a rare occurrence for the girls, but a visit to the great 1900 Exposition Universelle was something that no Parisian could ignore and few could resist. Geneviève would certainly not let it pass, and she could think of no better company for her visit than Marie.

On a gloriously sunny day in late summer Geneviève and Marie, accompanied by Marie's old nurse and sometimes confidante, Mimau, made their way in a most splendid, gleaming black, enclosed carriage towards the great complex of buildings that filled the site of the Exposition. The two young women had nimbly ascended the high step up to the carriage and from there, with eager arms, had effectively, though without grace, hauled Mimau up to join them. The red padded door had closed. The smartly dressed coachman, sitting at the rear and high above the roof, sent his command through the long reins that were needed to reach his horse and with a jangling from its harness, the trio joined the multitude of vehicles of all shapes and sizes that were heading towards the Exposition Universelle.

The streets of Paris could be filled by a confusing and frightening tangle of horse-drawn carriages—private, commercial, those for hire and those providing the omnibus service, crammed full on both the lower and the exposed upper deck—and the new phenomena of automobiles had joined the fray to increase the chaos. Geneviève had often watched these vehicles wildly and haphazardly crisscrossing or careering towards each other. But on this day, a holiday in fine weather that was irresistible to the crowds, the flow of the traffic was in only one direction, towards the Exposition.

The girls had been influenced by the wise suggestion of Morel, that rather than disembarking at one of the main entrances, they would first take a boat along the river. From the boat station near the Pont d l'Alma, they could cruise along the river and survey and wonder at the many international pavilions, built in the most grandiose fashion along the banks of the Seine. There were towers and pinnacles, spires and domed roofs from which fluttered the flags of the great nations, all vying in their own egocentric ways to create the most spectacular impression.

Just past the Pont Alexandre lll they returned to dry land, eminently placed, and according to Morel's plan, for the massive glass, iron and steel structure of the Grand Palais, built for the Exposition and practically filling the area between the Champs-Elysées and the river, whilst it faced, across the Avenue Nicolas ll, its smaller compatriot, the Petit Palais.

This was the area of the massive exhibition that both Geneviève and Marie had been drawn to. Engineering, industry, horticulture, the cultures of the dominions of France, the nations of Europe and the USA, and even the fairgrounds and the great Ferris wheel were not their priority, though the latter were certainly marked for their next visit.

This day, they sought the arts and it was in the Grand Palais, the greatest structure of metal and glass ever built, that these were housed. And though there were the fine and decorative arts of other nations within the glass structure, it was to the largest section, the Beaux Arts of France that they headed.

Under this enormous canopy of glass, Geneviève was taken up by an emotion completely new to her: it was of national pride. As she surveyed the thousands of people exploring with excitement, the great site that had been built within the city, and as she now entered the Beaux Arts section devoted to the creations of French artists and artisans, she believed herself fortunate indeed to be living in Paris and in a home which contained her mother's fabulous collection of the glass of Emile Gallé, of which here in the pavilion there were some magnificent examples. And with this emotion, she turned to her friend and uttered her pleasure and amazement and added the more personal comment, "And I'm even here with a Bonaparte!" Which Marie accepted with pleasure.

Geneviève, studying a Lalique necklace, was mesmerised by the brilliant sparkle of the diamonds set amongst the soft, deep, red hues of rubies. It brought forth a vision in her mind of the bejewelled mother who had so beguiled her on that rare visit to the convent home.

She was disturbed in her reverie by Mimau pulling upon her arm.

"Geneviève, I must tell you that I have noticed that there is a man who keeps looking at you. Should we be worried?" Mimau already seemed so, "Or is he someone you know?"

Geneviève turned to look, and there was indeed a man who quite plainly, and even with a slight smile upon his face, was observing her. She felt no alarm, that was not in her nature, but the insinuation in Mimau's attitude gave her some discomfort, though only for a moment as there came a dawning recognition. The man was very tall and had clothes that were of quality, though they were well worn. As many of the men, he wore a straw boater with a ribbon around its crown and which he raised respectfully, showing the thinning grey hair beneath. His moustache though was of a sandy grey mixture which, along with his complexion, showed that he had once sported hair, often designated "ginger" for men, and more agreeably "red" or even "golden" for women.

Geneviève felt again the sense of peace and comfort she had experienced at her mother's funeral when, for a moment, she had been with this man who was so unusually and in such a welcome way, taller than her. She immediately crossed over to him and looked up into his face.

"You are one of the artists who came to the funeral."

Her statement of fact was also her acknowledgement and greeting to him.

"Mademoiselle Geneviève, it is indeed a pleasure for me that we should meet again. I barely believed it possible. The heavens have smiled upon us at this great exhibition. Our meeting is a fitting tribute to the wonders of Paris."

Such intimacy, expressed with a tone of affection, would normally have surprised Geneviève and seemed out of place. From the wrong person it would have been impolite and even offensive, but with this man, whose name was still unknown to her, it seemed natural.

"Monsieur, I am, as well, pleased to meet you again, but I am embarrassed as I do not even know your name, and perhaps I should?" The sentence did end with a question, though more from politeness than conviction. She felt sure that the tall artist had not offered her his name.

"The embarrassment should surely be mine Mademoiselle, as I do believe that I strangely omitted to introduce myself at the time. It is strange that I did not, and it has been of concern to me since, as I never believed I would have an opportunity to make amends. My name is Jules Deschamps, and I could even say that I am Count Deschamps, though I have frittered away so much of my family fortune as to believe that I no longer deserve such a title, one that I fear I have not lived up to. But then I was summoned by the muse to the arts and they claimed all of me."

Geneviève, in her short time within the salons of Paris, was already noted for the quickness and often boldness of her wit. It was often because she spoke more quickly than she thought.

"And my mother must have been one such muse."

She then considered her spontaneous remark and was without regret as she strongly sensed it to be true.

A man still considering himself a Count, might have found the remark unacceptably impertinent. Jules Deschamps was not such a one.

"For two months, Mademoiselle, I adored your mother and painted her and was inspired by her. Then she became bored and turned to another. For the next twenty years, I tried to recover from the loss. Such was the power of Marguerite. Of course, sometimes our paths would cross, and I always heard news of her when I was in Paris, but I knew that I should keep my distance for my own survival. I can be candid Mademoiselle, as your own remark has allowed it."

The two had so quickly descended into personal areas of sensitivity that they simultaneously fell silent as if to draw breath. The discomfort of the moment was mitigated by the obvious presence of Mimau who was fidgeting nearby, still wondering whether there was cause for alarm, and also by Marie whose attention upon a pendant by Henri Vever, an exquisite, gold and bejewelled female figure with the spread wings of a butterfly, had now shifted as she noticed her friend in conversation with a strange man.

Geneviève made the introductions. Deschamps gracefully greeted Mimau, whose anxiety was soon replaced by an awkward pleasure at this imposing figure's charm. Turning to Marie, with an easy movement, he took her hand, then lowered his head halfway towards it whilst raising it the remaining distance, so that it was respectfully brushed by his lips.

"Princess Marie Bonaparte. It is a pleasure. I know of the scientific work of your father, Prince Roland. He has done much to add to our knowledge, and I would hope that there is an acknowledgement of his achievements somewhere in this great exhibition. It should be so."

In ordinary circumstances, a chance meeting of this kind would quickly lead to farewells and good wishes for the future. But Geneviève felt no wish to be relieved of the company of this man, and to the contrary, she experienced an attachment to him that, though surprising, filled her with pleasure. The warm feeling of relief that had been there as she looked up into his face was now transposed across their conversation as he increasingly took on the role of their special guide for the day.

The French section of the Beaux Arts, Grand Palais pavilion, was an intoxicating mix, that offered the artisans who created in glass, ceramic, bronze, and precious stones, an equal status to the painters and printmakers of fine art. This was to be the great achievement of Paris—to no longer rely on its painters, but to celebrate the arts in all their forms as they manifested through the sensual, curling lines of art nouveau. And it was Marie who noticed and said to Deschamps,

"Monsieur, do we have a new art here, that is feminine?"

"Indeed, Mademoiselle. For the first time, art truly requires the feminine for its very line. It is why on the pinnacle of the great entrance arch, the Porte Binet, we have, resplendent, the figure of a lady. She is known as "La Parisienne." And we can add to this—before you return to your homes, you must make one more visit—I insist. Sadly, I cannot accompany you, as evening approaches and I have a train I must catch. But you will still have time. When you leave this building, cross the river by the Pont des Invalides and there on the other side you can step onto the miraculous moving walkway."

"I will be very glad to have the walking done for me," interjected Mimau, who was feeling the effects of several hours walking and standing and for some time had been looking around anxiously for a seat.

134

The two young women were more interested in the invention of such a thing.

"It will transport you all the way to the other end of the site. You then cross back to the north bank by the Pont de l'Alma and there you will find a pavilion dedicated to our greatest artist—Auguste Rodin. And there, Mademoiselles, you will find even more of the feminine. And now I must leave you. It has been my great pleasure to be here, in the company of three most clever and beautiful Parisiennes."

Geneviève needed to ask one more question.

"The gentleman, Félicien. Do you see him?"

"Monsieur Rops was far hardier than I and continued to see your mother and survive. Indeed, he even outlived her, but only just. He died soon after her funeral."

"Then was he ill when he came there?"

"Indeed, he was."

And then he was gone. Geneviève watched the white hat, so much higher than those around it, until its distance reduced it to a speck and then it was only part of the ever-moving mass of a thousand others. Marie touched her arm and said softly,

"Come, Geneviève, let us try this magic walkway."

And so the three women, following Deschamps' directions, crossed the bridge and allowed themselves to be transported along the Rue de Nations, so that they passed the many international pavilions that they had first seen on their trip along the river. All the way people stepped on and off the moving platform, many, simply for its novelty. At the Pont de l'Alma, they crossed back and found the entrance to the Auguste Rodin exhibition.

Inside, the space was large and white with drawings around the walls and many plaster statues interspersed throughout the gallery.

Mimau had been Marie's childhood nurse. Now though, and especially on this day, she was a companion. But though the responsibilities of the nurse had passed, she was immediately

135

propelled by instinct to clasp Marie by the arm, turning her away from the nakedness before them and even reaching out with her hand to cover her eyes. Marie, in complete surprise at this action, pulled away. She felt angry, but it was also ridiculous so that she laughed.

"Dear Mimau, I am no longer a child!"

Several people turned away from the exhibits to view this new one with its element of theatre. Some were smiling. Marie was embarrassed.

She gathered herself.

"Monsieur Deschamps has declared that we must view the work of Rodin and that he is the greatest artist! Come Mimau; we must be bold!"

In fact, Marie had already seen enough to know that she wished to see more, and the interest that had been kindled in Geneviève's home by the pictures of Félicien Rops was finding new fuel for its fire. And she sensed too, that her friend, Geneviève, was one with whom she could readily share the interest.

Geneviève, hardly distracted by Mimau's outburst, had already progressed to a large plaster cast of a standing female nude whose contortions could either be sensual or expressions of pain. The fact that the mixture of these two things had already become part of Geneviève's experience, most explicitly through her abduction by the green-eyed Sister Brigid, increased the fascination. But it was too, as Deschamps had said, an exhibition of the feminine. There were other themes, and nude male statues as well, but the female nudes stood out. Geneviève was not sure why.

Marie was alongside her and spoke as if their thoughts were one.

"I believe Geneviève, that we are not meant to think of ourselves like this. But are these sensual forms not the physical essence of us, as women?"

"Not docile reclining nudes," said Geneviève, "but the body experienced—in pleasure and pain."

136

Marie took her arm and the two young women, now silent, strolled and looked at everything. Mimau was able to console herself as she had found a chair on which to sit and to rest her tired legs. From a distance, she too began to examine the sculptures as well as keeping a keen eye on Marie.

She watched as the two paused in front of a work that imposed itself as a centrepiece for the exhibition.

She could not hear, but what passed between the two as they surveyed the great statue of a man and woman embraced and united in a kiss, was a muted reflection upon a life to come, that would involve a husband.

The three women hailed a cab and travelled back to Marie's home in the Avenue d'Iéna. Geneviève stared out of the window but saw little, as a feeling was growing that had begun with her parting from Deschamps.

Marie sensed the emotion in her friend and her observations and intuition gave her a clearer understanding than was possible for Geneviève, who was now sinking into a state of confusion and misery.

Marie had noted the family resemblance and that Geneviève's father, for a moment, had brought his warm presence to her life, only to disappear again, into the crowd.

CHAPTER SIXTEEN

The ball

Geneviève was one of the first to be invited when the new Spanish Ambassador arranged a great ball to mark his arrival in Paris. It was the winter of 1902, three years since her mother's death and a year since she had reached the age of maturity. She was fully in charge of her own affairs.

The ball required a larger space than was possible at the embassy, so it was to be held at the home of the Comte de Feure, the Hôtel du Cèdre, in the Rue du Faubourg Saint-Honoré. This magnificent building was completely suitable for an event of such splendour.

Amongst the many servants employed by Geneviève to maintain the running and impeccable appearance of her great house, there was a small and increasingly intimate triad. It would have been unthinkable under the rule of her mother, but Geneviève's observations of decorum went only so far as to meet the critical assessment of her visitors. Otherwise, she cared little for formalities. And so there were the three of them: Morel, as elegant and efficient as ever; Sophie, her maid, always warm and lively, unless having trouble with a lover; and Geneviève herself.

The three were together in her dressing room as she began to prepare for the Ambassador's ball. The sampling of different garments was a source of mirth for Geneviève and Sophie. The maid would try on different dresses so that her mistress could judge their appearance. The fact that Geneviève was so tall and Sophie, though full-breasted and wide-hipped, was far shorter, only increased their laughter and happiness.

The two women shared a more private amusement at the expense of Morel. They would wait for the moment when his awkwardness at their state of undress overwhelmed him. He would then exit, showing as much dignity as he could and would wait outside the door until they were dressed and summoned him back to give his opinion of the garment. It became the practice of the women to see how many times they could cause his embarrassed exit and nervous re-entry.

However, the summons of Morel for his opinion retained a more serious purpose. Geneviève remained gratefully in need of his approval.

On this occasion, after a record tenth departure and re-entry, he fully endorsed a silk dress, trimmed in silver and gold and of the deepest green, and all three celebrated the choice. Morel then departed with pleasure and pride at his contribution, leaving Sophie to continue with the creative task of dressing her mistress to full effect. The corset, hardly needed by Geneviève but still a convention, accentuated the narrowness of her waist from which flowed the heavy silk material that had already formed a long and graceful line from her shoulder blades down to the floor and into the long train that gathered in a rich, silken ball of green, gold and silver. Beneath her red hair, her shoulders were bare with just the slightest straps to secure the dress and the low bodice hinted at the fullness of her breasts beneath the light and delicate material that covered them. Flowers and leaves of honeysuckle, created in silk, coiled gently around her upper arms, softening the allure of the nakedness of her shoulders. Sophie's hands, which at other times would caress the body of her mistress, were now industrious, fixing hooks and eyes and a delicate lace bow that rested in the elegant curve of her lower back. Geneviève, now ready for the ball, had never looked more beautiful.

Her carriage, with Sophie in attendance, headed first to Marie Bonaparte's home in the Avenue d'Iéna. From there, they would journey in Marie's carriage to the ball and Sophie would return home. Geneviève knew that her friend would be accompanied by her grandmother, Princess Pierre. Her encounters with the old lady had gone well enough, and she begrudgingly admired the formidable quality that reminded her of her mother. It was the case too that she was hopelessly ambivalent with figures of authority. By nature, she was a young, fun-loving woman, bright and spontaneous; the qualities that had served her so well in a host of salons and soirées, but within her resided the punitive figure, a parasite lurking and easily activated by one as formidable as Princess Pierre. The abandonment by her mother had left a dark, empty space, inhabited too easily by creatures of cruelty.

But it was also the case that Geneviève had needed, if not a chaperone, at least one other who was older, to accompany her to the larger social events and thus to satisfy the expectations of other guests, many of whom were ready to observe and only too pleased to disapprove. The paucity of family members left behind by her mother had not helped Geneviève in this. She had scratched around to gain some support and accompaniment from relatives of the late Count, but it was well known to them that he was not her true father and the great wealth that had descended upon her had severely tempered any generosity they might otherwise have felt. She, therefore, often attended the smaller gatherings unaccompanied and sometimes too, the larger more sumptuous occasions. Now though, she need have no such concerns and her arrival at the ball with Princess Marie Bonaparte and Marie's substantial grandmother Princess Pierre could give no cause for gossip.

Marie did not have her friend's experience of such events and was still in the midst of nervous preparations when Geneviève arrived. For her private amusement, Geneviève made the contrast with the burlesque scenes in her own dressing room, with the voluptuous Sophie and the challenged dignity of Morel, and she felt quietly happy to be so much less encumbered than her friend. In truth, she had seen that Marie was a troubled young woman with no mother, who struggled to survive the pressures of a controlling father and grandmother. But, Geneviève observed, survive she did, and through her aptitude and determination, had grown an impressive literary ability and the skill with which to express it. Geneviève had become very fond of Marie's mind.

From the Avenue d'Iéna to the Rue du Faubourg Saint-Honoré, Marie spoke with excitement about her latest book. She was reading Émile Zola's, "Travail." Geneviève, always ready to increase her prowess at the soirées, took note. Marie had already been a source of such supply at the dinners of the Villeneuves, as well as being a combatant. Geneviève did not mind such a challenge. She was largely, and unusually amongst her class, without envy. She was aware too that Marie's excitement at her latest reading might well be the displacement and, given the title, a mitigator of the worldlier thrills that awaited them at the ball. She knew that she felt such expectations herself and that it would be an occasion at which they would both be contending with an array of hopeful suitors.

Upon their arrival at the Hôtel du Cèdre, the carriage drew to a halt, and before the three women could pause their conversation, the doors swung open and on each side stood a footman in a powdered wig and full baroque attire to help them alight. Lifting the trains of their gowns, they then climbed the wide marble stairs towards the festive sounds and the brilliant light that flooded the great doorway and radiated out into the gardens, silhouetting the massive black shapes of the cedar trees.

Despite the grandeur of the guest list, it was apparent to Geneviève that she was greeted in the way that she had now come to expect: the same stares, admiring glances, and words between women, softly mouthed from behind fans or raised palms. Her reputation fitted her as perfectly as her exquisite clothes, and she allowed its aura to blend with a radiance that reflected her sense that she was, indeed, exceptional. And this evening, on entering the opulent ballroom and surveying the scene and the many faces turned towards her, she became immersed, without the slightest self-doubt, in the considerable pleasure of being herself. Never before had she felt so confident. It was as if the evening, the ball and the magnificent setting, all existed to complement her sense of perfection. And she was sure that this would be an occasion that offered her a prize, as was her entitlement, and to take home the pleasures of the dance, the wine and skilful conversation would not be enough.

At first, her gratitude and loyalty to Marie and Princess Pierre held her physically to them, but soon the great hall was full of a social swirl, and the many greetings and introductions lifted her and carried her away on a warm tide of welcome. She moved from couple to group, and to individual elderly ladies who complimented her on her beauty. And she knew that she had never looked better and that against the golden red of her hair, the green dress, donned with such affectionate help from Sophie and so warmly approved by Morel, was perfection. The green of the dress of her mother, the silk resting upon the shape of the breasts that had compelled her teenage gaze; the green eyes of Sister Brigid staring at hers as she brought her to climax; such troubling associations were now changing, in the libidinal tide of her womanhood, into experience. Her innocence was fast becoming a myth of childhood.

Paradoxically, the years lived without pride at the convent school left Geneviève with a natural grace of movement that overrode the formalities of dance, and with the lessons arranged by Morel she was a match for the most skilled of male dancers.

Beneath the many chandeliers, teaming with flashing crystals and glowing teardrops of glass, and surrounded by ornate, full-length mirrors that lined the walls of the great ballroom, their frames as lustrous as the colour of her hair, Geneviève claimed the attention of all. Young women looked on with envy; the married ladies, more secure in their titles and marriages and ensconced in the richness of their apparel, enjoyed the kindling of memories of more youthful times and the more adventurous of them allowed the thought of reuniting with their youth by taking one such as Geneviève into their bed. The young men, elegant in their tailed, black jackets and with shirts as crisp and white as thin ice, posed as casually as they could, masking the agitation of their wish to dance with the tall apparition whose clear pleasure in her own being only increased their desires.

Somewhat aloof though was Carlos Fernando Vincente, son of the Marqués de la Segura.

Though impressed by the sight of Geneviève and by her vibrant but graceful dancing, he had not awaited an introduction. Unlike the residents of Paris, he had no knowledge of her, a state which would have continued if not for a mutual acquaintance, who seeing them standing close to each other, took the initiative.

Don Carlos rarely left his native Spain, but when he did Paris was his favourite destination. On this occasion, he was a guest of the Spanish Ambassador. He was from a family whose fortune had greatly increased in the previous century through trade with West Africa, not only in the buying and selling of palm oil but also of human beings; native Africans who were shipped as slaves to Cuba.

His great interest, his love in fact, was the breeding of thoroughbred horses which took place on his estate in Andalusia, where he had also formed a reputation for breeding fighting bulls for the corrida. He had such success in this that his bulls were famous throughout Spain for their strength, enormous size and their pure aggression, so that even the greatest matadors had an unease about a contest with a Don Carlos bull and lesser matadors had discreet methods of avoiding them.

Don Carlos had much the look of a well-bred Spanish nobleman. He compensated for his medium height with an erect posture that some said he borrowed from the matadors for whom he was such a nemesis. His thick black hair was oiled and swept back above dark eyes, and his aquiline nose was distinctive, though not so large as to distract from the good looks that were, nevertheless, let down by the small chin that receded too quickly into his neck. For this reason, he habitually thrust his chin forward and upwards, a trait more to do with self-consciousness than confidence. Otherwise though, he was self-assured, the only son and always destined for position, wealth and the inheritance of the title of Marqués.

In this, his experience and development were in complete contrast to those of Geneviève. To Carlos, status and wealth were an unquestionable entitlement, not even seen as a privilege, and his concern for those of a lower status was non-existent. It was one reason that, even to the unease of his family, he retained slaves, hiding them amongst the servants at his Andalusian hacienda. In the Madrid household, which was the main seat of his family, this would now have been untenable, but there on his estate he could indulge himself in all that he enjoyed and one such pleasure was in having the complete submission of another.

Carlos had never troubled himself with the acquisition of a foreign language, but some knowledge had been instilled in him as part of his education. He was, therefore, in a rudimentary manner, with many mistakes which Geneviève found amusing and even endearing, able to converse with her in French. In fact, the faulty expressions in the language allowed

Geneviève to see, or perhaps imagine, something more vulnerable beneath the otherwise proud and even haughty demeanour of the man with the jutting chin.

Throughout the evening Geneviève received many requests to dance, but it was Don Carlos who increasingly became her chosen partner as the dances moved from the more formal to the more intimate coupling of the waltz. As a couple, their appearance was attractive, though most eyes rested upon her. The difference in height, and it was usual for Geneviève to be taller than her partner, was somewhat mitigated by the high heels of the Spaniard, who favoured boots that suited his love of horse riding.

The ballroom of the Hôtel du Cèdre had the expanse to allow a hundred dancers to display their skills in the most exuberant and extravagant styles. The gallery at one end, large enough for a small orchestra and the enthusiasm of the players, moved by the grandeur of the surroundings and the opulence of the occasion, was endorsed and celebrated by the dancers below.

Geneviève and Carlos, after a vigorous waltz, had paused to exchange some breathless words whilst they savoured the wine punch. It was dispensed from golden bowls by servants in full livery, who seemed charged to allow no glass to stay empty. As they talked, the contrast between the assured upright stance of Carlos and his hesitant and clumsy French, made Geneviève laugh, and with the replenishment of their glasses and the further sips of the delicious wine, there arose in her a feeling of pure joy, so that with no decorum she pulled her partner back into the centre of the dancefloor. And as they stood facing each other, his hands upon her arms, the orchestra played the opening bars of a polka-mazurka.

It was danced with such speed and ended with so great a crescendo, that Geneviève was sure it was the final dance of the night. But there was one more that could not be omitted and that could end the evening like no other. The gentle opening strains of the Blue Danube hovered in the air as Geneviève and

Carlos smiled to each other in recognition. Geneviève allowed the Spaniard to lead her into the first steps, gathering pace and movement, until with exhilarating force she felt him whirl her body around the whole expanse of the ballroom, amongst the multitude of couples, who were also smiling, laughing and giving themselves up to the grand finale of the ball.

It was an excited and happily weary Geneviève who, at the end of the evening, found her friends, Marie and Princess Pierre, and declared that she had danced her heart out and had, that night, met a man whom she really liked. Marie, who had danced little, but observed much, including an intense scrutiny of the Spaniard, kissed Geneviève and expressed her pleasure at her friend's happiness. Geneviève was too thrilled by the dance and her encounter to notice the doubt and concern in Marie's expression as soon as she looked away.

CHAPTER SEVENTEEN

Marriage

As Don Carlos was remaining in Paris for a whole month, there were several opportunities for the couple to meet and Geneviève increasingly looked forward to her times with the Spaniard, whose bearing, conversation, and interests were so different to the young men of Paris. Perhaps it was this difference that was the attraction. Curiosity was inherent to her, and she loved being drawn into ideas and culture that she found fresh and new. This, Carlos supplied, and at the same time, was utterly courteous in his approach and never fawning, the latter being a manner that Geneviève abhorred.

There was, too, another element that drew them together. It was far darker and for Geneviève, not yet in her consciousness, but was to cast the greatest shadow over her life.

Her faithful secretary, Morel, completely attentive but also never fawning, had researched and supplied her with his report. This would only be factual as emotion was not part of his role and anyway was largely outside his repertoire.

He informed his mistress that Carlos, the future Marqués de la Segura, had immaculate credentials and would make an ideal suitor, since he knew this was implicit in her interest.

There was one more factor which he included in a more anecdotal way. Don Carlos had become known, within his short stay in Paris, as a fine fencer with the épée. The information came to Morel through his involvement with the sword, though Carlos had not attended his own fencing club, Le Salle d'Armes Coudurier, but one on the other side of Paris.

Morel chose not to tell Geneviève the additional gossip. It was said that in Madrid the Spaniard had fought a duel with swords and killed his opponent. These were times when the duel to the death was no longer an acceptable or even a legal way to settle a dispute and the matter, through the influence of the Segura family, had been suppressed.

Over the following month, the relationship developed, and Geneviève was increasingly attracted to the indulgent attentions of this man who clearly shared her feelings. He spared no expense and flowers arrived morning and evening with letters written in his clumsy French, which always caused Geneviève to laugh and to love him more.

At the end of the month, to her great pleasure, Carlos decided to extend his stay by four weeks and by the end of that period, a firm date had been arranged for a visit to his family in Madrid.

The expectation of Parisian Society was that Don Carlos and the young heiress would soon be betrothed, thus leaving a number of men, both young and middle-aged and even an elderly Duke, mourning the loss of their ambitions.

Three months later, after more visits by Don Carlos and frequent gifts and letters, Geneviève travelled to Madrid with her maid Sophie and with the respectful approval of Morel, who made arrangements for the final leg to be in a carriage drawn by four magnificent black horses. He had in mind that such equine excellence would be received well by the Spaniard and his family.

If he was at all disgruntled by the prospect of his mistress entering a marriage that would certainly affect the happy and well-functioning unit within the Paris mansion and that might even affect his position and employment, he made no show of it, indeed, he seemed keen to facilitate the relationship.

Geneviève, in Madrid, was her usual, warm, and charming self. It was though, not easy for her to act with her natural spontaneity and good humour. The Segura family had the pride of Spanish aristocracy, without any of its flair. In the heat of the Madrid summer, the family of Don Carlos constituted a solid block of ice. She could only grant them the colour grey and did so with much disappointment, as her view of the colourful city was otherwise radiant.

Now came Geneviève's first concern about her suitor, doubt would still be too strong a term. When with his family, the young man who had so charmed her in Paris became as dull as his elderly relatives.

His father did provide an occasional glimpse of humanity, and Geneviève caught him looking at her, on more than one occasion, with an expression of yearning. After seven days spent with the family, she concluded that his desperate look was the result of the many years lived with his wife, Donna Isabella, who was clearly a complete stranger to anything approaching joy and was, indeed, more likely to be its enemy.

Geneviève had been ready to extend the wonder she felt for her own home to the Madrid house, but despite her efforts she could find little to enjoy in the dark furniture and gloomy portraits of ancestors that provided the décor. Instead, she turned to the description by Carlos of his Andalusian home and was eager to endorse his descriptions with her smiles and assurances. That horses were of little interest to her, and that bulls frightened her were not to become impediments to the life that he so ardently wished to offer her.

Feeling so valued, she gave little thought to what she might leave behind and no thought at all to the effect of a marital state upon her possessions.

Her naivety was interrupted by a brief but pertinent conversation with Donna Isabella. It was near the end of her stay, and Carlos was out riding and his father languishing in his own rooms, when the elderly matriarch sent a servant to request the presence of the woman she clearly assumed would become her daughter-in-law.

Geneviève was escorted to her sitting room to find her firmly seated in a straight-backed chair, dressed in black which was her custom, and with a small dog scratching around her feet. Geneviève had not been able to extend her natural love of dogs to this hateful animal that confronted anyone that it met other than its mistress, with a shrill, aggressive barking, conveying, for such a small creature, a surprising degree of menace.

"And," thought Geneviève, with a degree of shame at the failure of her usual generous attitude, "the dog is as ugly as its mistress."

Indeed, the face of the Marquesa, with her pallid skin unblessed by the Spanish sun and her downturned mouth above jaws set as firmly as a trap, displayed the imprint of the sourest of feelings.

There was, for a moment, an attempt at warmth though the effort was at most insipid. She spoke in fluent French.

"It is our pleasure that our house, which is one of the oldest in Spain, should be joined now to the house of Bolvoir in France."

The old woman spoke with such certainty that Geneviève was unable to protest that marriage had not, as yet, been proposed. She remained mute.

"We did not have to recover from a revolution, but our family, like yours has endured struggles to survive and to maintain our status. I know something of the Bolvoirs, though I never met your mother. I believe though, we would have understood each other."

Hardly knowing her mother herself, Geneviève could not comment, though she had glimpsed enough to be able to think, "Yes, I see you are a match—though not when it comes to art."

"We must always guard our entitlement. Rest assured, Geneviève, that my family will take great care that the wealth of your estate is preserved. You will do well to join yours to ours. I fear for you, my dear, a young woman alone in Paris with such responsibilities and many advisors who will only prey upon you. But in marriage, you will be protected. As your husband, my son will of course be your superior and in these matters will need full possession in order to manage the affairs of the Paris properties. No doubt, this can easily be arranged by my lawyers."

Geneviève had grown up without entitlement and with no knowledge or expectation of future riches. There had been great kindness as well as severity from the nuns who had fostered her, and the kindness had kindled her own generous spirit, so that when she came upon her inheritance it was accepted with an openness, devoid of desire.

At her core though, lay a deep duality. The infant girl who had been handed to the convent and who was never to feel the embrace and love of her own mother, bore the impact of a great absence. An absence that could surface like the tentacles of a huge sea monster, wrap themselves around her and draw her under, down to a state in which only deprivation could be expected.

Such were the tentacles of Donna Isabella and with such effect, that as the conversation continued, Geneviève felt something inside her begin to die. She had no answers to give and could only nod with mute acceptance. She felt a weakness deep inside her body, and an attitude of complete submission took over her mind. As well as a mumbled agreement to her

demands, she left behind, in the sitting room of the old matriarch, a portion of her soul.

On the final day of her visit, she conducted herself according to everything she believed was expected of her, but all was
performed in a compliant trance; the expressions of gratitude,
the compliments, the hopes for the future, the farewells, all
empty of true meaning.

It had been a considerable help to Geneviève that she had
the company of Sophie, though even Sophie, so effervescent
with life when it went well, became jaded to the point of gloom.

On their journey back, the maid seemed only able to gaze
silently out of the window. But then, due to her status, she
could not say what she truly felt, that such a family could not
produce a husband in any way worthy of her mistress and at
worst, it would end in catastrophe.

From then on, an air of depression settled upon the household of Geneviève de Bolvoir. Her "joie de vivre," her expectancy and excitement, freed from the austerity of life with the
guardian nuns, the finding of new talents and preferences,
became subdued so that an astute observer might say that
something much earlier, from a long way back in her life, had
caught up and was now demanding a reckoning. The young
woman who had celebrated the joy of her youth and beauty
at the Ambassador's ball, felt the bright light of her existence
begin to dim.

Her happiness was abandoning her as surely as the mother
she had hardly known. Within this atmosphere, but without
understanding, Geneviève longed for an ever-present figure in
her life and so, more out of need than love, she accepted Don
Carlos's proposal of marriage.

****

The wedding was planned for June 1904. Geneviève had
known Carlos for almost a year. They were to be married in

the Segura family chapel adjoining the Madrid house. In the following months, Geneviève searched increasingly for the enthusiasm that she believed she should feel. She made the mistake, understandable perhaps, of seeing its absence as a personal failure, as if some new defect had formed in her personality. Her now near constant state of depression was thus mixed with the inflicted cruelty of self-criticism, and this miserable cocktail permeated the atmosphere of the Bolvoir home and also caused a new reticence in her social life.

The young woman who had sparkled and added her own lustre to "La Belle Époque" of Paris, was now a shadow, rarely seen. Of course, the life of high society continued unabated. Her betrothal to the Spaniard was common knowledge, and amongst the women there was the assumption that her withdrawal signified her preoccupation with her fiancée and her forthcoming marriage. To the young men, she was no longer a marriage prospect and so of less interest.

Sophie, for whom pleasure and excitement were requisite in life and who had greatly benefitted from having Geneviève as her mistress and occasional lover, now began to share the depression, a state that for her was hard to bear. Her innate response was to withdraw and so, one morning as she helped her mistress to dress, she broke the news that she would be leaving her service.

She could not have imagined the reaction. Geneviève, sitting at her dressing table in front of the mirror with Sophie standing by her side, dropped the hairbrush she had been holding, her hair hanging loose around her shoulders, stared at Sophie's reflection and burst into tears.

Sophie, so easily attuned to happiness but so avoidant of its opposite, could not respond and stood motionless.

Geneviève knew exactly what she needed. She would have loved the young woman to lean forward, to place her arm around her, to stroke her forehead, to whisper reassurance, warmly and with love. It could not be.

155

She rose from her chair, the maid still standing there, so small in comparison, their bodies and laughter never again to be shared. It was now clear to Geneviève that everything had changed. There could no longer be such contact; she was betrothed to a man and her relational world had changed forever. It brought a gloom that she could not bear to acknowledge. There was a new formality with severity at its core. She pictured the loveless mother of Carlos and the desperately miserable father. She thought of Carlos and how, since their betrothal, his charm had faded, and she felt helpless and hopeless.

She and Sophie stood side by side, each gazing into the mirror, she looking at them both and Sophie just staring at herself. "How stupid we look," she thought, considering the difference in size, and the warm, voluptuous Sophie was gone to her and she felt utterly alone.

The idea of marriage had offered the healing of a wound, a place of love and comfort to one, who as an infant and child had never known the body of her own mother. Now she sensed a future of even greater melancholy.

With hair hanging loose and her dressing unfinished, she turned away from the mirror with its morbid reflection and headed instinctively to the only comfort she could still think of.

Morel was in his sitting room which also served as his office. It was now early winter, and the fire was lit and the room already warm. The large first-floor window looked out onto the garden where the grass was white and covered by a frost that sparkled in the morning sunshine. Inside, the room was comfortably furnished, but typical to Morel, only with that which he deemed necessary. There were two oil paintings from the collection of the late Countess, rococo works by Boucher; fine collector's pieces that meant little to him aesthetically. They were upon the wall when he was given the room, and he had been content to leave them just as they were. There was also a painting by Fernand Khnopff, a Symbolist work which he found unaccountably troubling and preferred not to look at. The only decorative items he had installed to reflect his personal tastes were the two duelling swords that were attached to the wall above his desk, their blades crossed and touching as if invisible hands were already engaged in the deadly contest.

He was, as ever, clothed in immaculate black and grey. The waistcoat which might have relieved the austerity of his dress with an embroidered pattern or even a watch chain never did so.

It was a widening of his eyes, followed by a keenness of look, that showed that the sudden, unannounced and wild appearance of his mistress had affected his usual calm.

Geneviève had burst into his room, her eyes brimming with tears, her body shaking with sobs, and had remained immobile in her misery, standing and gazing out at the glistening frost that was as frozen as the heart at which she now clutched. Her other hand reached up to her head and hair as if she was gradually realising the dishevelled state in which she had appeared before her secretary. Very slowly, the warmth of the room and the steady presence of Morel calmed the trauma in her mind and body, so that she collapsed into an armchair. Still she was silent, and still Morel waited until the moment came when she could at last begin to speak.

"Dear Edouard, let us go over the figures for the estate, for the last month, all of them please."

And Morel, comfortable in that which he could do well, and understanding the young woman's need for anything that might order her thoughts and her feelings, replied,

"Of course, Madame," and crossed the room to the ledgers that rested so neatly upon a shelf.

Geneviève, distressed and undressed, had abandoned all decorum and had no wish to restore it, only to calm the panic of her despair at the loss of Sophie; a loss that had breached a reservoir of grief.

Morel drew up a small leather armchair so that they both faced the fire, sitting side by side, and then began a detailed tour through the accounts of the Bolvoir estate.

Always the essence of decorum, he had been waiting since the engagement to introduce a topic which had at first occurred to him as a simple, necessary item, but over the recent months had grown into a matter of distinct concern. It was a worry that he could not convey as such, since it risked offending his young mistress and even questioning her judgement. He was also unsure about the cause of his anxiety, but nevertheless the unease had stubbornly remained, leading to sleepless nights and troubled dreams.

So, having dealt with the matter of staff payments and the need for new scullery maids, their ferocious cook having just driven two of them away in tears, he took the opportunity that opened before him.

"Madame, your wedding is now only four months away, and I have had no opportunity to discuss with you the financial terms of the marriage. Might we now take a moment for this?"

It was immediately clear to Morel that not only were the arrangements to be outside his remit, they were also beyond the control of his mistress, and she clearly had no wish to think about them. He could sense too, that this was not mere thoughtlessness; there were other forces at work. Geneviève was unable to discuss the matter further and was beyond persuasion.

They moved instead to the planned decoration of one of the guest rooms, but beneath Morel's formal compliance his unease had now become an anxious certainty.

****

At the news of the engagement, servants had brought messages from all the great houses of Paris and even the President sent warm congratulations. The marriage, after all, offered some symbolic value to the two great countries of France and

Spain, whose relations had been ambivalent during the previous decade.

But Morel had noticed in his mistress the increasing melancholy that had intensified after her return from Madrid and her stay with the Segura family. Don Carlos had made no further visits to Paris and was either in Madrid or his Andalusian estate, so at first the secretary saw the separation as the cause of Geneviève's mood.

Yet, he had also noticed a change in her character. The position in Society of his young mistress had given him a sense of pride, and quietly and resolutely he had worked to increase and maintain her status, mainly with his brief but pertinent words of advice. But the autonomy and happy spontaneity that had developed along with her social skills was now lost. She rarely went out and refused invitations, some of which were socially expedient to accept. He saw the detrimental effect as requests "for the pleasure of her company" ebbed away. Though the title of Countess had expired with the death of Marguerite and could not be passed through the female line, the family name, de Bolvoir, was still associated with great wealth and status, aided by the bearing of the young woman who had become its sole representative. Morel was seeped in the traditions of aristocracy, and his self-esteem had become interwoven with those whom he served. He had no wish to allow the decay and fall from grace that other great families had endured, and though, in France, the aristocracy had lost legal status, there was still the expectation that such a family prove its worth through its social presence.

He also observed the different way she inhabited her home. Geneviève had traversed the many rooms and corridors with the excitement of an explorer finding a strange land, and this had matured into a love of the many beautiful objects that surrounded her and which she now owned. Morel, who tended not towards such aesthetic pleasures, enjoyed them nevertheless through her eyes. Geneviève, walking through the opulent rooms, would look around and absorb every nuance of the fine décor and the exquisite objects and paintings. Now she only looked ahead, as if blinkers had been placed around her eyes.

By the time his mistress left his rooms, no longer distraught but with an aura of deep sadness, he was sure that her proposed marriage brought no hope of happiness and was, instead, an imminent disaster.

Morel had allowed his natural detachment from emotion to become the credo for his work. But an attachment with a need to protect had grown as steadily as had the personal development in the woman he served. So there came a point, three weeks before the marriage date, when he could no longer stay reticent. On that morning he requested a special meeting with his mistress.

When Geneviève arrived, he was dismayed to see that her appearance was no longer changed solely by her mood. After the departure of Sophie, Geneviève had employed a new principle maid, acquired from an agency for domestic staff. Whereas Sophie, alive and voluptuous, even in the uniform of a maid, had spread vitality throughout the home, running through the corridors and up and down the stairs, usually to redeem her habitual lateness, her replacement brought with her, along with absolute efficiency, the dissolution of joy. The new maid came as if she were an emissary of doom. The views of Morel, who liked to play his part in the selection of all new staff, had not been requested. He even surmised that the new lady's maid, a term ill-fitting for this older woman who appeared to be more like a strict governess, was the first name offered by the agency and that Geneviève, in her increasing state of apathy, had not the strength to refuse her. It was also as if fate had seized an opportunity to further drain the colour from the emotional opulence of the house.

He had seen the feminine ease, intimacy, and empathy that Geneviève had shared with Sophie. He was even aware, rather to his discomfort, that he had sometimes observed them with envy. When Geneviève now arrived, straight from her dressing room, he at once saw the imprint of the new maid, Jeanne. The long red hair, usually wound around and pinned so that it retained a look of buoyancy and with locks delicately curling against powdered cheeks, was drawn back from her face and tightly compacted, as if fixed with glue. On behalf of his mistress, he felt shame.

It had become outside his province to comment. The days when his acute observations would aid Geneviève to look her elegant best belonged to a time when such things were her concern. She seemed now to have no care for her appearance. And so he moved straight to the matter that concerned him. He had accepted that she had acquiesced to the Spaniard's lawyers and that the Bolvoir house and most of the fortune would be controlled by her husband. However, there was still the fate of a house in the Auvergne; a fine old building, set in rural surroundings, ten miles from the town of Issoire and, historically, the family escape from the stuffy confines of Paris in mid-summer.

Morel beseeched her.

"Please Madame, for your security, for your independence, for the sake of your family name, at least keep your Issoire house as completely your own."

Perhaps, once again, compliant in everything, she could only accede. Or maybe there remained a slight belief that she still deserved something. Geneviève agreed and took the opportunity as well to reward her loyal servant whose future had also looked in peril. He could stay at the Issoire house and gardens and manage them for her. Such a possibility had not occurred to Morel, his concern being only for the future of his mistress, but having recovered from his surprise, he gratefully accepted. At least, in this matter, he could negotiate with the lawyers and preserve the integrity of the Issoire house as the sole property of Geneviève de Bolvoir. In all other matters, he remained excluded. The will of Donna Isabella and her son had prevailed.

PART FIVE

PRINCESS MARIE BONAPARTE

CHAPTER EIGHTEEN

From an essay on J and his work. An evening with Marie Bonaparte

By Dr Paul Faucher (1935)

My next meeting with J brought a tremendous and most welcome surprise. As soon as I was ushered into his study, which is also his living room and consulting room, I saw that we were to be three rather than two. A dark head was visible above the back of an armchair facing the fire. The head partially turned, with the clear inference that the onus was on me to make myself seen. I did so and found myself facing no less than Princess Marie Bonaparte.

How exciting! It was not the first time I had met her, but to spend an evening in conversation was beyond my most wishful dreams, and of course enriched by the presence of our magnificent host. He was already standing and after a warm handshake,

"You do, of course, know Madame Bonaparte." This was issued as a statement rather than a question.

"I do indeed, and it is a privilege to meet you again, Madame."

For those who read this journal in years to come, and who may not be acquainted with the figures who grace (and sometimes disgrace) our group of French analysts, let me indulge myself by describing the illustrious personage of the Princess.

At the age of fifty-two, she remains a woman of beauty. She does, of course, carry the aura of a princess; we all know her to be one. And we hear that even Professor Freud will sometimes call her, "His Princess," even though she has been his analysand and sat at his feet. In any case, the use of the word by Freud is one of affection as they have formed a relationship which has the intimacy of like minds and which is bound by her tremendous allegiance to him and to psychoanalysis. To the rest of us she is a princess proper, indeed at least twice over, as she has it from Emperor Napoleon, being his great grand-niece, and also from her marriage to Prince George of Greece and goodness knows what else, those Royal families being so intermingled.

But we also respect her as a princess of psychoanalysis, which she has championed in our country, and along with Laforgue she laid the foundations of our Paris Society—the first psychoanalytic one in France—and about time too. We French have dragged behind, undoubtedly due to our national pride. We don't want to accept something coming from a mainly Jewish collective in Vienna. But no matter. Our very French Marie Bonaparte has worked her way through all that. Others were involved of course, amongst them my friend and teacher J, though his extreme independence of outlook always placed him somewhat on the fringe.

There has been so much argued in our response to what some feel to be the dictates of Vienna, even regarding the translations of Freud's works. Madame Bonaparte will truck little that deviates, but still her relationship with J continues, despite his excursion with Jung!

We do, of course, hear tales of our seniors: the parental figures who conceived and gave birth to our Paris Society. Freud in Vienna being our greatest patron and, one might say, the primal father. As I speak of these figures, using parental terms, I am well aware that my psychoanalytic colleagues can easily cast their interpretations and designate my excitement in these matters to that core issue in human development, the Oedipus Complex.

And I make no denial. To be in the home of J, so much a father figure, and to have the additional presence of Princess Marie, is akin to finding myself, fair and square, within the parental bedroom.

A dalliance has even been accorded to the two, in more youthful times. The Princess is known for her past lovers; amongst them, a prime minister of France, and though the private life of J is indeed just that, he still, in his old age, exudes a libidinal essence that would have needed consummation and satisfaction in earlier times.

I confess then to an oedipal excitement more appropriate to a five-year-old boy than a thirty-year-old, professional man. However, we, as psychoanalysts, know that such feelings remain in the unconscious mind for us all, and in my knowledge of that I am happy to admit to my awareness of them now.

I am also fascinated to observe in my patients how easily they can fantasise about parental substitutes, whilst finding it so hard, even audacious, to acknowledge the sexual lives that brought them into being.

And so, here I was, ensconced with the parental couple, though as the evening progressed my interest matured into less subjective matters as we once again entered the tale of the young Carmelite, Camille Beauclair—Sister Constance. And to my surprise and delight, Princess Marie was to become part of the story. No doubt, J had organised a meeting of the three of

167

us for this very reason. His fascination with the case of Camille has become transposed into a narrative for which I am the main audience. It is a fine thing that I am writing it down, as in noble tradition it will be passed on to those who follow.

It has given J such pleasure to interweave his history of Camille with the ancient myth of Eros and Psyche. And he began the evening in that very way.

"We had left it with Venus, hadn't we?"

The three of us were now sitting before the fire which was to be our shared focal point until Madame Bernard, J's house-keeper and exquisite cook, summoned us to the dining room. J sat in the middle with Princess Marie to his left, and on his other side he had positioned his beloved nursing chair for me to use. A privilege indeed. The lights were low and the flames from the fire sent a flickering light across his broad face. Madame Bonaparte, sitting in a large winged armchair was in shadow, adding to her already somewhat inscrutable presence.

J's comment had of course been made to me, though, without waiting for my affirmation, he continued.

"Poor Psyche had proved far too lovely for Eros to resist, despite the prohibitions and the terrible disapproval of his mother. Venus really should have been more secure—the goddess of love—the most beautiful winner in the judgement of Paris, and how many paintings there have been of that! And yet, she gets as jealous as a schoolgirl. Not only is Psyche a threat because of her beauty—she has just seduced her precious son. The gods of course can be as incestuous as they like."

At this point, I noticed some movement in the Princess's chair and she murmured something which I was unable to hear. J took no notice and continued.

"So, we have a mother who is both jealous and envious. Full of poison. Not unusual in our fairy tales either, though it normally falls upon the poor stepmother to be the evil one.

"Camille had been sent to a monastery in Issoire. Her kind Prioress, who clearly had a soft spot for her, hoped that a change of setting and a return to France might calm all those storms of emotion, so that she could be a proper nun again. And of course, this is what they want, to be a nun properly, no half measures."

I felt sure that I heard a muttering again from Marie, but though I strained to hear, it was indistinct. J hardly paused.

"I was part of the arrangement, as the Prioress wanted me to visit Camille at Issoire, something extremely unusual in the world of Carmel, but I'd helped the girl before and not only that, she kept on asking for me and they were desperate.

"But all was dependent upon the new Prioress. She had decided—it must have been on a whim—to let Camille into her house. Something must have caught her interest, but whether she was going to give me access was another matter.

"This new Mother Superior was about to become the Venus to our poor Psyche—Camille. And indeed, she had once been a Venus, many years before, a queen of beauty, a young goddess amongst the privileged players of Paris and with a fine personality. Her name then was Geneviève de Bolvoir. But fate and the years had taken their toll. Now she was Mother Geneviève, the austere Prioress of Issoire."

Marie Bonaparte, for the first time, interjected.

"It was such a change. I could hardly believe it. She had enjoyed life so much and it had been my great pleasure to be her friend."

At this, I was compelled to interrupt.

"Madame Bonaparte, you are even a player in this theatre of Camille?"

"Indeed yes," and the Princess sighed and signalled for J to continue.

"And Marie will continue to be so. But first, let me get back to Venus. Well, she's a sadist, no doubt. In her furious revenge, she sets Psyche impossible tasks and terrible tribulations to suffer. She may as well have trampled her beneath her elegant sandaled foot. Indeed, she was trying to. These gods are far

169

worse than humans, though some humans are monsters, we will meet one soon.

"Psyche undergoes terrible trials. Venus starts it off by having her whipped and tortured by two of her handmaids, Worry and Sadness. Then she's sent on impossible tasks. But she has a way of having bizarre encounters with others that help her out, so that each time, to Venus's growing fury, she succeeds in the seemingly impossible."

J paused for a moment in thought before returning to the real world.

"And Mother Geneviève sets Camille tasks. Not as malevolently crafted as those dreamed up by Venus, but still full of oppression and pain. The Carmelites are amongst the most austere, so it was easily enforced. All kinds of hard work and penance to kill off pride. But Geneviève imposed nothing she hadn't experienced herself, such had been her own need for suffering."

"Such a tragedy," said Marie from the shadowy depths of her chair.

"She even had them self-flagellate together, highly dubious of course," continued J.

"Yes, of course, perversion," enjoined the Princess.

J responded with a rather enigmatic sound and stretched out his legs dangerously close to the fire.

"Inevitably, all this attention upon Camille was just bringing them closer together. So, Camille, without any intent, was working her magic again and causing her prioress deep trouble."

We were interrupted here by the maid who announced that our dinner was ready to serve and so we left the highly personalised comfort of J's study, with its many books and artefacts, his analytic couch and the worn, but still plush armchairs, for the more functional surroundings of the adjoining dining room.

Our dinner, prepared by Madame Bernard, was as sumptuous as ever and J had selected from his cellar, actually a stone cubby hole he had requisitioned in the basement of the apartments, a Giscours Bordeaux.

The subject of Camille and Mother Geneviève, and Venus and Psyche, was put to one side in this new setting, and in the changed context of our meeting.

I have noticed before that J discards his normal garrulous manner during meals which he enjoys so much as to give eating his complete attention, so that all matters of the mind and soul are abandoned. As Marie was careless of this, or perhaps her attention remained fixed upon her own thoughts (she in fact ate very little) she was the only speaker. Firstly to J, but deprived of response, to the room, and finally to me, and of course she found me a most attentive and respectful listener.

Her preoccupation was with lay psychoanalysis. Should there be non-medical analysts? Her own position was clear. She had no medical training and saw this as no impediment whatsoever to her practice. In this, she was able to cite Freud himself who in no uncertain terms has stated, not just to her personally but to the whole world, that psychoanalysis is much better off without it being the province of the doctors. There are those in medicine though, who feel threatened and we have all been shocked that the Americans now insist upon a medical background. No doubt this will not improve Freud's already ambivalent view of them.

Though I have undergone full medical training, I assured her of my agreement. I did not doubt that J's view would be the same, though his concentration on his Confit de Canard and the Flaugnarde that followed could not allow him to respond even with a facial expression. But then, no doubt, the two have discussed the matter before.

During the desert, on which J feasted and which Marie hardly touched, her attention was switched to something further from home, yet clearly close to her own interests. It began with her fascination in the work of Edgar Allan Poe, and then fiction was replaced by fact as she recounted the actual case of a few years ago, of the terrible sadistic murderer, Peter Kürten, known as the "Vampire of Düsseldorf" and sometimes, most aptly, the "Düsseldorf Monster." Though his crimes could only be likened to the combined rape, pillage, and murder of a mediaeval army of mercenaries and were of the most extreme sadism to women, she did not temper her account. With forensic psychological interest, she described his spontaneous ejaculations at the sight of blood and his requirement of blood for orgasmic satisfaction. It caused me to wonder whether this was an assault upon J's enjoyment of his Flaugnarde pudding and might be revenge for his previous silence.

It certainly curtailed my own pleasure, and I found myself desperately looking forward to the cognac.

It is the case, though, that cruelty had been raised earlier in the tale of Camille, which was now as well, a tale of Geneviève.

On our return to J's study, it was the Princess who took up the story. Once again, I was unable to see her face which was hidden by the wings of the chair. Her voice, though, was clear and she spoke with emotion.

J was sitting between us and fussing with his Partagas which seemed unwilling to light. I had, for the moment decided not to smoke having been completely taken by the feisty manner of her opening delivery.

"The swaggering little man thought he was a big cock! But really, he was just an anus and full of anal sadism too. To him, everyone was a piece of shit that he could nip off with his nasty tight sphincter."

I should say here, that as analysts, life's baser elements, so often repressed, are the very stuff of our work. It was, nevertheless, a surprise to hear such language from a mature lady of high standing. It was also a relief. Clearly there would be no undue discretion in Marie's description of the events.

"Poor Geneviève—to all who met her and saw her on the Paris scene, she was utter confidence and bonhomie. But we know so well how turmoil can live concealed and the earliest wounds can fester.

"She had this awful mother who had abandoned her from birth. She only brought Geni, that is what I called Geneviève, back into her life because she was dying, from syphilis amongst other things, and she needed someone to leave all her money to. She'd have hated it going to the state.

"But maybe, just maybe, she wanted to repair the damage to her daughter. Perhaps a scrap of guilt languished in some neglected corner of her soul.

"The psyche can suffer terribly from life's misfortunes, and there are those who exude tragedy from the depths of their beings. Others seem born with a vitality that defies the damage. Geneviève was such a one. I was a princess, but she was the Princess of Paris and all was at her fingertips. So, what went wrong?"

Marie posed the question in the knowledge that she had the answer. J, having recovered control of his cigar, was content to allow her that and for her to continue with the history of her friend.

"Would we not be happier without marriage and the requirements of the sexual instinct? Sometimes I believe so, but few can resist. Of course, it can be fine, yet so often it rekindles that first desperate contact between a baby and her mother, though in the case of poor Geni, its disastrous absence. It is something we shared, for in my own infancy my mother died. A terrible thing, it left me expecting the same fate, and it had a terrible consequence for Geni.

"Falling in love exposed her to the most primitive needs. Needs that had not been met by a mother or father. I'd had a father, horribly distant at times, but he loved me in his way. And I had my grandmother and a nursemaid and all the servants. A kind nursemaid can make such a difference. But Geni

173

went to the nuns. Some would have been kind, but of course everything has to be shared out with other children and with all their observances—they are really there for Christ, not for bawling infants. And you see, and this is very important for Geni, there is always the feeling, 'What did I do wrong? What is so bad about me that I should not have a mother?' And we know the nuns can be a guilty bunch, such a mood would not have helped.

"So Geni grew up and fell in love. Freud has told us about the compulsion to repeat. I have discussed it with him myself. Why should we make things happen over and over again? Events that caused us such pain and yet we keep bringing them back, as if constantly trying to put them right, and, sadly, forever failing to do so. It is what happened to Geni. Her choice of man was a disastrous repeat of the rejections. She chose a sadist and it turned her into a masochist!"

Marie made this summation with such emphasis and flourish that her whole head and shoulders emerged from the confines of her chair, and one arm gestured with such force as to almost knock the cigar from J's hand. I know from J's love of a good cigar, and this one was now burning slowly and evenly, that such an event would cause considerable distress. However, he had clearly become as enthused by the story as Marie and simply moved his hand to vigorously flick some ash into the fire.

"I was invited to the wedding. It was 1904. Geni was twenty-four and I was twenty-two. The journey was huge and tiring for us, from Paris to Madrid, but I knew I must go. I went there with my old nurse Mimau who had come to know Geni well. She was with us at the Paris Exposition. What a day! We saw there the sculptures of Rodin, pure instinct, expressed and refined by art. Wonderful!

"What a contrast. The wedding was a dull affair and Rodin was nowhere to be seen, felt or imagined. Just grim religious artefacts in their chapel and then a ball, if that's what you can call it, in their house. Geni and I had attended the Spanish Ambassador's ball eighteen months before. Such a difference. Geni had lit the place up. It had even caused me to cast away my own worries and dance with abandon. Even my grandmother danced the Polka. But sadly, that is also where Geni met the anus, Carlos, the son of the Marqués de Segura.

"At the wedding ball, the mother of Carlos sat presiding as if upon a granite throne. She never moved, and she certainly never danced. Her husband did: once with his new daughter-in-law, Geneviève, and I would swear that I saw tears rolling down his cheeks. Poor man. What a lifetime of misery, and I could see that the same was in store for Geni.

"The groom was strutting around. He had romanced Geni with flair in their early months, but it was different now. He seemed to spend most of the time talking to male friends and then sitting with his mother. Geni had few friends there and as you know, no family. A remarkable thing. I do believe that she considered me to be the family guest. This was all bequeathed to her by her mother of course, who had dismissed the few relatives that she had and whose friends had all died of syphilis or drug addiction."

Here, J withdrew his feet from the fireside and leaned forward in his chair.

"Marie, you give our young friend the wrong impression. The Countess was well known in Paris and was a friend of Mallarmé, one of our greatest poets, and even Charcot. I, as a student doctor, saw her at one of Charcot's clinical sessions in the Salpêtrière, where he treated her as someone rather special. He even asked her for her opinion of his patient, one of his famous young hysterics called Madeleine. I remember the answer was astute and we were all very impressed as she had no medical training. It was rare for a layperson to attend such meetings and I know she attended his soirées too."

"Alright, Jean, I know that sometimes contempt gets the better of me. But my grandmother told me tales of Marguerite.

The woman was beautiful and bright and could charm people, but her destructiveness shows that she was taken up by the Death Drive. You know that she was rumoured to be in league with the Satanists."

"Granted, Marie, I have heard such rumours, though I cannot follow your link to a Death Drive. But that is for another time."

It is of course known to my colleagues, that Freud increasingly proposes a Death Drive. An internal force that aims, from birth, to return us to our previous lifeless state. A view not easily held by all. I, for one, find it rather restful, knowing that death is inevitable and a return to the organic earthly components from which we emerged, rather romantic. But then I am a young man. And death is far off. J is known not to favour the theory, hence his remark. Freud has also linked the passive component of the Death Drive to some kind of primary masochism, and I could see that Marie had this in mind. She was not ready to leave it yet.

"My story of Geni is about masochism. You will see. I also believe that your young nun Camille was not of the Death Drive but of the drive for life! And of love, which Freud calls Eros. It is why it became so important for Geneviève that your girl came into her life, and why I believe Camille had that dream about Eros. Yes, your Camille was of the Life Instinct."

I had always considered the patient Camille Beauclair to be the complete province of J. But I could see that Marie Bonaparte, through her knowledge of Geneviève de Bolvoir and her own ideas, was laying some claim to his territory. I assumed that he was man enough to take it!

Marie relaxed back into her chair and continued.

"We were guests at the house for three days. I was overjoyed to be leaving, though dismayed for the state of my friend. Geni tried so hard to believe she was happy. She thought it wrong not to be, but how can one force such a thing? When we left, the two of us embraced and she would not let me go. But I could tell. This was not just the embrace of a dear friend, but a clinging to a lifeline. For all my faults, I knew I was worth more to her than the sum of all those in the Spanish family put together. In fact, even that does not say enough. In Don Carlos, there was more than just deprivation; there was outright cruelty. This was to come. But first, he had to get her to his Andalusian estate.

"This happened soon, as Geni was very willing, believing that any change would be better than the gloom of the Madrid house and its matriarch. And also, Carlos had painted the estate within Geni's mind in the most glowing colours. And, I dare say, without Carlos it would have been a heavenly place. Southern Spain is very hot but has great beauty. There are usually mountains to be seen and they were close to the great river, the Guadalquivir. It's a fat lazy thing that drifts for hundreds of miles through Andalusia. I was later to visit there myself with Geni's man, Edouard Morel. By now he was one of the only good things in her life but distant, an employee caring for her house in Issoire, and no longer her secretary."

I knew by then that this current entry to my journal was to be a long and detailed one. I wished not to lose any of the details nor the nuances in the conversation. It was thus that I asked for permission to write a few notes. J was aware of my journal and not averse to occupying its central space. Any man with a long career will surely be pleased to know that there is one who will wish to record it, so that its achievements will not decay and disappear in the process of time. Since Marie gave no objection, J indicated some paper and pens upon his desk and having collected them and returned to my seat, I was settled again, and Madame Bonaparte continued.

I will, however, now rest my pen. Midnight has passed; the good food and wine that gave such pleasure are now exacting their toll and sleep is required to restore me to the state needed for clear memory and writing. I have my notes to aid me and a free morning tomorrow. I will continue then.

CHAPTER NINETEEN

From an essay on J and his work. Continuing the evening with Marie Bonaparte

By Dr Paul Faucher (1935)

Now refreshed, though my sleep was troubled, and with the aid of my notes, I return to my journal.

Princess Marie had taken up the story of Camille through her knowledge of the young nun's new prioress, Mother Geneviève. A woman with as remarkable a history as Camille herself.

She continued.

"In Andalusia, things did improve for a while. Carlos, freed from his attachment to his mother, became the man who had courted Geneviève in Paris. He wanted her to know how much he loved his estate and his horses and Geni re-found some of her more natural responses to life. She even came to see and to share the beauty that is inherent in the body and movement of a horse. And these were the finest horses, tall elegant creatures that would be displayed at festivals—they are always having them in Spain—and also sold for great sums of money.

"Carlos taught her to ride, and on one occasion they rode until they reached the grasslands where he bred his ferocious bulls. They were not to confront these creatures in the bullring or stir their aggression, so the experience was without danger. However, Geni came close enough to study their magnificence."

I have scribbled just here my notice of an enthusiasm in Madame Bonaparte as she began to describe the fighting bull. Linked perhaps to her well-known interest in the phallic aspects of sexuality.

"These bulls were magnificent, and though calmly grazing and indifferent to nearby humans, they still transmitted their massive power, and as Geni told me later, though by then she was hardly allowing it, she could even feel the heat from their bodies, smell their musty odour and sense their physicality. They have great wide shoulders and height, these bulls, and as Carlos and his forbears had been sure to develop, they had the largest horns, like great daggers to the matador. And we know about the testicles. A great bag that hangs between their legs."

I did not note it down, but Marie's enthusiasm for her subject was still evident.

"What moved Geni was seeing such power in an animal so self-contained and peacefully grazing."

Here, J briefly interrupted.

"I was to hear something similar when Camille told me about her beloved Sister Africa. She'd been a primitive native in Senegal and loved big cats and knew them as powerful spirits."

"And we will hear more about the African too," declared Marie, triumphantly.

"When they rode back, they paused in a rare space of greenery, a cleft by the banks of the Guadalquivir. They were alone. The sky was as clear a blue as you could ever see. The sun beat down, but just there, by the river, there was the slightest breeze and there was shade, and the river, slowly drifting through its long course to the Atlantic, made no sound so that all that could be heard was silence. And there they lay together and made love. It reminds me of a time when …"

But Marie, thinking better of it, paused and continued,

"And do you know, this was the first time. Carlos in Madrid, with the lurking presence of his mother, was impotent. But just now, reassured by his bulls and horses, and with Geni truly in awe at their grace and power, they consummated the marriage. Geneviève was no longer a virgin. Even later, after all that followed, she could refer to that time as one of beauty and pleasure. In fact, I believe Geni had a very healthy Eros. Her only problem was the man she had chosen.

"It would never happen again. Carlos seemed to spend the next few weeks regretting his encounter with the feminine as if enfeebled by it. How sad. A woman like Geni could make a man feel so good to be a man. But not for this poor creature; governed by his mother, and with a father all but physically castrated. They were never again to make love, and on the few occasions they had sex, the prerequisite was cruelty of speech, which then turned into physical beatings.

"And Geni put up with it. She was a masochist. Was there some part of her that enjoyed it? I suspect so, though she would have enjoyed far more some real love. But the cruel deprivations of her childhood were now to fuse with her libido and be repeated. I do believe that she would have suffered like this forever, but for one factor. Though she could not save herself, she found another whom she could save.

"Carlos had servants at his hacienda. They were local peasants. Some travelled in when needed, and there were others who were housed in quarters, some plain rooms within a stone outbuilding. But in the cellar of the actual house, Carlos kept his favourite. Or, should I say, the one he used most. Her duties were to serve him. Not to clean, or to cook, or to wash the dishes, or make the beds. Such things were too impersonal. Carlos wanted direct subservience from one who would fetch for him, bring him his drinks, serve him his food, attend whilst he washed and dressed and when he undressed. The fact that these duties were carried out by a female only increased his pleasure and feelings of dominance. The servant was a young African girl, no more than sixteen years in age. And of course, not a servant, but a slave.

"Geneviève, after her brief reprieve, was descending again into depression. But, despite her apathy, she could not bear what she saw. Her husband's cruelty to her merged into his abuse of the young African. She could do nothing about her own suffering but felt compelled to help the girl.

"One night in July, after a day of intense heat which was hardly cooled by the darkness, there came through the open window, a pitiful sound—a cry of pain and then a sob of sheer misery. It repeated so that Geni, unable to sleep, lay awake, waiting for it to cease. But it did not, and the cries of pain increased in their loudness and frequency so that Geni could no longer wait in the hope that they would stop and that she could force them out of her mind. Slowly, impelled by a power she could not resist, she rose from her bed, slipped into a light dress and sandals and left the bedroom.

"Much of the hacienda was laid out on the ground level with a courtyard at its centre. She entered the courtyard and could see an open door on the other side. It was a room where Carlos kept his favourite items: his guns, his swords, his mementoes, his photos, and paintings from the corrida, and on this night, his slave. Geneviève looked across at the doorway. The flame of an oil lamp was flickering from the violent movements within and cast upon a wall the shadow of a figure whose arm was rhythmically rising and falling. At each downward move-ment of the arm, there was the sharp sound of an impact and the cry of the girl.

"Geneviève crossed the courtyard and reached the open doorway. The shadow of the figure was huge, and the sounds of violence and pain were at their height. She crossed the threshold and it was no longer shadows, but the physical presence of Carlos reaching back his arm to strike. Geni knew the switch that he held. He had used it on her. It had been ritualistic then. Acutely painful for her and for him, it was his only way to achieve climax, though that was not to be shared with her. And she had allowed it, absorbed it, seen it as an offering to his fragile masculinity and also as her fate.

"There was no ritual to what she saw now. It was an assault that left the young African cringing, huddled against the wall. The thin smock that she wore had been torn away by Carlos and thrown across the room. All over her body were the raw welts from the beating and the bruises from the many that had come before.

"Carlos, so intent on inflicting pain, did not at first see Geni. Unable to find a voice with which to shout, she crossed the room and grasped the arm that was raised to strike. He whirled round—his surprise, in an instant, turning to fury at her action. There was sweat upon his brow and the hair, normally oiled back behind his ears, hung wild and loose around his face. Geni looked and saw the dark eyes narrow and the top lip curl in hatred and contempt. She knew then that her presence would bring no release for the African, but that she had simply included herself in the savagery.

"He hissed at her in Spanish. She had learned the language well enough to recognise the insults and the condemnation of her as a woman. She felt the strength that had carried her from her bedroom and across the courtyard now fail her in measure with each contemptuous word. And still, the words came, until, for Carlos, they no longer could suffice. Her whole being was shaking, and there was such a weakness in her legs that she was just a loose bundle as he threw her to the ground. She fell next to the girl and lay still. She expected there to be blows. Once more the arm rose and fell and struck the girl, who now, despite the pain, could only whimper. Geni scrambled to move closer, placing her arm around her and covering her with her own body. She waited for the switch to descend. She felt fear, but most of all there was utter dejection, and then her mind and body parted. She left her body to cover the girl and allowed her mind to wander. She thought of her descent. She had been happy at first in Paris, she was sure of that. She remembered Sophie and the warm intimacy of their conversations, sometimes after lovemaking, with Sophie proclaiming that her mistress would have even greater pleasure with a man. She thought of the sinewy nude sculptures of Rodin that had both scared and excited her and the many paintings of lovers in the great house that she used to own but that now belonged to her husband. And all had come to nothing."

Marie Bonaparte paused. There was just the occasional crackling sound from the fire. I suddenly worried that it must be late and wondered whether I would still get a cab. The silence continued. J sat motionless, his legs stretched out, his cigar long since finished. It occurred to me that perhaps my own mind and body were separating as I felt strangely insecure and ill at ease.

Marie lent over the side of her chair to a small bag from which she took a handkerchief. She dabbed at her nose, not her eyes, but I have noticed in my patients that such actions are often the substitute for the wiping away of tears, tears of grief or great sadness. I realised then that it was great sadness that filled the room. We had heard of the tragic decline of a fine woman and of her sinking to the greatest depths.

"Is the heart able, in its despair, to simply end its life?" Marie still held the handkerchief though now she seemed unconscious of it.

"I believe that Geni nearly died that night. Her life force, her Eros, had lost its battle. Carlos was gone. He chose not to beat his wife in the presence of his slave. Perhaps some twisted vestige of decorum. Geni had waited for the switch to strike her, ready to suffer for the sake of the girl, but there were no more blows. It reminded her of a time with a nun, when she was a girl at school and how, then too, when the blows stopped there was silence and looking around, she was alone. Now she was just with the African girl. She asked her name—'Diatou.' She touched her and looked at her wounds and said, 'I must bathe them for you,' yet neither could move.

"Geneviève turned onto her back. Through the open doorway, she could see the night sky that teemed with stars. 'I must turn off the light,' she thought, and she hated the pale, yellow light that came from the oil lamp. She raised herself, and on her knees, she moved across to the lamp and turned down the wick. Now the stars in the sky were even brighter and more numerous. She was still on her knees and it made her think of the nuns who had raised her and cared for her as a child. She thought of how often she had seen them just like this, on their knees, revering a greater power, and she remembered how safe she had felt with the sisters and how long ago that was. It seemed such an ancient memory, but it gave her comfort.

"She turned to the girl, who also lay on her back and who was watching her. Her nakedness seemed not to count. Geni turned back to the stars and suddenly needed to see the moon as well, so that she rose, and stumbling a little, left the heat of the room for the warm air of the courtyard. There was no moon that she could see, so she turned back to the girl. She found her smock and helped her to put it on. Then she took her to the small fountain at the centre of the courtyard and she gathered the hem of her own dress, pulling it up so that she held a handful of cloth that she dampened in the slight bubbling stream, and with that, she gently bathed the areas of skin where there was blood. And she thought, 'I must make her safe before he returns because he is of death, not life.' She moved to the wall at the side of the courtyard and sat leaning against it. The girl was watching her with wide eyes. Despite all that had happened she seemed composed. 'It happens so often to her,' thought Geneviève. She rose and beckoned Diatou to follow her, placing her finger upon her lips to command silence.

185

"The hacienda of Carlos was miles from other dwellings. A safe place to keep a slave, and somewhere he could feel confident to lead his life in whichever way it suited him. His confidence was such that there were few locks upon the doors. Geni knew that the stables were unlocked, and she headed towards them. They would first have to re-enter the house. Geni led the girl by the hand. Carlos would not be asleep and could be in any room. They had to pass one that was his office and from underneath the door there was an ominous strip of light. 'He is there,' she thought, 'drinking perhaps, wondering what to do with us next—or in the morning.'

"Geni was sure then, that there must be no more mornings with Carlos. She crept as quietly as she was able and the girl that followed her was as silent as a shadow. And it was as two shadows that they went through the house. But not yet free. The main door to the house loudly creaked and groaned, so that Geneviève froze, the door just half open. Very carefully, she pushed it enough for them to slip through, expecting, any moment, the furious Carlos to burst from his room.

"The stables were fifty yards away and now they ran. Geni had kicked off her sandals so that they were both barefoot. They reached the stable doors. It was now that Geneviève realised that her plan was useless. There were no saddles in the stable—she had never harnessed a horse—she knew not if Diatou could ride. There, in the shadows of the stable, she watched her plan collapse before her and the old feeling of helplessness, the weakness in her legs, the subordination to fate, crept back into her being. She felt herself surrendering and hopelessly and helplessly she leant against the wooden wall of the stable and slipped down until she was sitting, ready to wait for the dawn and the wrath of Carlos.

"It was Diatou who, in French, whispered fiercely in her ear, 'We must go, we will walk and we will run.' And with great physical strength and courage, she pulled Geneviève from the ground. 'It is too far,' was all Geni could say, but the girl responded, 'It is nothing—I have walked through the desert—and my lion will protect us.'

"The thought of the power of a lion, however uncanny and out of place such a creature would be on an Andalusian night, raised Geni up, as surely as the strong arms of the African girl. Yes! They would walk.

"A light appeared in another room of the house, a room that looked onto the stables. Geni turned. Any moment she might see the face of Carlos, looking out. 'Yes,' she whispered, 'We will walk and we will run.'

"Firstly, they ran, their bare feet pounding the dirt and the scrub until they had reached the end of the hacienda's long driveway and they were upon the main road. And there, shining big and full and straight ahead, was the moon.

"Now, nearer to dawn, there was the slight cooling of a breeze, as the two headed towards Seville."

Marie's tone had changed, her voice was quieter now, and I could tell that for a while at least Geneviève and Diatou were free.

"Geni had come from the nuns and now she went back to them. And anyway, where else could they go? There are many convents and monasteries in Seville. They reached the city as the sun rose high in the mid-day sky. The feet of Diatou were hardened and not damaged by their long walk, but Geni's were bleeding and so painful she could hardly continue. There was to be no searching for a choice of convent. They stopped at one of the first. It happened to be Carmelite. The Carmelites were little known to Geni; she had been brought up by a non-reclusive order. If she had known more, she would have feared the Carmelite exclusion of the outside world. But they were not turned away. Love, after all, is paramount. The two would have appeared as beggars, but the obvious pain of Geni and the strange apparition of a sixteen-year-old African, made them take notice. The nuns took them in and heard their story. There was a building attached to the convent, it's a monastery really since they are Carmelites, and this was used for the lay staff or for rare visitors to stay. Here they were settled and cared for. They could wash and were given the smocks that the nuns slept in, to wear.

"And so, word reached me. A wire was sent beseeching me to travel to Seville and rescue poor Geni and bring her back to Paris. Rescuing people and things seems to be my lot! I might soon have a much more difficult one to accomplish. Well, I am willing—for a good cause. And I have the money! I wrote to her man, Morel, who had been her secretary in the Paris house. He was looking after her remaining property in Issoire. I got him to meet me en route and we continued to Seville. An even worse journey than Madrid. Far worse in fact and the heat was unbearable. But we made it. We got her and brought her back to my house in Paris.

"She was changed, very changed. She was defeated by life, so let down by Eros, and desperately searching for something. The childhood with nuns and the kindness of the Seville Carmelites offered it. She soon believed that her only salvation was through Christ and the strict observations of Carmel. And that's where she headed. She had some job, becoming a nun, but we managed to get the marriage annulled. The offering of her Issoire house as a monastery may well have swung things for her. I tried to change her mind but had no chance.

"Twenty-five years later she was the Prioress at her old Issoire house and giving your Camille such a hard time!"

She reached over to J and placed her hand upon his knee. I had never known him to be quiet for so long. He placed his hand upon hers.

"What happens to Eros, Marie? Such forces range against it. The news from Germany is terrible. And now Austria. Will you need to get him out?"

"If he'll let us," replied Marie, and I could see that in their minds, Freud's danger from the Nazis was mirroring the tale just told, of Geneviève and Diatou.

I asked, "And what of the girl, Diatou?"

Marie answered, "She stayed in the Seville monastery and helped with daily tasks. Afterwards, she moved to the Carmel at Cordoba, not so far from Seville, where she became a novice and went on to take her vows."

"Where, years later, she met and was loved by Camille," added J.

It was now very late. The fire had burned down to a few softly glowing embers, and unlike the heat of southern Spain, our Parisian winter was exerting its chill. We were all tired. J helped Marie on with her coat. With the benefits of wealth and status, she had instructed her driver to await her pleasure outside. And so, quietly now and with few words, I was taken home in the limousine of Princess Marie, who bid me goodnight and continued to her own home in Saint Cloud.

She made just one more remark concerning our topic of the evening: that it was by no means the end of the story.

CHAPTER TWENTY

The sacrament of marriage

M arie Bonaparte was just twenty-three when, in 1905, she received the telegram from her friend Geneviève. The message expressed great distress and a completely unambiguous need to be rescued. Marie was a young woman herself but had gained her maturity, and along with that, control of the enormous wealth that she could now fully inherit from her mother. She was a character of considerable complexity, often suffering from neurotic conflict and hypochondria, but there was already an adventurous quality which together with her intelligence was later to make her a pioneer and considerable force as a psychoanalyst and one who was very close to Freud himself.

She lost no time in preparing for the journey to Seville. She would need a companion, and in the circumstances, she wished that to be a man and Geneviève's faithful secretary Morel was the obvious choice. She sent word to the Bolvoir house in Issoire, Geneviève's last remaining property, which had been left in Morel's care. Morel was to meet Marie en route in Madrid and from there they would continue their long, hot, journey down to Andalusia.

As they travelled, Marie had addressed Morel as one who had his own special knowledge of her friend. She was exasperated and could speak of little else than the disastrous marital choice that Geneviève had made and the cruelty inflicted upon her. So much had come through to Marie in her letters, but the existence of the slave and the events of the night of the escape were only told to them when they finally arrived in Seville and sat with a still shaken and exhausted Geneviève in the annexe of the monastery.

Later that evening, Geneviève had called Diatou to join them and holding her hand, had introduced her.

"This is Diatou, and she grew up in a village in Senegal. She has told me about it and how they would live and how they would find spirits in the trees and plants and especially in the animals."

And then in turn she introduced Marie and Morel to Diatou.

She said with a smile, "This is a real princess," and Diatou had given a little bow to Marie.

Morel, who for many years had observed the rituals of class difference, knew when such a gesture was not of pure deference and when pride was retained. He could see this was the case with the girl, whose large eyes were wide and observing, but who gave little indication of her thoughts and feelings.

"And this is Monsieur Morel," said Geneviève. "Edouard has served me and looked after me, and I need him now more than ever."

Morel was taken aback. He sensed a displeasure in Marie Bonaparte that his mistress should show such vulnerability to one she employed. But as Geneviève spoke, her eyes filled with tears and she reached out, so that she grasped the hands of them both.

"At last, I feel some love."

She paused, and then,

"In the midst of my despair, it has come. But can it really last?"

And the tone of her voice trailed off into melancholy.

Turning to the girl again, she said,

"Diatou will be staying here at the monastery and will work for the nuns. She will be safe here."

And Morel, well attuned to the ways and the power of the aristocracy, had thought of Carlos and had wondered whether such safety could truly be so.

But their lives had moved on. His tenancy and management of Geneviève's remaining property at Issoire had been a pleasant time. And it was his pleasure, that after her delivery from Carlos and a short stay with the Princess, Geneviève fully moved into the Issoire house.

Morel had served his mistress in the strange position of secretary, accountant, and trusted advisor, even in the choice of dress, and he had almost become a friend. If the matter had only been the choice of Geneviève, friendship it would have been. But Morel saw things differently. He had developed and grown and been promoted within the culture and traditions of class and the aristocracy and had imbued these to such an extent that he believed that entering into an informality of friendship with his young mistress would be to disrupt, not just the structure of the Bolvoir household, but that which maintained his own wellbeing. The loss that accompanied this position was accepted as a necessary sacrifice. He was now ready to serve her again as her secretary and advisor and looked forward to her gradual recovery.

He was, though, to be disappointed. Geneviève rarely left her bedroom. A maid was employed to care for her daily needs, but her services were hardly used. The maid herself became depressed, and within two months gave in her notice.

Morel made the arrangements to replace her as Geneviève was indifferent. He watched helplessly as she became increasingly reclusive.

When she asked him to arrange a meeting with a priest from the town he was relieved, though it was not something that figured amongst his own remedies for life's troubles. He had served her mother and had known her contempt for the Church and to see her daughter now seeking its help needed some adjustment to his outlook. It was though, his natural way, to accommodate, and he travelled to Issoire and found there a young, fresh-faced and enthusiastic Father Pierre. Morel assumed that it was also his role to explain to the priest the events that had caused Geneviève to now seek salvation through the Church.

Geneviève was reaching into the past for something that had been steady, reliable, and that had never let her down. She had grown up in an institution managed by nuns. They had been her providers and in the school rooms, her teachers. Their religion had been the sustenance that held and directed their way of life and this they had offered to the girls in their charge. Geneviève had accepted this but had rarely been moved by it. In fact, she was far worldlier than she or the nuns could have imagined. The worldliness was to be met, engaged with and embraced when her dying mother summoned her to Paris and the House of Bolvoir and placed her in a world of Belle Époque exuberance in which she became a new and shining star.

During that time, she hardly said a prayer, but the kindness of the Seville nuns who had interrupted the quietness of their lives to receive her and the girl, and who had made them safe, had rekindled memories of those nuns in her childhood who had been kind to her. It seemed, now, that such evidence of love was all that could sustain her.

And in reaching back to those times and to the people for whom religion was all, she began to think of sin and the life of riches and of pleasure that led up to her romance with Carlos.

The duality that had always lurked waiting, seized upon the memories of social success. Surely, one so worthless as to be rejected by her own mother could not sustain, nor even deserve them. And were they not pointless pleasures anyway?

Though she was unaware of the fact, her experiences of soirées and balls and of the liberating bustle of Parisian life with its openness to sensation and new experience, contained within them the natural spontaneity of childhood. Responses within friendships, the enjoyment of culture, flirtations with men and with women, were all part of the natural play of life.

As she confessed to Father Pierre, and as she increasingly formed in her personal doctrine, all such feeling and emotion should now be held in abeyance. The ordering of a religious life and the sacrifices that it entailed should be the sole priority. In the increasing vigour with which she approached this, she had little idea that she was drawing a cloak of protection around herself which existed to repel all feeling other than that she deemed acceptable to God. And in doing so, she left little room for any feeling at all.

Father Pierre, in his naive and well-intentioned attendance to this woman, whom he found so interesting and who seemed so amenable to his teaching, was easily able to convince himself that her looks played no part. Instead, she became for him a young weeping Madonna, as beautiful in her sadness as any he had seen in the great paintings and with an added frisson of the Magdalene. After all, as she told him so often, she had sinned.

A bemused Morel would take her regularly to Mass as well as shepherding the priest to and from the Issoire house. He was relieved that his mistress had, at least, found a purpose in her life.

The great triumph for Pierre was that not only had Geneviève returned to the faith, but she was also now enquiring about the ways of becoming a nun and the requirement of order and control in her life caused her to think of the Carmelites.

They too had been her saviours in Seville, and to join the order became her only aim. Father Pierre set the process in motion.

The massive obstacle was her marriage, as she could only take vows if the marriage be annulled. She could not lie; non-consummation would not be used, though it was so nearly the case. She begged Marie to exert all her influence. Marie was not actively religious, but her contacts were considerable. A princess herself, great-grand-niece to the Emperor Napoleon l, and the daughter of Prince Roland, a distinguished naturalist. And it was through the contacts of contacts, and not without gifts and favours, that a dialogue with the Vatican began. But even this seemed not enough to annul the sacrament of marriage in the eyes of the Church. It was Marie's acute intelligence that found the way.

Geneviève, secluded in her Issoire house, received a letter from Marie.

My Dear Geni,

I have cast my mind back to those fateful days when you were courted by Don Carlos. How much can change between those days of early romance and then the sharing of lives in matrimony that allows the most hidden qualities of a person to emerge and to gather a force which might otherwise have remained dormant. All, of course, still to come for me, though I fear the storm clouds of courtship are approaching! I am, unfortunately, very eligible!

But I then thought much further back than that. Even to your infancy, my dear. I was told much about your mother by my grandmother, a character who, through her own ruthless determination, felt some affinity towards her. She did not know your mother personally, they only met briefly two or three times, but she certainly knew her by repute. Your mother was known to be utterly against the church, to such an extent that it was rumoured that she had an ongoing assignation with an excommunicated priest who was a master of the dark arts and as evil as they come. Oh Geni, there is even more, and one day we must talk about it—along with this wish of yours to be a nun.

They talk about the "sins of the fathers," but I wonder about the sins of the mothers!

Anyway, my conclusion is this. Your mother would never have had you baptised. It is in no way feasible. She would not have stepped inside a church unless it had been desecrated and turned over to Satan! And she would not have allowed her daughter, even one whom she was about to so cruelly abandon, be designated to the Catholic Church through its sacrament of baptism.

It means, Geni, that your marriage is not sacramental in the eyes of the church. I have enquired and researched. For one such as you, who wishes to now take her place in the Catholic church and who (stubbornly!) wishes to become a bride of Christ, there can be release from a non-sacramental marriage, in order to enter one that is so. It needs a papal dispensation and will still require all our efforts, but despite your strange wish to become a Carmelite, I cannot bear the thought of you still being married to Don Carlos. (I have to say that neither, at times, can I bear the thought of marrying anyone myself and the prospect of childbirth terrifies me—it killed my own mother, you know, but that's for us at another time.)

Now we must just keep thinking about you. There must some-where be a certificate of baptism because the nuns who brought you up would have required that and no doubt you had to produce one when you married. It will be a forgery—for sure. Find it and send it to me. I will have my people scrutinise it!

Enough for now, Dear Geni, you know I love you—my dear friend. Don't let the Carmelites take you away.

Marie.

The baptism certificate did indeed prove to be suspect, as the signature of the priest did not stand comparison with other certificates issued by the same hand. But what really made the difference was noticed by Marie herself. It was she who examined not only the front of the certificate but its reverse.

She had been studying the writing, feeling and turning the paper over in her hands and then had placed it, face down, upon her desk. It happened that her desk lamp was lit and cast upon it a very bright light. She noticed, in one corner, the faintest outline of a design. It was an inverted pentagram surrounded by a circle. Marguerite, Countess of Bolvoir, had bowed to the despised necessity of obtaining a certificate, but not without secretly desecrating it with a satanic symbol. Such an act, which relieved her of the pain of compliance, left her as well, with a degree of triumph.

Even that was not enough. Marie promised an endowment to the Church, and there was also one from Geneviève: that the Issoire house should become the property of the Church on her death. That it be used before then as a monastery, was her extra gesture when it was beholden upon her to give up her worldly possessions as a Sister of Carmel.

Geneviève was a postulant, novice, and then made her Solemn Profession in a Carmel convent in Paris. Ten years later, her obedience and devotion, as well as the strength of her presence, aided, it can be said, by the donation of a beautiful country house, placed her securely as the choice to become the Reverend Mother in the new Carmel of Issoire.

PART SIX

CAMILLE AT ISSOIRE

CHAPTER TWENTY ONE

A dreamless sleep

She had ceased to dream. Since her arrival at Issoire, there were no dreams at night, and the day-dreams that had been so clear as to be almost visions were now rare glimpses of vague, shifting shapes. She longed to leave the monastery and to walk through the beautiful garden to the gate and to the river where she had watched the water nymph and her graceful dive from the clutches of the beast that pursued her. It had frightened her, but she had known the excitement of fear mixed with pleasure.

Her timeless creatures of instinct had stirred a vitality she could no longer feel. It was as if she were sleeping.

Nothing could wake her—not even the tasks that Mother Geneviève was so purposeful in imposing. There were boring, repetitive duties to perform and when she was upon her knees for hours, not praying but cleaning the stone floors of the corridors or the chapel, there was pain as well. There was pain from the scourge that she used, occasionally and almost with indifference, as something simply expected of her. She obeyed the commands of her Mother Superior and observed her duties as a Carmelite nun, but without the vigour and love that had filled her first years of monastic life. Then, she was attuned to every moment, and each day with its challenges and hardships had brought spiritual reward.

There was no clarity now. No involvement; no reward. She lived in a demi-world, as if she were sleep-walking, though without a dream. She longed to be woken.

The Sacrament of the Confession was again part of her life. Once a week, Father Pierre travelled to the convent from the town and absolved the nuns from their doubts and mis-demeanours. Camille spoke and confessed. She could pro-duce sins enough without including the longing she felt for her dreams. Through the mist of the present, she recalled the moment of clarity in her Cordoba cell when she had declared, "I will not share it—nor will I confess it." It seemed long ago.

What had she done wrong? Had she opened and gazed into a forbidden vessel? Had she usurped a part of her soul that belonged only to God? Had she tried to fill it with the creatures of her dreams; her winged god, the racing cheetah, a horned man-beast, and a beloved, African goddess? They had no place in her marriage to Christ for whom she should sacrifice all. Were her dreams just the sinful product of pride? She had been so happy to contest all vanity when she became a nun. Worldly values were easily forsaken for her great love of Christ and a little less surely, the Virgin Mother. But it was pride that Mother Geneviève had seen within her and so ardently wished to crush. Camille had said, "Mother you are beautiful," and amazed them both and brought down the full force of retribution.

"I have reminded her of her beauty," thought Camille. "And why does she wish to forget it?"

The Prioress had begun to tell her. Something sad, per-haps tragic, in her past and then she had clamped down upon the words and offered instead the scourge as all that she would share.

At the Issoire monastery, there were twelve Sisters and three novices. Camille did not know that once the house had been a worldly possession of her Mother Superior. But from conversations in Recreation, she learned that Mother Geneviève had been a novice leading to her profession in a Carmel near Paris and had continued there to become a novice mistress. When the Issoire house was consecrated as a monastery she had moved there to be its first Prioress. That was two years ago. There were two older nuns there from the beginning, but the others were unusually young. Camille was now twenty-six.

The monastery in Cordoba had been in the ancient part of the city, but the Issoire house was in the countryside, and Camille knew from her journey there that there were no dwellings nearby. There was though, a gatehouse to the grounds and she had occasionally seen the figure of a man who lived there and whose work was to maintain the gardens and carry out repairs to the house. Through a window on the top floor, she had watched him work. She never saw his face. He seemed always to place himself so that it could not be seen. And he never looked.

She was unsure whether he had a grace of movement or whether she imagined it. She longed so much for her winged god.

And she missed her Sister Africa, terribly. She wondered whether Julia missed her. She seemed so strong and sure of herself. Her night in Julia's cell could have done them great harm. Julia had been pleased to tell her story and had held her in her arms, but it was Camille who had entered the cell and stood frozen in the moonlight waiting for her to wake. Such intimacy was utterly forbidden. And then she had been seen leaving and running through the corridor. It had been reported of course, but she was known to be ill and fevered and Julia, with calm assertiveness, had declared that Camille came no further than her door.

"Such strength, to lie like that," thought Camille, and she knew that Sister Julia was like no other nun. But then she added, "Neither am I," and she saw and savoured their sharing of pagan spirits, whether from the primaeval soul of Africa or the pantheon of ancient Europe.

But to all observers, including Mother Geneviève, Sister Constance was now obedient. That she also seemed listless was of no concern to Sisters who had not known her before and were unable to make a comparison and for whom the professed life contained no real place for an independence of spirit.

CHAPTER TWENTY TWO

From an essay on J and his work. The sleep of Psyche

By Dr Paul Faucher (1935)

Princess Marie was not present at my next evening with J, though I feel sure that the three of us will meet again. Her old friendship with Geneviève has now made her a participant in the tale of Camille, and I look forward to hearing more of her insightful comments as well as her memories. She is though an extremely busy woman who travels widely and internationally and is at present away from Paris. I wonder what J thinks of that. He has impressed upon me the need for our reliable presence with our patients and has told me off on more than one occasion for taking a sudden or extended holiday.

This evening I described the case of a male patient who had developed an all-consuming terror of stepping in puddles caused by rain. It made it completely impossible for him to leave his house after rainfall, but most worryingly he had begun to watch the sky obsessively, and the slightest darkening of the clouds had become an additional cause for self-internment. Our discussion of the case had centred around a childhood memory of my patient in which, as a four-year-old boy, he had seen a man in the street take out his member, which to the four-year-old looked immense, and urinate against the wall of a building. He had been with his mother at the time and had turned towards her looking to be reassured by a look of horror upon her face that would match his own feelings, but instead, and it was a shock to him, he saw that his mother had watched the scene with interest. J had wondered whether the look of interest on the mother's face had actually been imagined by my patient and that he had displaced his own interest in the full-grown male penis onto his mother. Whatever the case, the incident would surely have awakened his feelings about the sexual mother, a most exciting and terrifying being, who, of course, would be just as interested in the penis of the boy's father. The fears and temptations of the Oedipus Complex had therefore been set into irresistible motion.

As we know, for some neurotics, the act of venturing outside the home can stir the possibility of falling prey to forbidden temptations. My patient, now an adult, is tormented by the return of oedipal wishes and fears when he goes out and is reminded of this childhood experience. All of course completely repressed by him and only escaping as a phobia about dirty pools of water. I look forward to our next sessions in which the validity of such interpretations can be tested.

We had then dined and returned to the study for cigars and cognac. I relaxed into my normal seat whilst J retreated into the shadows of the room and took from a shelf a large volume which he placed on his desk. He switched on a lamp and a golden patch of light brightened the desk and an area of carpet around it. The yellow glass of the lamp glowed to reveal the metal stem with its graceful curve and the intricate floral motifs at its base. I could see it was of a fine art nouveau design and remarked upon it, to which J just mumbled, "Gallé." He was too immersed in searching through the book to say more.

He found what he was looking for and carried the heavy volume back into our familiar space before the fire. He then dropped it into my lap without a care for the damage such an action may have caused. Fortunately, I had expected something similar and had my hands well placed to soften the impact. He then fell back into his armchair as if the whole operation had exhausted him. I am, in fact, a little concerned about J as I have seen him at meetings within the last two weeks and he has been without his customary vigour. I dearly hope that this is simply a temporary tiredness, though even J cannot defy the rigours of old age forever.

There was an image covering a full page, with text on the facing page. Just for a moment, I believed he was again showing me the statue of Saint Teresa by Bernini. There was something similar in the imagery, but most of all, it was the mood. I exclaimed immediately,

"It is another image of love! Is it again by Bernini? Surely it is."

J seemed satisfied with my response but needed to correct me.

"Antonio Canova, Italian, 1757–1822. Yes, love indeed, and this time we do not have an angel and an ecstatic saint, we have Eros himself, or Cupid for the Romans, or call him what you will, sometimes he's simply known as Amor—love in name and love in action."

"And he is with Psyche?"

"Indeed he is and it's a crucial time in the story. Many artists have painted the myth, but Canova's sculpture leaves them far behind. We have several Cupid and Psyche paintings by our own Bouguereau. Very beautiful, very romantic, as is everything he does, transporting her through the air, and she looking as well one might when lifted to the heights and flown away. Can you imagine what it would be to fly? We walk around Paris feeling so full of ourselves, and we rarely even look up. What would we see? A whole other world of feathered flying creatures that might well be looking down on us with some pity. They can travel from Notre Dame to the Eiffel Tower in the time it takes me to get down the stairs. Especially with the infernal lift broken again!"

The broken lift has been a repeated problem for J who lives on the fifth floor. I had to climb the stairs myself that evening. I wonder whether this may be a cause of his tiredness.

He continued.

"Anyway, yes Bouguereau. All very beautiful. But I go for the images that Camille eventually described to me. And she had waited so long. That Mother Geneviève had been an absolute pain. But she came around. Events made that unavoidable.

"But Bouguereau is just too sweet, and when Camille describes the creatures of her dreams, their beauty mingles with power, and they are of the earth as well as the heavens. Do you know that Bouguereau even had the gall to make a painting of Cupid and Psyche as children! A couple of ghastly ornate cherubs!"

I ventured, "But I suppose that does include the infantile sexuality that is the very basis of the theory of our work."

My intervention was utterly ill-advised.

J sat forward in his chair, and addressing the fire as if it was now the only object worth speaking to, he barked,

"That, my boy, is not infantile sexuality! It is psychological idolatry!"

I had never been addressed as "my boy" by J before and received it with mixed feelings.

"Anyway, Paul," and J was now conciliatory, "Look what you have before you—'Psyche Revived by Cupid's Kiss.'"

The statue was of great beauty. Seeing that the text on the opposite page continued overleaf, I turned the page and found more images taken from different angles.

"He made it on a revolving platform so that it could be seen all around. Not a bad idea for a sculpture, though he's been criticised because there's no single point that claims the view.

Not a problem to my mind since we have it in our Louvre and can happily walk all around it, as I have on many occasions. Though clearly you haven't, even though you live in Paris!"

J was in such an irascible mood that I felt fearful about saying anything. But as I continued to view the images, I ceased to care about my grumpy mentor as the beauty and love in the sculpture took me over.

We were both quiet for a while and then J continued in calmer tones.

"Venus has given Psyche a bad time. The tasks and the trials, all of which with extreme luck and help from others she has managed to fulfil.

"Now, the final one is to go down to Hades and find the queen of the underworld, Proserpina, and bring back a portion of Proserpina's beauty—for Venus. As if she wasn't beautiful enough. An insatiably vain woman. And Psyche manages it. She carries the beauty closed up in a vessel, a vessel that she's been forbidden to open. Of course, in the end she can't resist, and she opens it to steal just a little bit for herself and finds worse than nothing. All it contains is a curse of endless sleep. And so that's what happens. She collapses into just that. And that's how we see her in most of the paintings, helplessly prostrate and sleeping, normally laid out in a leafy glade.

"So! Let's go back to Camille, our Sister Constance, who is now in Issoire."

"She'd looked into forbidden places too. And hers were truly full of beauty and other marvellous things as well. The creatures and images from her dreams, and as a nun her love of these was forbidden. It was all pagan. In a way, she became cursed. After being sent to Issoire and to Mother Geneviève, and separated from the African, she stopped dreaming and it was as if that part of her was put to sleep. She felt half-dead. Nothing mattered and all she could do was pray for something to wake her, though even that was fraught since prayer was not meant to be for the purpose she had in mind—the recall of her lost Eros. Of course, in Mother Geneviève's eyes she was now behaving herself."

I looked at the images before me. In immaculate, smooth white marble were two figures: a youthful winged god gently cradled a young woman who lay before him. One arm was around her back and the other supported her breast. His wings, large enough to satisfy J, pointed upwards to the sky, whilst he looked down lovingly upon her. Her eyes were open, and she looked up at him and the closeness of their lips spoke of the kiss that would surely change everything.

J was calm now.

"He'd flown off and left her because she had dared to look at him, but he loved her far too much to let that continue. And his mother had been so cruel to her. Now it was the final tragedy— a curse of eternal sleep. Which sadly some do—sleep their way through life. Anyway, that was not to be Psyche's fate; Eros had to save and reclaim her. A kiss and a prick from one of his arrows and she was restored, and there she is in his arms."

I said, "I feel so deeply for Camille. How will she be restored? She has lost and been separated from so much. How terrible to lose one's dreams."

J arose from his chair. He wobbled a little and then steadied himself.

"The problem and the solution lay in Mother Geneviève. But Paul, forgive me, I am tired. Come again next week and we'll continue. And in the meantime, take a trip to the Louvre. I can't believe that you've not seen the statue. Remarkable!"

And with J's final reproach in my ears, I left. But it was without feelings of reproach towards him. I could see that he was surely not himself. I hope to find him in better health next time.

CHAPTER TWENTY THREE

Camille and Geneviève

The autumn was giving way to winter and the trees were almost bare. Pausing for a few moments on the way from her cell to the staircase, Camille looked out and watched the man again as he bent down to gather the dry, crisp, dead leaves, throwing them onto a bonfire before resting his back and wiping his brow. The wind chased the smoke from the fire across the garden to disappear amongst the tall, dark yew trees, but some found its way through the weathered wooden frames of the windows and mingled sweetly in the corridors with the smell of incense.

She continued down to the ground floor and made her way to a door that opened into the annexe of the house, an area which had been extended into a natural rising in the level of the garden so that its outermost wall and the paved, stone floor cut deep into the earth. It was always cool in summer, and in the winter months it was cold, and patches of damp made forlorn patterns upon the lower walls. This was their chapel.

All was simple and white and grey and the altar cloth, with its embroidery of silver and gold, offered the only decoration. Above the altar, the dying Christ hung from a large wooden cross, His eyes downcast.

There were periods of Divine Office throughout the day. Some were formal gatherings of the Sisters in the chapel. Others could be said privately. This was such a one and Camille found herself alone. Her bare feet felt the cold of the flagstones as she stepped towards the solid hard benches, but she did not sit down. Instead, she knelt in the aisle, close to the altar, so that she was almost in line with the downward gaze of Jesus. She held her hands together, her knees upon the hard floor, and looked up at Him. She liked it when she was alone there. It was rare and could only be by chance.

When she looked at the figure upon the cross, He seemed to move. It had been the same before, in Cordoba, and before then, when she had spent long periods sitting quietly and observantly in the churches near her home in Paris. She would keep looking until the figure would begin to vibrate as if energy pulsed from the body. She knew then how easy it would be to feel that she observed a miracle, just a little bit more movement, some tears or some blood. She had also watched the Virgin who had seemed even more animated, but she was not pinned to a cross, and though she tried to wish otherwise, Camille always felt less at ease with the Holy Mother. Her Son had been her chosen love since she was a girl. He had not always been on the cross then. There had been the many picture books with images of His kindness to children, of making miracles, or gracefully summoning the fishermen to be by His side and to join Him.

Since she had become a Sister of Carmel, the main images were those of Christ crucified and suffering. She wondered about this, and as before, there was the question of why it should be and the memory of a different, free and air-born god, who could fill her body and even her soul with joy and who did not speak of pain.

Since she came to Issoire, she had struggled to re-find her love of Jesus. Her struggle had pleased her Prioress, but without her dreams she was left with nothing; just an impenetrable darkness of doubt. It was despair that now brought her to the chapel and a hope that faith might be restored through prayer.

To kneel was not enough, so she placed her hands upon the stone and lowered her whole body to be prostrate before the altar and crucifix, just as she had done months before, in her cell in Cordoba. They had thought then that she was in crisis, but for Camille the crisis was now, without her dreams or her visions, without Sister Africa and without Jesus. She placed her cheek upon the cold floor, but the coldness of stone was all that she could feel. There was nothing else. She remembered how it was the same cheek that the winged god had breathed upon and it was his warm breath that mattered most and, prostrate before the crucifix, she knew that Christ was no longer enough. Nevertheless, she prayed. It was her favourite prayer said in French, and there was some succour from the memory of how she had loved it in the past, so that tears filled her eyes and then she wept, and her whole body shook with the sobs.

The nuns never touched each other, but kind words could do much to convey love. There were such words that Camille thought she was hearing. She discounted them as her imagination, but they were there again.

"Sister, what makes you so sad?"

Geneviève had entered the chapel of her own accord. She too enjoyed the accident of finding herself alone there and for a moment believed that this was the case. She had looked across as she entered and seen no one, until she heard the sobs and there, almost hidden by a row of benches, was a figure lying face down upon the ground. It caught her completely unguarded and the surprise opened her to a wave of compassion. She knew too, in an instant, that her emotion was also due to her recognition of Sister Constance.

She moved to where Camille lay. The brown habit was spread out as if it had spilt across the floor and her face was turned so that one side rested upon the stone, whilst the other, wet with tears, was exposed.

Geneviève wanted to kiss the cheek. Resisting the impulse took all her will. She sat upon a bench very close.

Day after day, Geneviève, as Mother Superior, went about her business. There was much to do and her own acts of devotion, her counsel to the nuns and her order of the affairs of the monastery, gave little time for stray thoughts and feelings. This is how she liked it, and she relied on her routines to maintain her in the present and to keep her memories at bay. But the advent of Camille had ruffled the edges of this calm existence and then made inroads towards the core. Amidst the disturbance, there was the thought, "Perhaps it is time for something like this." Such a thought could not have occurred before the coming of the errant Sister from Cordoba who had dared the intimacy of calling her beautiful and had done so with spontaneity. She had been shocked and scolded her of course. But something began that morning that could not be stopped. The same evening, she had thought of the green dress she had worn at the ball when she first met Carlos. She remembered the feel and the crinkly sound of the rich material and the knowledge of how it complemented so perfectly the golden red of her hair and how admiring had been the looks of her secretary and maid and then, at the ball, of the assembled guests. "Now my hair is grey and shorn, and so it should be. Such pride will undo all I have achieved," and she had used the scourge to drive out her vanity.

She arranged meetings with Sister Constance: spiritual consultations to crush the rebellious will that had caused such havoc in Cordoba. "Bring my gift to you," and Camille had dutifully brought the scourge, and Geneviève had set the example by chastising herself and then commanding Camille to do the same. She had, without complaint. Camille had become so dead inside that even pain was welcome, but she knew that she was doing this more for her Prioress than for herself and really it was of little consequence to her.

And it was no solution for Geneviève. Now she was increasingly beset by memories. The scourge upon her back reminded her of the sexual arousal followed by the beating from Sister Brigid, and then the grim memories of the sadism of Carlos.

And now she looked at the young nun lying before her in such pain; she thought of the naked figure of the native girl who had been the slave of her husband and how she had used her own body to protect her from the blows.

She had believed the exclusion of her previous life to be a spiritual requirement and her personal triumph over the past, but the spirit of memory had found her, alighted, and would not leave. It was there during the prayers and the troubled nights, watching her and waiting.

She saw it as a threat to her faith which she confessed to Father Pierre on his weekly visits. It made no difference. But, at the same time, the difference Camille had brought had become a temptation she increasingly welcomed. She asked herself, "Is it just because she said I am beautiful?" Perhaps the audacity of the statement was enough. But no, "It is because she really meant it and was able to say it."

There in the chapel, she moved from the bench and knelt next to the young woman whose sobbing was now silent yet visible in the movement of the cloth of the habit, draped across the supine body. Geneviève prayed aloud and for Camille the tone and the sense of the presence of the other helped her to open her eyes. She saw the large, imposing shape of the woman next to her and listened to the soothing words of the prayers that were spoken in French, the mother tongue of them both. She remembered the peace that she had felt in Cordoba when the nuns, fearing for her soul and her sanity, had laid her fevered body to rest in the little cot in her cell, with its plain hard mattress and its crucifix upon the wall, and had blessed her. As did Geneviève now, as she rose to leave.

"Bless you, Sister. Join us soon."

Geneviève continued to summon Camille for spiritual counselling. At first, she was sure that she intended to return her to a faith and obedience that would reduce her unhappiness. There seemed to be progress. There was little sign of the fevered disturbance that had caused such consternation in Cordoba, only the melancholy. Geneviève wrote to the Cordoba Prioress to let her know that Sister Constance was a dutiful and obedient presence in the Issoire Carmel.

Her concern though was the growing feeling of pleasure with which she anticipated their meetings and with it an unease about which of them was the true beneficiary. The young nun would enter the room and stand silently and respectfully until bidden to sit. Geneviève chose extracts from the scriptures as starting points. They were usually about sin, particularly pride, and she would try to develop the themes and encourage Camille to speak of her own sinfulness. In this, she was disappointed. Camille was unable, or perhaps unwilling, to share any more than the most mundane sins and seemed to be harbouring a private world that was not for her Prioress to enter.

"Sister, you know that we give ourselves freely and completely to the Lord. For Him we give everything, and we can keep nothing of ourselves away from him. If we do, we fail in the very task to which we have devoted our lives."

And Camille had answered,

"I have no fear of keeping anything from Jesus as he already sees all. I know he loves me and will always grant me his blessing. But Mother, does it mean that I need share everything with you? Does our obedience mean that we can have no thoughts and feelings that are kept for ourselves? If I were to offer up everything, would I not be like a slave?"

At the word "slave", both Camille and Geneviève thought of Diatou, Sister Julia, though neither could possibly know that it was in the mind of the other. That she was known to them both was still to be realised.

So, each thought of the African in their own way and each did so with love. And love was troubling Mother Geneviève. Over the many years of monastery life, had she only paid lip service to love? "To obey", had superseded "to love", and she feared she had lost the meaning of the word. For now, she was feeling the stirrings of a love that brought her memories of her early months with Carlos, when he had been gallant and honourable, and the deep attachment she had felt for her maid Sophie, and the loving service of her secretary Morel, and the love and compassion she had felt for the slave girl. In the moonlight, on a warm Andalusian night, scared and exhausted and with bare feet, they had walked together and then, with the girl supporting her, she had limped up to the gate of the convent in Seville, looking for safety. This was the love that was returning, and she felt it now for the young nun before her. And with the love came the beginnings of a grief that had waited a lifetime to be released.

Why should this be with Sister Constance? Because she was so different and had spoken outrageously? No, not just the words. She saw in Camille a spiritual depth and was beginning to sense that it was of a free will, without creed or dogma. There was something else too, which she was yet to realise.

And so in the third of the spiritual consultations that were meant to mend the soul of Camille, Geneviève wept like a child, and discarding her shame, as one who pulls off a heavy cloak and throws it aside, she asked Sister Constance for her forgiveness.

And Camille knew, without definition but with intuition, that the plea for forgiveness was not about the sins committed by her Mother Superior, but about the sins that had been committed against her. And this, she told her.

217

For the Carmelite Sisters, a deference to those who were senior was paramount. Nothing changed visibly between Mother Geneviève and Sister Constance. But an equality founded in love existed silently between the two and transformed the lives of both. It did not interfere with their religious duties; indeed, the spirituality of their lives was enhanced. Geneviève knew happiness for the first time for many years, and Camille ceased to depend on her dreams. They were still missed but no longer essential. The passionate sharing of Geneviève's grief had restored a closeness to another that had begun with Sister Africa, from whom she had been so painfully torn away. In this, there was a reunion, one that was soon to become even more complete.

CHAPTER TWENTY FOUR

A letter from the Prioress of the Carmel, Cordoba, to the Prioress of Issoire

From: The Reverend Mother, Marie Cecilia, Prioress of the Carmelite Monastery of the Holy Resurrection, Cordoba, Andalucía, Spain.

To: The Reverend Mother, Geneviève, Prioress of the Carmelite Monastery of The Holy Mother of Bethlehem, near Issoire, Auvergne, France.

December 10th 1929

Dear Reverend Mother Geneviève,

I thank you for your recent letter, and I was deeply relieved to hear that our Sister Constance has found a place of conciliation in your Carmel at Issoire and that she has been able to resume her life of devotion to Christ and her obedience to the rules of our order. We are ready as well to accept that she may remain at Issoire. It will, of course, be for you and me to decide though we would not wish to make impositions that risk her recovery.

My letter, therefore, is firstly to thank you for this wonderful news about our Sister.

There is an additional matter. I have another request. Let me first reduce its burden upon you by reassuring you that I am also writing to others in our houses of Carmel. I pray that from one, there will be a generous response.

I almost held back from including you for fear that this may do actual harm to the progress of our Sister Constance. However, the changes that you have described persuade me that I might put aside my concern.

We have here in Cordoba, a Sister who has a past as strange as any I have known. She is Sister Julia and she was born in Senegal in Western Africa. When she was a girl of fifteen her mother sold her into slavery. The family had lost all their male members and were desperate to survive. It nevertheless fills me with dismay to imagine the pain of a girl so cruelly abandoned by her mother.

You and I have not had children, and we have transformed our instinct to mother into our caring for the Sisters who depend on us for example and guidance. I feel blessed in my position that I can perform such duties and with the inspiration and grace of our Holy Mother, can do so with love.

I feel now, with great concern, a need to protect this same Sister Julia.

I shall explain.

We first received a letter from a man, someone from the aristocracy.

In the letter, he informed me that twenty-five years before, he had employed as a servant, a young Senegalese girl called Diatou. He had rescued her from a life of potential slavery and out of kindness, had taken her into his home near Sevilla and given her honest work to do.

She repaid his kindness by stealing jewellery of great value and taking flight. The police were called and sent out to find her but to no avail. The aristocrat persisted in pursuit and insisted the case be kept open for several years, but with no reports of the girl he had to accept that justice would not be done and he should bear his loss.

The girl had completely disappeared and had perhaps found her way back to her country of Senegal. A long and difficult journey, but by no means impossible.

Our Sisters rarely go out into the world, and though our Cordoba church adjoins the monastery and we welcome those who wish to worship with us, we are always hidden by a dividing wall. But, at some stage, someone from the outside world must have noticed an African nun. And, of course, a Carmelite with such dark skin would be a striking and unusual sight. Something to remark upon.

And so, it came to the notice of our aristocrat from Sevilla. He had no hesitation in deciding that the African nun, Sister Julia, was the criminal who had betrayed his trust and kindness those many years before. And now her strange disappearance made absolute sense. Only a monastery could provide this. Clearly, the intervening years had done little to mend his sense of injury or lessen his need for recompense.

In his letter, he conveyed great respect for our order and our need for privacy but nevertheless demanded that the thief be handed over to the authorities.

Sister Julia has been with us for many years and I already knew the true nature of her story. She came to us from a Carmel in Sevilla which had offered her safety along with the wife of the aristocrat who had helped her escape. Both were in a terrible state and the wife even feared for her life. Julia stayed with them for two years, performing menial tasks, before joining us in Cordoba as a postulant. It was felt safer for her not to remain in Sevilla. The aristocrat's wife had already returned to her native France.

This aristocrat, Carlos Fernando Vincente, heir to the Marqués de la Segura, had purchased the girl Diatou from Mauritanian slave traders. He had enslaved her and regularly beat her in the most sadistic fashion. It is a sad fact for us that at that time, despite our prayers, such hate and cruelty had been triumphing in a place not half a day's travel away.

I had no intention of giving her up to a man who only wished her harm, and it is unthinkable that there could be such denigration of one who has taken holy vows and devoted her life to Carmel.

I wrote back, reminding him of the nature of our existence: that our lives are given over to obedience and prayer, that we can have no actual contact with him and that we certainly have no interest in jewellery, stolen or otherwise. I stressed that the reclusive nature of our lives was paramount and should be respected. I also offered to pray for him, as he had nursed this wound for so long; a proposal that I now realise was very unwise.

I finished by stating that though we were aware of our own sinfulness and the sinfulness of all men, we harboured no criminals in our monastery.

For three months there was no response and I believed that the matter was over. Until one morning, in the middle of Lauds, there was a terrible pounding at our outer door. We have a secluded pathway that leads there, and one of our Sisters hurried along it and opened the small grill in the door. She was astounded by the hostility of the words that came through. She told us, with considerable dismay, that they were accompanied by a spray of spittle as he spat out his words. That we were "harbouring a criminal", that we caused him and his family great offence and humiliation and that, if need be, he would summon the police to break down our (cursed) doors and seize the woman who would be thrown into jail along with any (cursed) nuns who tried to protect her. I suspect that our Sister at the door had not heard such obscene language in her whole life.

She closed off the grill and hurried back, full of fear, and with her alarming report. Yes, she was truly frightened.

And so am I. It is something that we rarely contemplate; that our way of life and the structures that maintain it can be so usurped. True, our Church has not the ascendancy in these matters that once was its right, and our monastery status, though still respected by nearly all, is not enshrined in law. But I have never felt as vulnerable as I do now, and I fear for our Sister Julia. She has already suffered great injustice and might now face a fate that is incomprehensible within our ordered lives and our wish to do no harm to anyone.

It is my urgent task to arrange a move for Sister Julia, as far away as possible. No legal documents have as yet been served upon us, so I must move quickly, as this will surely happen.

You have already helped us greatly by accepting our Sister Constance. She once felt a closeness to this same Sister Julia that caused us much concern, and indeed, it was a factor in her fall from grace. Such intimacy can never be allowed and devalues our true devotion to Christ. There was an occasion when Constance attempted to enter Julia's cell during the Great Silence. It was a measure of her extreme disturbance and knowing this we have readily forgiven her. Sister Julia acted with great calmness, gently turning Constance away from her door.

If the two were to live again under one roof, I believe it to be acceptable, given my trust in Sister Julia and your own account of the recovery of faith and discipline in our Sister Constance.

Thank you for your kindness in fostering the loving relations between our two houses of Carmel. If this can be extended even further, I will thank the Lord for allowing us to have such blessed friendship in Christ.

Marie Cecilia

Reverend Mother of the Cordoba Carmel of the Holy Resurrection

CHAPTER TWENTY FIVE

Awakening

Within an hour of Geneviève receiving the letter from the Cordoba Prioress, she had written her reply. She was ready to receive Sister Julia immediately and fully concurred that arrangements be made in great haste.

Geneviève was warmly pleased that she would see again the African girl who was now a professed Sister, but she also felt a colder touch of fear. There was the reality of the return of Carlos into her life. The distance between Cordoba and Issoire and the anonymity of monastery life were there to ward him off. She hoped it would be so.

Mother Marie Cecilia would have been dumbfounded by the knowledge that the Prioress at Issoire was the ex-wife of Don Carlos. If she had known, she would not have written. But she was to be the agent of fate in a tale that was as yet unfinished.

"Not just fate, but God," thought Geneviève and she knew she must do all in her power to protect the African Sister.

And now, as well, there was her own closeness to Camille, who had been so close to Julia that her Cordoba Sisters and Prioress had feared she would disown her vows.

"We will be three," and she smiled as she remembered "The Three Musketeers". She had read the novel in her first year in her Bolvoir home in Paris. It was in Morel's sitting room, gathering dust and leaning against "The Count of Monte Cristo", the two propping each other up and the only books there apart from the ledgers. They were on the shelf beneath the crossed duelling swords that Morel had fixed upon the wall. She had borrowed the novel and enjoyed reading it and engaged with the cut and thrust between the heroes and villains, though there was something about Milady de Winter that caused unwelcome thoughts about her mother. The sword fighting had excited her, and her interest in her suitor increased when Morel informed her that Carlos was known as a fine swordsman.

"My memories again," she thought, and then ruefully, "Perhaps I should be thinking more in terms of the Holy Trinity."

Later that day she summoned Camille.

In the presence of Camille, her great sadness had been released, and there was now an intimacy between the two that did not depend on words. Neither were words really possible within the structure of their daily lives. The spiritual counselling had ceased. Its course had led to transformations that were hardly foreseen by either woman; changes that were not due to discipline or faith, but to an understanding made possible through love.

For both Geneviève and Camille, love now permeated the monastery at Issoire, and for Camille it was the return of a joy that had at first drawn her so ardently to Carmel. There was no need to deny the dreams and imaginings that had filled her mind in the preceding months. She knew now that love could take many forms and that the love her body had yearned for was as natural as the wind she listened to at night through the window of her cell and the night time calls of the owls hunting in the nearby woods. All was of nature, as was the fluttering of wings in the bushes around the garden of her childhood home, a fluttering that had become the beating of magnificent wings at the advent of her full emotions as a woman. She could see now that her love of Jesus had contained the dawning of her sexual feelings, had wrapped them up and disguised them and thrown their full force into her adoration of the kind and crucified, Son of God. "Perhaps His story contains all the passions of a life," she thought. "We cannot be sure He never loved a woman. Perhaps He did, but it was His love of mankind that He needed to leave us." And the thought made her happy.

It is unlikely that Father Pierre, in his weekly visits to receive the confessions of the Issoire nuns, heard all the thoughts of Camille or her Prioress, but on leaving the monastery he too felt an uplifting of his spirit and that all was well with the world.

As Camille entered the office of Mother Geneviève, she reflected that it was six months since their first meeting. It had been there in the same room that looked out onto the garden, with its statues celebrating the classical, pagan gods, all installed by the late Marguerite, Countess of Bolvoir. Camille had been right to think that the statues had been too heavy to move. For her years there as the Prioress, their presence had troubled Geneviève, though a little less since the expression of her grief. For Camille, they stirred wistful memories of her encounters with the creatures of myth.

The formalities had still to be obeyed and she stood silently.

"You came to us from Cordoba and there is one who will soon be following."

Geneviève was also standing. She was close to the window and she turned to it as she paused to arrange her thoughts. Much of the night, she had pondered how to tell Camille about the coming of Sister Julia and how much to tell her of the reason for her arrival. It was her wish to say everything and to follow the emotion she had already shown, by telling all of her story, starting right from the beginning. She longed to do so, but she knew she must now act again as the Mother Superior; the order of their lives in Carmel required it.

She was now clear as to what she would say. Her own time with Julia need not be mentioned. She turned back to Camille.

"The Sister who comes from Cordoba is Sister Julia of Saint Jerome."

Geneviève knew, from the letter of the Cordoba Prioress, that to continue speaking at this point would be a deceit. Emotions were no longer to be denied. She had been told of Camille's attachment to Julia, so she paused.

Camille had moved to Issoire without hope of Julia following. The order of their lives left no space for stray good fortune. The parting had become a hard, cold fact; an ache of loss that was borne throughout each day. Gradually, the suffering had lessened and more so, since her Prioress had shared her own sadness. But now, the prospect, so suddenly evoked, of reunion with Julia brought back the pain of the separation, as if the two states existed in binary attraction; tragedy and happiness rotating; irredeemably drawn together.

She reached out and placed a hand upon the desk to steady herself, but it was useless and her knees buckled and her body, made helpless by emotion, collapsed onto the floor.

For Geneviève it was an opportunity to hold Camille, to lift her from the ground, to embrace her within the allowed confines of physical help. It was her awareness of the very strength of her wish, that prevented her from carrying it out. But with compassion in her voice, she bid Camille to stand again.

This was their life. Their hardships, their physical weakness, the strength of their emotions, should always be acknowledged; this she could now see. But their endeavour to rise above their suffering was what marked them as servants of the One who had suffered for them all.

"Dear Sister, you must love her very much."

Camille, as one about to climb a great staircase, stared up at the towering figure of Geneviève and reaching for the table, slowly pulled herself up until, trembling, she was once more standing before her.

She said, "It hurt me so much to be taken from her."

And in that moment, she remembered their last minutes together. The Great Silence was over, and she had fled back to her cell, past the shocked Sisters on their way to the morning observance. And just before that Julia had said,

"My story is not finished—and I do not know yours."

And Camille had answered, "I don't have a story, I didn't have a mother," and had been shocked by what she said.

And now it was her turn to express the emotion that had been stored for years; the grief at the loss of a mother who had died as she gave birth.

And she spoke her thought and realised,

"It is what we share, Julia and I. Our mothers abandoned us."

And at the same time, Geneviève was remembering how, at six years old, she watched the slowly disappearing, impassive rear of the coach in which her own mother, beautiful and cold-hearted, was departing. "Did she see me waving?" And she knew then of the indelible imprint left when the one who is most needed exists only as an absence; a tantalising phantasm that usurps the worthy expectancy of desire. So, she said,

"It is we three."

The next day, she again summoned Camille and assigned to her the initial reception of Julia. She did so with confidence and pleasure. And Camille expected the arrival with excitement and awe.

As if a single, potent, magic word had been spoken, or the impresario of a theatre had waved his hand to command a change of scene, the imagination of Camille became restored, and even the bare walls of the corridors and the simple austerity of her cell were now imbued with anticipation.

And what was that? What was stirring within her to add a quality, an extra intensity to all the activities of the day? Her prayers were directed as ever to God the Father, Jesus, and the Virgin Mother. But her contemplation, with the concentration that played such a part in clearing away the mundane, the worldly and the physical, felt driven and enhanced by the expectation, ever-present, of the coming of Sister Julia. She could readily direct her thoughts and emotions towards the Saints but did so with an awareness that each saint contained something of the Sister from Senegal. And because her prayers and meditation felt so fulfilling, she was ready to allow this. The more fundamental element in her training ruled against it as a corruption of her aims as a nun, but she had travelled far from the point at which this would have caused conflict. Her spiritual life in Jesus and the devotion that had taken her to Carmel had been regained but also broadened out to include Sister Julia, to whom she was certainly devoted, and those other elements that she could now recognise and own as belonging to her own most personal, unique, and private inner world. "It is mine to possess, I will not confess." And she was pleased with her challenge to her Mother Superior; that not all was a sin to be spoken of and exposed, and she knew, as well, that Mother Geneviève would no longer challenge her in this. And she thought too of her knowledge that Julia had told an absolute lie: that Camille had never had access to her cell, and she felt not the slightest guilt for this, not for herself, nor for Julia. Indeed, it increased Julia as a figure of strength.

It seemed to her now that her love for Julia, who was sometimes an African cat, and for her magnificent winged god, and her thrill at the creature of pure lust that had thundered across the field towards the nymph that had escaped him with the most graceful curved dive, all these were a source of energy that enhanced her love of a God who had surely made all things possible. These were her companions for now, and she was deeply grateful that they had joined her on her journey.

She sensed too, that as the years continued, they in their turn would change and take their place in her own personal pantheon, as spirits and daemons that had helped her on her way. "One day," she understood, "I will not need them, and all will be spirit, but for now they are my beloved friends."

Camille was not concerned with the threat of Carlos who was unknown to her. This part of Julia's story she had not heard, and Mother Geneviève had not shared the details of her own past tragedies, only the emotions. So, Camille could only believe the forthcoming presence of Julia to be a gift of God.

But Geneviève, despite the relief that she now enjoyed, could not free herself from intrusive thoughts; a spectre of destruction had forced itself into her mind, if not actually into her life—yet. Carlos needed to re-possess his slave. Her escape had usurped his utter expectancy of control of the female. He could only think in terms of reversing it. But she knew as well that this was not enough to explain his relentless pursuit and that, most profoundly, it was because of her. It was she who had released the slave, but it was also she who had left him, abruptly, in the middle of the night, defying his power and his status as her husband. And most of all, there was the annulment to their marriage. It would have been impossible without the great influence and wealth of her friend, Marie Bonaparte. A technicality and many good offices and donations had succeeded, but to all who observed and gossiped in the wealthy and aristocratic homes of Paris and Madrid, it could only have been the grounds that they all knew as acceptable to the Church—non-consummation—and so Carlos had been left and divorced because of his shameful impotence. So close to the truth and if it were not for a moment of love by the banks of the Guadalquivir, that would indeed have been the grounds.

PART SEVEN

THE THREE

CHAPTER TWENTY SIX

Sister Julia

The arrival of Sister Julia was to be in the afternoon. Camille remembered when she had made the journey herself. In the early summer, six months before, in the midst of her private imaginings, she had looked out of the window to see the Pan creature and the water nymph. She had lived then in two worlds, and the routine of her daily life in Carmel had seemed so dull in comparison to the rich excitements of her fantasies—her possessions. Though wistfully, she could miss the intensity of such experience, her life now was one of growing contentment. The creatures who had found their way into her dreams and staked a claim in her waking life had departed but had enriched her by their stay.

Camille believed the arrival of Julia to be a test; one that was enhanced and elevated by the woman at its centre. She did not believe she would fail and that to have Julia's presence would be one more factor to increase her love of God. She knew that once Julia had settled into the monastery they would rarely speak, but she could instead become an icon, a symbol through whom Camille could achieve an even higher sense of spiritual being. Such was her expectation.

It was now winter and there had already been snow. It had fallen during the night and stayed attached to the branches of the great, dark green yews and cedars that surrounded the garden. Whiteness streaked the tree trunks as well, and the ground was covered with a brilliant coating that sparkled in the pale December sunlight. Occasionally there was a stirring of wind so that with a sigh and soft collapse, clumps of snow would make their languid fall from the branches.

Camille, passing the window near her cell on the top floor, looked out in the way that she loved, and there, sure enough, was the man. He had a spade and was clearing the path through the garden. She was sad to see the virgin purity of whiteness removed from the path and the gravel replace the transitory beauty of the snow. Her mind moved from the whiteness of the snow to the white capes they wore at times of ceremony, and she thought of seeing Sister Julia dressed like that and how beautiful she had looked.

Watching the man clearing the snow she wished she could join him. If he were not there, the nuns would do this themselves, but always he was there for these things. She imagined being next to him, maybe with other Sisters, working together, moving their spades, throwing the snow to one side. But such closeness to a man could never be. She felt the sadness and the loss of this as she descended the stairs and walked through the corridor towards the chapel.

In the afternoon there was work to do, she had begun the embroidery of a new altar cloth for their chapel, and there were the usual observances, but near the expected time of Julia's arrival she could do nothing but sit and wait in the large, dark entrance hall. She sat on the seat on which she had glimpsed the great silhouette of Mother Geneviève when she herself had arrived at Issoire. Now the Prioress had entrusted her with the reception of Julia.

Above her hung the portrait of Saint Teresa. She thought about the Saints. She had taken her own religious name after Saint Constance, and she had investigated Julia's name and found it to be from a fifth-century Carthaginian Saint who was enslaved, tortured, and martyred by the Romans. She wondered whether Julia had chosen the name herself or whether it had been decided for her. She could see that it was a good name for the African. "I will ask her." But then what if Julia chose silence and held only to the rules of their monastery life? Just the briefest of greetings as they passed in the corridor or worked together; perhaps a little extra when it was time for Recreation.

She compared such prospects to the memory of lying in Julia's arms with the moon slowly moving its pale light across the floor of the cell. Throughout the Great Silence, Julia had told her story and Camille had felt entranced and contained and safe in her arms. She thought, "It was the most wonderful night." And she was filled with a terrible anxiety that it could never happen again. She felt her new confidence disappearing.

Since the man had cleared the path, it had snowed again and the path was once more covered. There was a silence outside as if the snow had cast a soft white veil upon the ground and over the shrubs, gently muffling any sound. She believed that the foot-falls upon the snow outside would not be heard and she feared being surprised by a sudden knock on the door, so she moved to the window and unbolted and opened the shutter. It was an act of boldness; the entrance hall was lit by lamps and the shutter was never opened. It creaked in resistance and dust fell as it swung heavily upon its hinges. "Have I broken a rule?" and she wondered whether it was again, the effect of Sister Julia.

At last, they came. She saw them through the window—two Sisters carrying cases and tentatively stepping upon the slippery snow. They were followed by the tall figure of Julia who carried nothing. Camille saw the dark skin of Julia's feet upon the snow, sinking into it and then lifting it in a fine spray as she walked towards the door.

"She has come barefoot as a true Carmelite," and she thought too, of the girl from Senegal, Diatou, with bare feet in her native land, and also of the barefooted woman racing by the side of the cheetah in her dream.

Camille did not wish to hear the sound of knocking or the ringing of the outside bell, so she quickly opened the door.

She knew them all. There was Sister Elizabeth, and also Sister Gertrude whose facial twitch had become such a source of anger and contempt in her most challenging days in Cordoba.

She greeted them and ushered them in, but she could not bear to look at Julia. Overwhelmed by the impact of Julia's arrival, she could only ignore her.

She said what was expected. "The journey—it was so long—you must be so tired—God bless you," and they, as if realising this was more than an ordinary meeting of nuns, seemed tongue-tied and embarrassed. But perhaps that was only as she saw it. She felt she was moving and speaking as one in a trance. She thought, "It is she who is doing this." And still, she could not look at her.

Julia's two companions would stay three nights and then return to Cordoba. There was a cell they would share during their brief stay. Camille led the way up the stairs to the top floor where their room had been prepared.

They were both tired and sat upon the narrow beds. Their cases with their few possessions rested upon the floor, waiting to be unpacked.

Julia then spoke for the first time, quietly, in her soft, deep and clear voice.

"Let us leave our Sisters to rest. And I must rest too when you have shown me my cell."

And now, like a wraith, her sense of self so engulfed by Julia's presence, Camille led her to a door that faced the window that she so enjoyed looking through. She opened the door and they entered. Of its own accord, the door swung closed behind them and Camille, gathering her courage, at last looked.

The dark brown eyes were wide and questioning, but it was as if the answer was already known. The mouth was relaxed, the face soft and framed by the brilliant white of the wimple.

With the hint of a smile, Julia said,

"Are you still crazy, Sister? Not even a greeting," and she held out her arms, and Camille felt tipped into them by a force she had no wish to resist and her own arms, in turn, encircled Julia. Raising her face, their lips met, and her legs became useless and all bodily control was lost. There was only the joining of their kiss and the joyous helplessness as the chill of Julia's lips, so recently touched by the snow, became warm again and for Camille the whole world began to melt.

Time was irrelevant and she did not know how long they embraced. Eventually, she felt Julia firmly, but gently, move her hands so that she held Camille by her shoulders and then moved her slightly away. Their faces were still close. Now she was smiling.

"My loving, Sister Constance—how much you love me." And she gently kissed Camille upon the forehead. "And I love you. Whenever we can, we will show it. But now we must see to our love of Christ. Come, you must show me around this lovely old house."

And Camille felt that she was in the company of the most loving parents: the body and the emotional power of Julia, the mother, and the blessing of Christ and God the Father and that they, including her as their child, had an intercourse that she felt deeply within her own body and that reached right into her womb, and left her knowing something of the ecstasy of the Saints.

To generalise about passion in the lives of the nuns would perhaps be a mistake. As for any group of people, passion will be a force felt more by some than others. There was, though, the potential for this emotion to be at the very heart of the Sisters' lives. Indeed the heart, because love of Christ and a marriage to Him was the foundation to their calling, though the ardour of some may have been more towards the Blessed Virgin. And what could be more passionate than the Christ, dying slowly upon the cross for His love of mankind, and His loving Mother weeping helplessly beneath it? What could be more consuming than stripping away all irrelevance in life, to bare the soul and devote a whole existence to God?

Passion was in the air breathed by the Sisters of Carmel. It gathered in the hallways and rooms of the monastery, was manifested in the rich and intense smell of incense, was stirred by the ringing of bells that sorted the order of their day, and was expressed through fervent prayer and in the singing of hymns with their words of adoration and worship.

Camille believed that she and Julia would embrace again. Julia would never be like the others. She worshipped as them and obeyed the observances as required, and Camille had no sense that this was against Julia's wishes. She was a Carmelite, but one who came from a different continent, not only through her birth but in her being. They might kiss again, but the opportunity would be rare, and the passion, which for Camille was an element of the soul, would find its expression through the spiritual concentration in her cloistered life.

Julia's meeting with Mother Geneviève did not have the passion of that with Camille but was nevertheless filled with emotion. For Julia, there was also the surprise at her recognition of her new Mother Superior. Her life as a Carmelite nun had given no opportunity to know of events in the outside world, even those that pertained to the wider aspects of Carmel. The woman who had rescued her from her slave-master had quite soon disappeared from her life. That she should suddenly appear again as a Reverend Mother shook even the calmness of Julia, one who had experienced and grown strong through the most severe challenges. But Geneviève had the advantage of knowing exactly whom she was to meet, despite the many intervening years.

Geneviève, who would normally be treated with due deference in any interview with a Sister, believed that this particular meeting should in itself be treated with deference, and with a sensitivity and a respect for an experience they both had shared and in which they had greatly helped each other.

There was, therefore, a sense of equality between the two that would not otherwise have been there, though it should be added that there existed a certain element in Julia that rarely allowed for superiority in the other.

The affection between the two was duly expressed in words and was felt in their pleasure at sharing a spiritual path that allowed them once more to be together.

Monastic life at the Issoire Carmel continued with Sister Julia smoothly taking her place.

CHAPTER TWENTY SEVEN

From an essay on J and his work. J is missing

By Dr Paul Faucher (1935–1936)

I am sitting at my desk. It is the usual time for recording my most recent meeting with J, but there is nothing to write of except my anxiety. J has disappeared. A week ago, I arrived at his apartment in L'avenue des Gobelins and had no response to the door-bell. Out of concern, I rang some other bells and eventually gained access to the entrance hall. The lift was still not working so I had to walk up the five flights, thinking all the time about the strain this has been causing J and the tiredness he has recently been suffering. I rang and banged on the door of his apartment to no avail. A head peeped out from another door on the landing to see what the commotion was about. My feelings were certainly in commotion and this must have been evident to the neighbour, who tried to calm me by saying that J was probably having a vacation, but then only made things worse by stating he had not seen him for two weeks. I cannot help but connect such a sudden disappearance to his poor health. There is no sign of his housekeeper, Madame

Bernard, but she is not resident in his home. Indeed, I have no idea where she lives, and she would normally only be there on occasions when J especially needed her. He was quite happy to do much of the dusting himself. It is really her cooking that he values and the occasional thorough cleaning of the apartment, an event that he finds an infuriating nuisance and so keeps to a minimum.

I have of course enquired amongst colleagues, who knowing his eccentricities shrug and tell me not to worry. But because of our regular meetings and growing intimacy, I know his movements better that anyone—except perhaps for the Princess. So, I have been to her house in Saint Cloud, as well as her other residence in Rue Adolphe Yvon. All to no avail. As is so often the case, and just now it is a source of great irritation, she is away. At least she has staff whom I could talk to. She is in fact in Lucerne, presenting her paper on Femininity and Masochism. I left a message with her servant that J is nowhere to be found and I fear greatly for his health.

So, in this allotted hour, I have nothing to write of except my concern. For the sake of habit and discipline though, I will record a few thoughts. They come to me now as I mention Bonaparte's recent publication as I believe them to be relevant. I would, as normal, have expected from J another instalment of the Camille Beauclaire story. I now understand that Madame Bonaparte's interest in this saga is not only as a past friend of Camille's Mother Superior but also as a theorist. Knowing the title of her paper, I can see that her comments about masochism in respect to her old friend were part of her broader thinking.

What a subject masochism is. With a remarkable force, our patients repeat the identical self-destructive acts and unhappy relationships over and over again. The Princess has been telling us of Geneviève and the drive to submission that seemed to govern her, despite a natural joie de vivre. I think she believes that Geneviève, unconsciously, always knew her

244

future husband was a sadist. We know how well people can size each other up in an instant, only to discover what they already knew, months or even years later. Well, it happened very soon in Geneviève's marriage.

Despite her own considerable activity, I know Marie sees passivity in the whole biological existence of the developing female. That she is indeed "broken into" and inherits the passive role of the child-bearer, and how passive to the cruel dictates of fate that can be—so much loss and illness that is caused through childbirth. Marie's own mother died very soon after her birth. And she sees it even on the cellular level, the male sperm breaking into the female germinal cell. How interesting to take things back to so elemental a beginning.

One must surely see with Geneviève the added influence of the abandonment by her mother. Instead of a life-affirming breast-mother there is only the negative, and the only thing that can be attached to is a rejecting absence. Such tragedy, to be acted out again in later life. And Geneviève's anger at all this—turned against herself? Perhaps.

I believe that in Marie's view, full female sexual pleasure can only be attained through vaginal intercourse, though she seems less anti the clitoris than her beloved Freud. Hearing her description of Geneviève and Carlos making love on the banks of the Guadalquivir, one might well imagine a complete reception allowed through love. But Geneviève's very femininity seems to have filled Carlos with terror, sadism being his only remedy. Surely, if coitus is successful, active and passive merge into one consummate experience where there is little difference. But then fear of the loss of gender role can spoil it all. I do hope that I have the chance to discuss this with Marie at some stage.

But in thinking that my alarm returns. Will J be there with us? Just now I can only hope, but I have a grim feeling that all is not well.

CHAPTER TWENTY EIGHT

The gardener

There was a pounding upon the oak door of the monastery. For a moment all was silent and then it resumed, loud and insistent, echoing through the corridors and even reaching to the chapel.

For the Issoire Carmelites, such intrusion into the quiet ritual of their lives was cause for alarm. Any contact with the outside world was pre-arranged and subject to the utmost vetting. This present demand for entry was at daybreak, shattering the quietness of the house and gardens.

In an earlier century, when the nuns were chosen enemies of the state, such a visit could signal fatal danger. In 1794, during the Reign of Terror, sixteen members of the Carmel of Compiègne, the "Martyrs of Compiègne", were deemed traitors and guillotined. Together, at the foot of the scaffold, the nuns sang a hymn and each one continued to sing as she went to her death. The first to die was the novice of the community, Sister Constance. The last to mount the scaffold was the Prioress,

Mother Teresa of St. Augustine. The old house at Issoire did not have this in its memory, but to be a Carmelite was to know the history and to inherit its tragedies.

As the pounding continued, now joined by the ringing of the entrance bell, Mother Geneviève swept through the corridors, her dignified progress belying the anxious pounding of her heart.

Sister Marie turned and moved from the small grill set within the door. What she had heard caused her to look anxiously towards the Prioress.

Geneviève did not pause to speak but continued to the entrance. Through the grill, she made her own enquiry.

"Sister, you must excuse this disturbance at your holy house, but I represent the law."

"Speak then," said Geneviève.

"Sister, you harbour one who is accused of a crime for which they must answer. I have authority to demand entrance if she is not given up."

Geneviève, in the monastery that had once been a Bolvoir house, far from Spain and clothed in the holy traditions of her Carmelite order, had not believed this could happen.

"Name the accused," she demanded.

The voice was conciliatory.

"Madame, I very much regret our intrusion. If only it were otherwise, but I have with me a warrant and with it the right to force entry. Tell me, Madame, that it will not be necessary."

Geneviève replied.

"Monsieur, are you alone?"

"I have with me two others who have travelled from Spain where the crime was committed. In Paris, they obtained their authority and the warrant. There is a nobleman here Sister. You must open up."

"I am the Prioress, Monsieur. Who do you name as your criminal?"

"My apologies, Mother. We seek one who is known as Diatou from her native Africa."

"What is the charge?"

"It is theft of precious jewellery."

Geneviève quietly mouthed her words of disgust.

"What use for jewellery would we have here?"

For sure, Carlos was present. He had travelled for days to achieve his goal, and she knew he would never give up. A serpent of dread that had slept for years, hibernating in the dusty unseen corners of the old Issoire house, now awoke and wrapped its cold coils around her and she felt the strength that had taken her so long to regain, start to ebb away. She was to face an enemy and to do so without arms. The law superseded the rights of the nuns, and the spiritual aura of her monastery was just a pleasure for Carlos to defile.

"I will grant you entry. It is only you who may enter."

She slid open the bolts that secured the door, top and bottom, and turned away so as not to see the Spaniards who waited outside. A cluster of nuns were in the inner doorway and the corridor beyond. They were not to be seen and she gestured them to leave.

She heard the policeman enter but knew he was not alone. She turned. A cold gust of wind slipped in through the open door. It ruffled the great sleeves of her habit, crossed the floor and reached the hallway where the anxious nuns of Issoire shivered as they strained to listen.

The doorway framed the bright winter light. The harsh light disturbed Geneviève's vision until her eyes adjusted and she faced the man, scruffily uncomfortable in his uniform, who held out the official papers. He clumsily withdrew them to first make the sign of the cross. It was unnecessary for the monastery, but a compensation for his intrusion. Again, he offered the documents.

Geneviève took them and moved so that she was away from the light. The policeman stood in the middle of the large entrance hall, but he was no longer her concern. Standing in the shadows, she was near the bench on which she had sat when Camille had entered the Issoire house six months before. Saint Teresa, in her dark and heavily varnished portrait, looked out and beyond such worldly travesties as the one played out before her. Her tasks were completed. Geneviève's had begun. She looked up.

The two other men were middle-aged and richly dressed in dark colours. She knew Carlos immediately, and in the midst of the shocking advent of his presence, she sensed a remorseless act of fate, one which threatened to reverse all progress made and strength gained. An old sensation: of the weakness of submission, entered her body, causing her legs to tremble and her arms to ache. She felt the fear from the night of their escape again and here they were once more, subject to his will. It was his perfect revenge. The betraying wife and the slave she took with her—he had them both.

She looked again at the papers in her hand but there was little point. Carlos, with his title and his connections to the embassy in Paris would have his way. The papers would be genuine.

"I'm afraid you must obey the law, Mother. There is no choice in this."

Then a new voice followed that of the policeman. It had a thick Spanish accent and a recognisable tone of contempt.

"And you would not wish, Madame, your holy house to harbour a criminal."

Geneviève refused to look at him. She continued to address the policeman.

"You know very well, Monsieur, that we are Sisters of Carmel. We do not accept the presence of strangers here, especially men who wish us harm."

The policeman raised his shoulders in helplessness.

"What can I do, Mother? This is not easy for me. I beg you with great respect, please don't make my task harder. You can change nothing."

Again, there was the familiar threatening voice; this time with a sneer.

"And Madame, you risk your whole existence here if you insist in obstructing justice. A bunch of reclusive women are hardly above the law."

Geneviève, in their marriage, had not confronted Carlos until the final night when she had grasped the arm that was striking the girl. And after that her defiance had been to flee and to take his slave with her.

"This is the real theft for Carlos," she thought. "To steal his slave and to steal his power."

She now turned to him.

She had wanted him to have grown fat and unhealthy, but he was not. Twenty-five years older but little changed. The hair that would now be grey was died black and was still thick and oiled and severely drawn back behind his ears, and he had introduced the flourish of a small pigtail, secured with a ribbon in the manner of the matador. She remembered his admiration for the Seville matador, Juan Belmonte, and there was a likeness. And just for a moment, she recalled her love for him, when as a proud and handsome conquistador, he had engaged her in courtship. Their night at the ball had been the happiest of her life. The long, cruel tragedy of its loss had turned her to an austerity that was its opposite.

When Marie Bonaparte fetched her back to Paris, those twenty-five years ago, Geneviève had spoken of everything. They had stayed up a whole night whilst she described the pain of her life with Carlos, and the descent from the love and security in another's arms to the hard, stone floor, where she lay with her body protecting the girl who was his slave. And Marie had declared that surely Carlos was a man fearful of his own weakness.

But the Carlos now haughtily standing within her holy house was not there to show weakness. His black cloak was fur trimmed and there was a flash of red satin lining as he threw it

251

back over his shoulder. His white shirt was brilliant against his dark skin, and the buckles on his belt and boots gleamed softly within the shadows of the hall.

She could not resist him. To do so would bring danger upon the monastery that had restored her life. There would surely be a court case and perhaps justice would prevail. But she knew better: justice was already absent and would remain so. If Julia was tried at all, it would be in Seville where Carlos had his friends and his power. And surely all he wanted was to drag her back to slavery. There would be a trade: a trial and prison or servitude. Either way would give him revenge, but the latter would be his desire.

She called out, "Sister Julia should join us."

For a moment she thought of offering herself to Carlos—to take her instead. It was a wild thought, but it was amidst a sinking feeling that at its very deepest could submit to slavery. But Carlos did not want her back in any form. He wanted revenge. His consummate insult was to penetrate the very sanctum in which she had been secure.

Sister Julia emerged from the passageway and into the entrance hall. She had put on the white choir-mantle the sisters wore on the most solemn occasions.

"Why does she wear this?" thought Geneviève. "She looks magnificent. A brilliant African angel."

Diatou had never lost her pride; even when Carlos had used his riding whip and she had sunk to her knees beneath the blows. Then she was fifteen; now she was forty. As she walked into the vestibule, it was with an energy that was conserved and waiting. And behind her was Camille.

"Sister Constance, you are not needed."

Geneviève spoke the words softly. She acknowledged Camille's love for Julia and at the same time she was resigned to her own love for Camille, and in that moment, as she looked at the two nuns, she felt the force that joined the three of them.

For a moment it brought her peace and a strength began to ebb back into her mind and body.

Carlos instantly shattered the peace in his broken French.

"There you are. In fine robes now—but you won't need them where you are going. Thief! And your Prioress is a thief too!"

"Only if you believe Sister Julia is your property!"

The strength that had ebbed away from Geneviève was now returning like a riptide. She felt a force growing within her that she had never known before. As it gathered and grew, it drew its power from her pure rage at the incredible fact that this man would desecrate her house and violate one of her nuns.

Thus, she added,

"Little man!"

Such contemptuous words from his ex-wife left Carlos in uncharted waters. He allowed no one the chance to speak to him this way. His life had been ordered to accommodate his supremacy. He thrust out his chin, but now there was a hint of uncertainty.

And Diatou, Sister Julia of Carmel, was now speaking. At first with a whisper, then louder and resonant.

Camille had heard Geneviève's instruction to leave but it was impossible. All duties and observances had been abandoned by the nuns who clustered anxiously around the doorway and along the corridor. The pounding upon the door, the continual ringing of the bell, followed by the voices of men in a place where only priests came, pierced the soft spiritual membrane that surrounded their monastic life. And the outside walls, with their barred and shuttered windows that blankly faced the world, had not deterred these strangers.

Camille had guessed their purpose. She followed Sister Julia into the presence of these men as if she too were summoned. She stood by her side.

Julia was speaking in her native tongue; not French, nor Spanish, but of her childhood in Senegal and Camille understood nothing except for one word that was repeated. It was the word that she had learned when they had lain together in Cordoba, and she had heard the tale of Diatou and the lion that spared her.

Julia looked only at Carlos and her voice rang out with a strength that echoed through the hallways of the old house. Camille heard the word "Gaynde" and, with a growing excitement, she knew that Julia was summoning the spirit of the great lion that had walked around her, almost brushing her body with his mane and his warm sides.

Feeling the wild strength rising in Julia, Camille remembered that she too had been visited and been blessed. She remembered her beautiful male god with his great wings, and how he had placed one arm around her waist and risen up, so that the two had hovered with ease and grace, as high as the tips of the trees outside the Cordoba monastery.

But as her eyes drifted longingly towards the outside door and the garden beyond, she spied a new figure, framed in the doorway.

The appearance was so sudden and unexpected she thought her visions had returned and that she had summoned a hero to rescue them. But this was not a creature of mythology. He was a man and there was something that she recognised. But how could she know him? The feeling of unreality caused her again to doubt her perception until he took the steps that brought him fully into the entrance hall. His movement reminded her of the question she had asked herself when she had looked through the window, high up in the house, and watched the man who tended the garden. "Does he really have grace, or am I only yearning for my winged god?"

Julia's voice had now reached a pitch that filled the hall so that Camille again turned to her. Something strange had happened to Julia's eyes. They were like a cat's when about to spring. She too had looked upon the figure in the doorway. The bright light from outside formed a halo around the dark silhouette and to Sister Julia, who had become once again Dia-tou of her village in Senegal, the flickering light of the halo was like the great mane of the lion that had stalked off into the trees, but never left her side.

Mother Geneviève also gazed upon the figure whose sudden presence, though utterly unexpected, did not surprise her. Of course, she should have known he would be there. For many years, Edouard Morel, in the only capacity left to him, as caretaker and gardener of the estate, had dressed in coarse and hardy clothes, practical and with a conservatism that was his gesture of respect to their community of the religious. But now he stood in black britches and a full sleeved white shirt, unfastened at the top, and she remembered the elegance of the young man who had greeted her when she was eighteen at the doorway of her mother's house.

Carlos looked puzzled. His companion, less invested in the proceedings than his revengeful friend, watched this new entrance with interest. The policeman looked around at all the participants, unsure as who to approach next. Geneviève had handed the papers back to him and he waved them in the air in a gesture of helplessness.

Morel knew exactly what he wished to do. He walked straight up to Carlos and moved very close to him so that their faces were only inches apart. He then spat fully into his face. Pausing just long enough to recharge his mouth with liquid, he moved so close that their noses were almost touching and spat again. He then stepped back and with the flat of one hand struck Carlos across the face. In his other hand, he held two fencing swords. Geneviève recognised the handles of the weapons that had been Morel's only personal artefacts in his office at their old home. "Fine swords," she thought, "no doubt."

The challenge to the duel had been made in a way that no man with Carlos's conceit could refuse. He stood there with spittle running down his face and with the imprint of Morel's hand beginning to leave its pink impression upon his cheek.

255

The pink disappeared as his dark features reddened with the realisation of his position. His ascendancy had unaccountably been reversed, and instead of the ease of victory and dominance that he considered his right, he now had to fight to save his pride.

His companion had instinctively made a move towards Morel but had stopped as he recognised the change of circumstance. Morel's action had transported them to a place that bore no resemblance to the scene of just minutes before. It was no longer one of powerful aristocrats and a policeman enforcing their will upon anxious nuns. It was now a confrontation between two men which spoke not of trials and penalties and suffering in the future, but of a resolution to an insult which would be completely of the moment and devastating in its finality. The insult and the challenge it contained, took precedence over everything. It was an extreme point in a life— one that overrode all other considerations. Both Carlos and his companion knew the cold reality of this, utterly. And so did Morel.

Morel knew that it could not be to first blood and must be a duel to the death. There was no alternative. A wounded Carlos would only return later as set on revenge as ever.

But he also knew how small his chance of success was. For many years he had handled nothing but the tools of a gardener and handyman. Away from Paris and with a change to his existence dictated to him by the fate of his mistress, the fencing had ended and his considerable skill, proven time and again to many combatants at la Salle d'Armes Coudurier, had become an abstraction; a potential once realised but now without substance. Whether ability lived on, in his mind, body and the hand that held the sword, was unknown to him. It might, but he was sure that his foe would have continued to fence. The Spaniard's reactions would be slower now through age, but experience and craft would more than compensate.

A month before, as he cleared the snow from the paths in the monastery gardens, the habit of his normal downward look had been interrupted, as three nuns passed him by. Two, reacting to the presence of a man, made to cover their faces, but following behind, taller and with an almost athletic elegance of movement, was one who made no such gesture and looked coolly at him as she passed so that the dark African skin of her face was exposed; he recognised the slave girl from Seville and knew that, now a woman, she was for some reason, reuniting with Geneviève.

And on this morning, he had watched as the limousine drew up outside his cottage and as the three men disembarked to walk through the little wooden gate towards the monastery. One was a policeman in a scruffy uniform; the others were dressed expensively, one in a dark grey topcoat and Carlos, like a creature from a bygone age, with a heavy black cloak hanging from his shoulders almost to the ground. Morel had recognised him immediately.

He had left the cottage and followed them. He knew that if they were allowed into the monastery, they came with power, as well as dark intent. They entered and the door remained open so that he could hear all that was said.

It was obvious to him that for Carlos, heir to the Marqués de la Segura, this was the summation of many years of brooding, waiting, and hating. For his mistress, the past had suddenly returned, as dangerous as before. All that she had built, the Monastery of Issoire, her life as a Sister, and now Reverend Mother of Carmel, was threatened by the need for revenge of a man for whom the dark clouds of insult could never clear.

In the entrance hall, Geneviève watched the developing scene. She had felt fear, then rage and now, with the advent of Morel, there was excitement, but fear again for the danger he was in. And there was also her position as the Prioress of a Monastery and rising through the intense emotions, this now asserted itself.

"You are in a house that is dedicated to Christ and to prayer and to the love of mankind. We can have no swords here."

The policeman, fumbling for some course of action that could help him in his duty to prevent an illegal duel, was enlivened by her statement.

"Monsieurs, such a fight, even between gentlemen, cannot be allowed."

The companion of Carlos had fluent French.

"Monsieur le gendarme, I respect your position, but here we are far from the towns and the cities where your laws have their force. You must understand, Monsieur, that my friend is a man of high birth who has been insulted in the most extreme way. There is no law that can give answer to such insult. There is only the duel to which he has been challenged and which must be accepted. I can assure you that whatever the result we will not hold you accountable. Furthermore, this gentleman here," and he indicated Morel, "will need his own second, and it can only be you."

And turning towards Geneviève,

"And Madame, we will, of course, step outside."

Snow had begun to fall. The covering of the previous days had melted, but a thin layer of white was already spreading outside and was beginning to shape itself around the branches of the many shrubs that encircled the house.

Carlos still seemed stunned by the shock of Morel's violent challenge. He said nothing and seemed remote as if gathering together the events that had led to so unforeseen an outcome. His companion had taken one of the swords from Morel and was examining it. He held it between fingers and thumb, testing the weight and the balance and then gently touched the point with one finger. The sword was an épée de combat, a duelling sword with a finely engraved bell guard to protect the hand. The slender blade was triangular with a length of about ninety centimetres, leading to a point as sharp as a needle. With a look of approval, he handed it to Carlos.

Everything then moved very fast. The companion called the two men to take their positions, and it was with the speed with which the executioner dictates the last moments of the condemned man.

Carlos, with the sword in his hand and with the familiarity of the feel of the weapon, was reviving. He now looked alert. He had discarded his cloak and the coat that he wore underneath, so that both men were in shirts and breeches.

The three women were in the entrance hall but close to the doorway and watching. Julia was almost standing outside; Camille was close to her and Geneviève, with her height, was standing behind and looking over their shoulders. For two of them, there was the awareness of their centrality in a battle between two men. For the two men, it was now purely about the contest.

The companion gave the formal commands: "En garde! Allez!"

For a moment the blades of the two swords just touched, a gentle kiss between two, perfectly crafted, strips of steel. Though for many years only items of decoration, Morel had maintained them in their true functions as weapons to maim and to kill.

It was he who moved first, engaging his opponent, as if testing his resolve through the touch of his sword. In that moment, the two men seemed joined together in an intimacy as their blades flirted and danced.

Geneviève watched the tips of the blades but lost sight of them in their flickering speed. And as she watched Morel, she thought,

"He is left-handed and I never noticed—in all the years." An omission that she believed would only add to her feeling of guilt if Morel was to fall.

The first lunge was made by Carlos. He had tasted enough of the preliminaries. His footwork was fast and strong, together with an outstretched arm, the point of his sword searching for Morel's heart. It was skilfully done and Morel backed away, his crude defence only just sparing him. Again, Carlos attacked and this time his sword point teased open Morel's shirt so that the cloth that covered his heart dropped downwards and hung in a great fold over one hip. Blood appeared upon his bare, left breast.

Camille, watching intently, thought of the near-naked Jesus in His loincloth, bleeding upon the cross. She thought too of the winged god she wished would save them but could only imagine blood amongst the feathers.

Carlos paused. He could see that this man was no match for him. He felt a sense of superiority surging back, as sure as the blood was seeping from Morel's wound. He decided to exact his revenge in as slow, painful, and humiliating a way as was possible. He decided to play.

Morel was now backed against one of the large shrubs that bordered the garden. Carlos engaged his blade. He made several passes. He thrust and he parried with a mannered nonchalance. He then flicked the point of his blade upwards.

The move was just a blur to the onlookers, but the result was clear. Morel's cheek was opened to the bone.

Julia saw her lion wounded and the incredible prospect of its death. Geneviève saw the destruction of her life and the end of the one who had cared for her more than any other.

Morel knew he must now end the deception. It was his remedy for the years without practice and it had served its purpose. As Carlos again paused, considering where to inflict the next wound, Morel swung his body around. His feet changed position, the right foot now, in an instant, leading the left whilst his hands met to transfer the sword from the inferior left hand to the right. In a consummate, graceful move he was now in his natural position.

For a fateful moment, Carlos and his sword ceased to be as one. The change of stance and sword arm of his opponent had subverted the space of combat. Morel knew that his ploy would only be effective for a moment and he acted accordingly.

He was now naturally positioned inside the guard of Carlos. He moved his sword to the left and downwards to engage with Carlos's and to keep it aside and then with a sharp upward movement of his wrist he set his blade on its return curve towards the Spaniard's throat. The point entered just below the chin, and he followed on so that half the length of his sword slipped through the neck where it trembled on the other side, exposed.

In the garden, muffled by snow, there was only silence. The human figures were transfixed as if in a tableau. Carlos was upon his knees, his eyes wide open, directed up at the sky but already unseeing. Morel stood in his natural right-handed stance. As Carlos had sunk to his knees, his sword had slowly disengaged from the Spaniard's neck. He now held it pointed downwards. All around them on the brilliant white ground were fresh spots of bright red blood and small patches of pink where the blood had already mixed and thinned with the moisture of the snow. It was so obvious that Carlos was dying that not even his companion made a move towards him; as if only distance could show respect in the moment of death.

It was Sister Julia who made the first move. She had been in front of the others in the doorway. The soft sound of her bare feet in the snow gently broke the silence as she stepped towards Carlos. Taking hold of the hem of her white over-mantle, she reached towards him and placed the cloth upon his neck. She gazed at the crimson mark on the garment before letting it drop from her hand. Standing above him, her own body tall and upright, she spoke words that none there could understand. She then made the sign of the cross and turned and walked inside. Geneviève and Camille stood aside to make way for her and Camille would have followed her, but was in awe at the scene that she still surveyed.

It was Geneviève who next moved towards Carlos. He was still upon his knees, his shoulders now slumped and his head no longer facing upwards but hanging down. There was a gurgling from his throat, and blood was pouring from the fatal wound. Geneviève knelt by his side and placed a hand upon each of his shoulders. She then eased his body around and let it collapse into her arms. One arm supported his neck and the other rested upon his legs. She knelt there, her size seeming massive now, surrounded by the brown Carmelite habit that spread itself across the snow.

Camille observed this with wonder. The helpless body of Carlos seemed diminutive as it lay in the lap of Geneviève, and she thought, "It is a pietà."

Geneviève looked down at the face of her ex-husband. If there was still some vision in his eyes, he would have seen the look of sadness in hers. She cradled the chin that he had needed, so desperately, to jut out against the world. She thought of his mother and the weakness of his father. She remembered the banks of the Guadalquivir where, for just one time, Carlos had been overtaken by love, and the grand ball in Paris where they had danced, and she had felt held and safe and transported in his arms. She remembered the beatings, the curses and the humiliations, and she knew exactly why, as Carmelites, they thanked Christ for his endless forgiveness.

CHAPTER TWENTY NINE

From an essay on J and his work. A letter from Issoire

By Dr Paul Faucher (1935–36)

At last, I have received word from J. A letter that I copy here in full and which completes this part of my account of his work. One that has been quite taken over by his story of Camille. It is hard for me to imagine our evenings together without the presence of Camille and her Sister Africa and the Mother Superior who once graced the salons of Paris. But I would not be surprised if J has another fascinating case held in reserve. Or maybe each of us will only have one such as this in our lives as psychoanalysts.

The letter:

January 26th 1936

My Dear Paul,

I am so sorry. I hear that I have caused you some anxiety. A message has just come through from Marie. I should know better after all these years. Reliability is so important in our profession, isn't it? I think I am getting forgetful. I have tried to deny it, but for recent events, it can sadly be the case. And causing you such a worry when you are a bit of a hysteric anyway! And yet, I have not been completely at fault. My concerns do sometimes take me away from Paris and this is one instance for which I know you will forgive me. I will explain. Perhaps, indeed, it will bring some closure to my ongoing tale of Camille, over which I know I have kept you in some suspense as well as preventing us from talking about your own analysands, whom, after all, are the ones we are really meant to discuss.

I am, in fact, not dead or even terribly ill, as I believe you have imagined, though I do have some concerns for the rate and regularity of my heartbeat. But then at my age... Neither have I absconded for a holiday. I am in fact on my annual visit to the Monastery of Issoire. This will surprise you, no doubt. I have kept certain things from you, simply holding them back until later for the sake of narrative. I'm afraid that as you well know from my love of the myths, I do enjoy a good story.

Let me first round off the related tale of Eros and Psyche.

We left Psyche cursed into a deep and endless sleep. She'd looked into that vessel of Proserpina's. Forbidden territory, but she couldn't resist! So much like our Camille, who really had to follow where her dreams and imagination led her even though it meant breaking all the rules. And, of course, she stumbled on because she was fuelled by love. Camille and Psyche, in their different ways, had both been touched by Eros and could never give him up. And the happy thing about this story—rather unusual in a myth—was that neither did Eros give them up.

Camille had her long curse of sleep, just like Psyche. For her, it was no dreams and no visions, but like Psyche, Eros was still around to wake her, though he was now mixed up with compassion and he had moved aside to allow Jesus back into the picture as well. Camille could continue her marriage to the Church with a love that was fuller and wiser.

And Venus forgives Psyche, and Jupiter makes her immortal and allows Eros to marry her, so they have their marriage too. I think we probably can't get anywhere in life without a marriage of some kind.

So, yes, I am here at Issoire. Not in the midst of nuns of course. The Carmelites go about their daily business much in the old traditions, and, indeed, my business on these annual visits is only with three of them. Not that I see much of them either, but the years, the history, and the events, have forged a bond of a kind that I believe we all value. The three, well perhaps not the African, though she is always interested, but the other two are quite amenable to my psychoanalytic comments, and especially so is Sister Constance, dear Camille Beauclair, who first saw me as a girl because her father thought she was going mad with religion. You will remember. And I'm not here just for them. You will know Paul that unlike our Professor in Vienna, I have no aversion to religion and I positively love being so close to these women who really spend most of their time praying for us. If I am to die soon, I would like to be here when it happens!

I am only allowed as far as the reception hall, which is a lot further than most men get. Even then they try to rig up a little screen they can hide behind. All very coy to my mind and Camille tends not to bother with it. She, of course, has told me much of what I have passed on to you. I believe that they kind of smuggle me in as if I was a priest and, indeed, they rather treat me as one. Yes, I do hear confessions of a sort, and try to make helpful comments. But mainly we meet now as a kind of nice ritual, a little tradition we've had since I turned up, just after the most terrible affray, and had to help sort things out.

Back then, it was the winter of 1930. January, to be precise, and all three nuns were together at Issoire. Camille had recently been sent there, and six months later she was followed by Sister Julia. It had been proposed that I give a consultation or two to Camille, who had been causing much anxiety about her state when she was in Cordoba, and who, quite simply, kept on asking for me and refusing the priest. She had a very kind Prioress, Marie Cecilia, if I remember rightly, who quite broke the bounds in various ways and tried to arrange for me to see Camille when she moved to Issoire. But there we had the angry Prioress, Geneviève—remember, Marie's old girlhood friend? The angry Venus mother, and very bitter she was and wouldn't allow us to meet. But then there is Camille's charm. No—quality is

265

a much better word; she really is rather special you know, and she somehow found her way into Geneviève's heart and began to melt all the ice that had filled it up. Terrible pain actually. And so, Geneviève relented and I was summoned to speak, not just to Camille, but even to Geneviève herself.

You know, we become a healer in the mind of the analysand. They bestow power upon us and it really helps the whole thing to work. Both Freud and Jung know all about this. For Jung we become an archetype, the wise old man or woman, the doctor, the healer, imbued into the collective unconscious over generations and placed into the outside world when needed to be found. And for Freud, we become the historical parent, with all their positive and negative aspects, but within that, there is always the power of the parent to make things better and to love and to care. Oh, yes, believe me—we can't do it all through love, but it certainly helps, and maybe, sometimes, in itself it can cure. And I expect that is why I can get along with the Carmelites. They believe the same thing.

I eventually came there, expecting to speak with the two nuns through a grill, which I was ready for, but found instead that there had been carnage. That dreadful ex-husband of Geneviève had turned up with some trumped up charge to ruin her life and take back his African slave. After all those years—such narcissism. You know about the background. Marie had helped get Geneviève away from him (though she couldn't stop her from becoming a nun!). Dear Marie, she does so much. A fine analyst too.

So, I arrived, to find that the previous day the Spaniard had been run through and killed by Geneviève's man, Morel. He'd been the secretary and was now the gardener and the guardian angel. Always faithful and clearly still with his skill as a swordsman, though it left him with a great scar on his cheek. I'm staying with him now. I always do on these visits. Very convenient, as the town of Issoire is ten miles away and I'm not allowed to have a room in the main house. Morel lives in the groundsman's cottage. It's a little stilted between us. He's not a man of many words and as you yourself have so often suffered, I am. And he doesn't have much culture. Just what he has

266

picked up along the way. A natural poise and elegance though, even when he's in his rough old handyman's clothes.

When I arrived, the nuns were in absolute need, for once in their lives, to speak to someone from the outside world. Desperate in fact. Don Carlos had arrived with a friend from the aristocracy, been challenged by Morel, and couldn't decline. Honour had it to accept, and his friend had acted as his second, so was complicit too. There was a French local policeman there who was completely overawed by the whole thing and was also taken up by the tradition himself. So, he didn't stand in the way and I doubt whether it would have changed anything if he had. And there in front of the three nuns, Morel killed him. It was a duel and as far as Carlos's companion was concerned, the result had to be honoured. He arranged for the body to be removed back to Spain with as little fuss as possible. The family of Carlos had been ruled by a ferocious matriarch, but she had died and his father was ancient and by all accounts, a miserable recluse. They had to accept their loss. They already knew that Carlos engaged in duels and had previously had blood on his hands.

Anyway, I will be leaving for the long journey back to Paris in two days and I suppose I will be here again in a year's time, as long as my old heart still works. But, to the end, it will remain full of love for Camille—Sister Constance. You have probably guessed Paul, that I do love her. I never had children as you know, and I would have loved a daughter. And indeed, I love those that she loves. I do find the Senegal Sister rather tricky, but for Jung she would be the most interesting. I have a few words to say to him about her when we next meet. Camille says that she is really a cat.

So, this word, love, keeps coming up doesn't it. The three women had already worked it out that they were united by its absence, and they didn't need me to tell them. One way or another, they had all been abandoned by their mothers and so they turned to Carmel. Rather an austere choice I have to say, but then, maybe, not surprising. But in the midst of all the discipline and sacrifice, the Carmelites are about love. And Camille, as a person, brought love into the lives of them all.

267

And by the way, I almost forgot. Geneviève is no longer the Mother Superior. After all that happened, she wanted to stand down. You know, I believe that she is the least natural as a nun. So much has been her reaction to deep disappointments, and it just occurs to me— what a consummate revenge against her mother, to become a nun and even a Reverend Mother! I think she has now decided to just live out her life as simply as possible in what had once been her family house. And Morel will still be there, though their contact will be minimal as she's no longer the Prioress.

Maybe he was always the one she should have loved. He certainly loved her and risked his life for her. They will hardly speak, but surely, in her mind and heart, he remains her faithful "gallant".

And those two, Camille and her Sister Africa. They had defied the rules before, why not again? Though I have to say that Camille was the true nun amongst them and I believe she always will be. But the paradox is that it was she who raised Eros. He may still be hanging around to cause more mischief, but I believe she has his measure and will love according to her vows. It's good to see, though, that there's still a twinkle in her eye.

Last thing. Who is now the Prioress? Amongst the Issoire nuns, it had to be Camille or Julia; they stood out completely. Camille gave it to Julia. This we could talk about and she made it into a joke.

"I so much wanted to call her, Mother Africa."

Your friend,
J.

ACKNOWLEDGEMENTS

It has been very helpful to me in the writing of this novel to have had encouragement from my wife Candida, family and friends and I warmly thank them for their involvement and for offering their interest along the way.

I have benefited especially from the active participation of Paula Charles and Mary Hughes.

Paula Charles, as with my first novel, received the chapters as I wrote them and gave me her generous and sensitive support throughout. Paula is also the superb artist Lynn Paula Russell and I was delighted and privileged that she made the painting after the Bernini statue of 'The Ecstasy of Saint Teresa' that we have used for the cover.

Mary Hughes also read the chapters as I was producing them and gave me invaluable advice that came from her experience as a religious. She generously gave her time to consider the many questions that I needed to ask her. If I have made any factual errors it will only be through a lapse in my attentiveness to the information she so carefully gave me.

Special thanks as well to Clare Yates who made the initial proof reading before it went to the publishers and to all those at Aeon Books who then took over the process. I have again greatly benefitted from the calm assurance of the editor of Aeon and Sphinx books, Cecily Blench.